PRAETORIUM

Caesar's
house

SUBURA

Basilica
Aemilia

FORUM
ROMANUM

PALATINE
HILL

SERVIAN WALL

Circus
Maximus

VIA APPIA
to the Necropolis →

ROME
61 BC

GLADIATOR

STREET FIGHTER

'There is something of a
mystery about you, my boy.
You are no common slave.
You have courage, determination
and toughness beyond your years.
Your father would be proud
of you, wherever he is.'

'My father is dead.'

Books by Simon Scarrow

GLADIATOR: FIGHT FOR FREEDOM

GLADIATOR: STREET FIGHTER

SIMON SCARROW

GLADIATOR

STREET FIGHTER

PUFFIN

PUFFIN BOOKS

Published by the Penguin Group
Penguin Books Ltd, 80 Strand, London WC2R ORL, England
Penguin Group (USA) Inc., 375 Hudson Street, New York, New York 10014, USA
Penguin Group (Canada), 90 Eglinton Avenue East, Suite 700, Toronto, Ontario, Canada M4P 2Y3
(a division of Pearson Penguin Canada Inc.)
Penguin Ireland, 25 St Stephen's Green, Dublin 2, Ireland (a division of Penguin Books Ltd)
Penguin Group (Australia), 250 Camberwell Road, Camberwell, Victoria 3124, Australia
(a division of Pearson Australia Group Pty Ltd)
Penguin Books India Pvt Ltd, 11 Community Centre, Panchsheel Park, New Delhi – 110 017, India
Penguin Group (NZ), 67 Apollo Drive, Rosedale, Auckland 0632, New Zealand
(a division of Pearson New Zealand Ltd)
Penguin Books (South Africa) (Pty) Ltd, 24 Sturdee Avenue, Rosebank,
Johannesburg 2196, South Africa

Penguin Books Ltd, Registered Offices: 80 Strand, London WC2R ORL, England

puffinbooks.com

First published 2012
001 – 10 9 8 7 6 5 4 3 2 1

Text copyright © Simon Scarrow, 2012
Map and diagram by David Atkinson

The moral right of the author and illustrators has been asserted

Set in 13/21.3 pt Bembo Book MT Std
Typeset by Palimpsest Book Production Limited, Falkirk, Stirlingshire
Printed in Great Britain by Clays Ltd, St Ives plc

British Library Cataloguing in Publication Data
A CIP catalogue record for this book is available from the British Library

HARDBACK
ISBN: 978-0-141-33364-9

TRADE PAPERBACK
ISBN: 978-0-141-34345-7

www.greenpenguin.co.uk

Penguin Books is committed to a sustainable
future for our business, our readers and our
planet. This book is made from paper certified
by the Forest Stewardship Council.

For Lindsey Davis – who also inspired my interest in Rome

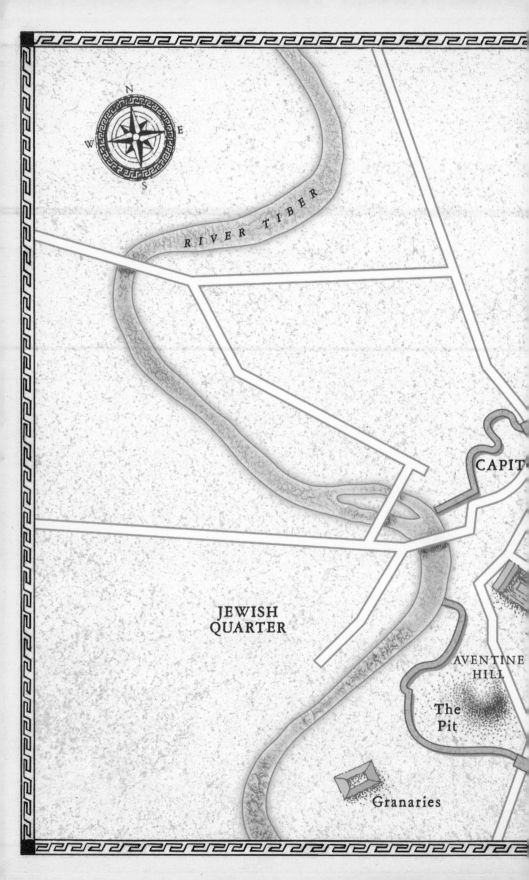

PRAETORIUM

Caesar's
house

SUBURA

Basilica
Aemilia

FORUM
ROMANUM

PALATINE
HILL

SERVIAN WALL

Circus
Maximus

VIA APPIA

to the Necropolis →

ROME
61 BC

1

Marcus knew he had made a fatal mistake the moment he backed into the corner of the yard. He felt the heel of his sandal scrape against the cracked plaster of the wall and instinctively took a half step forward to win a small space in which to move. It was what he had been trained to do at Porcino's gladiator school – always give yourself room to move in a fight, otherwise you surrendered the initiative to your opponent and put yourself at their mercy. It was a lesson that Taurus, the stern and cruel chief trainer, had beaten into the trainee gladiators.

At eleven years old Marcus was tall for his age, and the hard training had made him strong and tough and had given him some skill with a sword. Even so, he knew the odds were against him as he faced his opponent, a wiry man in his thirties, fast on his feet and with a keen eye that anticipated almost every move that Marcus made in their fight.

Blinking away a bead of sweat, Marcus thrust aside his anxiety. He knew his only hope was to do the unexpected – something his opponent had not been trained to deal with. From the way the man moved and handled his short sword, it was clear that he'd been trained as a soldier, or perhaps even a gladiator, like Marcus. When he had drawn his sword on the boy the man had begun with a few lazy thrusts and feints. The initial sneer on his face had quickly faded as Marcus confidently parried his sword blows aside. There had been a brief pause as the man withdrew a few paces to cast a fresh look at his young foe.

'Not so wet behind the ears then,' he growled. 'Still, you're just a little whelp in need of a good hiding. And that's what I'll give you.' Then he closed with Marcus in earnest and the clatter of their sword blows echoed off the walls of the court-yard. Outside, in the Rome back street that passed behind the yard, the hubbub of voices dimly carried to Marcus's ears, muffled by the blood pounding through his head. He paid them no attention and concentrated on his opponent, watching for any flicker of movement that would indicate the next attack.

The man was good. He wouldn't have lasted more than a

few heartbeats against an expert like Taurus, but it was only a question of time before he defeated Marcus. Despite the boy's quick, darting movements, the man soon edged Marcus into the corner, trapping him against the walls.

For an instant Marcus surrendered to the fear that the man would win and cursed himself for letting it happen. Forcing the thought from his mind, he settled into a crouch on the beaten earth and cobbles of the yard. He moved his weight slightly forward so that he was poised on the balls of his feet, ready to spring forward, or aside, in an instant. His sword was held level, a short distance from his side where it could lash out to attack, or block any strike the man threw at him. His left hand reached out to keep him balanced.

There was a brief pause as they stared at each other.

Marcus was aware of movement behind the man as the figure watching from the doorway on the far side of the yard shifted his position.

As his gaze flickered aside the attack came. With a roar, the man sprang forward and slashed his sword at Marcus's head. The boy ducked to one side as the tip of the blade hissed through the air a few inches from his face. At once he made a cut towards his opponent's sword arm and sensed a faint jarring as the edge of the sword nicked the man's skin.

With a curse, the man fell back and raised his arm to look at the wound. It was only a shallow scratch but the blood flowed freely, the droplets scoring jagged crimson lines down the man's forearm as he stared at the cut flesh. He fixed Marcus with an icy stare.

'That is going to cost you, boy. Cost you dearly.'

Marcus's blood went cold at the menacing threat, but he kept his eyes on his opponent.

The man lowered his arm, tightening his grip in case the blood flowed into his palm and caused the weapon to slip. He strode deliberately towards Marcus, lips curled back in a vicious snarl. There was no attempt to pull back his blows this time. The clash of blades rang loudly in Marcus's ears as he was beaten back against the wall. The tip of the sword struck the plaster to one side of his head, and chips exploded off the wall. The blade ripped back, high, ready to strike down on Marcus's head.

'Stop that!' a deep voice called across the yard.

But the man's blood was up and he aimed another blow at Marcus. At the last moment Marcus desperately leapt forward, inside the arc of the blade. He went low, throwing his full weight into his attack as he punched with the guard of his sword between the man's legs, into his groin. There was a deep groan and the man stumbled back with an agonized expression. He let out a cry of pain and rage, balling his left hand in a fist as he swung it hard. Marcus tried to duck the blow, but it glanced off his skull and the impact snapped his head to the side. Bright white sparks filled Marcus's vision as his body flew through the air. Then he landed heavily and the breath was driven from his lungs. He rolled on to his back, gasping, as the walls and sky spun round above him. The man lurched into view, groaning as he doubled over. Then Marcus felt the tip of a sword touch the bony notch at the base of his throat.

The man's eyes narrowed and Marcus feared he would thrust the weapon home to cut Marcus's throat as the tip tore through the top of his spine. He would die, and his heart was flooded with regret and shame that he had failed to win his freedom and find his mother. She had been enslaved at the same time as Marcus and taken to a farming estate somewhere in Greece, and if he died she was doomed to end her days there. Clenching his eyes shut, Marcus prayed to the gods that he might yet be spared.

'Festus! That's enough!' the voice called out again. 'Cut the boy and I'll have you crucified before the day's out.'

There was a slight pause before the light pressure of the

sword tip eased and Marcus dared to blink his eyes open. He was cold with shock and his limbs trembled as he lay sprawled on his back in the corner of the yard. Above him he saw Festus gritting his teeth in frustration and, beyond, the smoke-smeared sky. Even though it was late in the spring, clouds hung low over Rome and threatened rain. Festus straightened up, reversed his sword and snapped it back into his scabbard before turning towards the doorway to bow his head. Marcus scrambled to his feet, breathing hard, and stood apart from Festus as he bowed too.

When he straightened up he saw the other man striding across the yard towards them, a thin smile on his lips. He stopped in front of Marcus and looked down, appraising him, and then turned to Festus, his chief bodyguard.

'Well? What do you think of him?'

Festus paused before replying cautiously. 'He is fast, and skilled with a blade, master, but the boy still has much to learn.'

'Of course he does. But can you teach him?'

'If it is your wish, master.'

'It is.' The man smiled swiftly. 'It is settled. The boy is in your charge. You will train him to fight. He must learn how to use other weapons beside the sword. He must be able to use the dagger, throwing knife, staves and his bare hands.' The man looked at Marcus again. There was no hint of good humour in those cold eyes as he continued. 'One day young Marcus may become a fine gladiator in the arena. Until then, I want you to continue the training he began at Porcino's school. But you must also teach him the ways of the street if he is to be an effective bodyguard for my niece.'

'Yes, master,' Festus nodded.

'Then you may leave us. Take the boy's sword with you. Then find my steward and tell him I want my finest toga cleaned and scented for tomorrow. The mob will expect nothing less from one of their consuls,' he mused. 'I want to look good when I stand beside that fat fool, Bibulus.'

'Yes, master.' Festus bowed again, then hurried across the yard back into the house. When he had gone the man turned his full attention on Marcus.

'You know that I have many enemies here in Rome, young Marcus. Enemies who would harm my family as gladly as they would dare to harm me, Gaius Julius Caesar. That is why I need someone I can trust to protect Portia.'

'I will do my best, master.'

'I want more than your best, boy,' Caesar said firmly. 'You must live to protect Portia. Every waking moment your eyes and ears must be open to every detail of your surroundings, if you are to detect threats before they can cause harm. And not just your eyes and ears. You must use your brain. I know you have quick wits. You proved that back in Capua.'

Caesar paused for a moment and they both recalled the fight when Marcus had beaten Ferax, a boy almost twice his size, before killing two wolves that were set upon him after Marcus had refused to finish him off. But it was neither of those deeds that had won over Caesar. It was when his niece Portia had fallen into the arena, at the mercy of the ravenous wolves, and Marcus had saved her life. For that, Caesar was indebted to Marcus. At the same time, Caesar shrewdly recognized a chance to invest in a boy who might one day be a gladiator who was popular with the mob, and some of that popularity would rub off on the gladiator's owner. So Marcus had been bought from the gladiator school, transferred from one master to another like a common beast.

He leaned forward and tapped Marcus lightly on the chest. 'I may be consul, one of the two most powerful men in Rome, but even I can bleed just as easily as the next man. I have men who protect me, and men who spy for me, yet somehow I sense that you may prove to be one of my most useful servants. For now, you will guard Portia, but I may have other uses for you.'

Caesar's eyes narrowed as he stared at Marcus. The silence made Marcus edgy and he swallowed nervously. He was not yet sure what to make of his new master. At times Caesar could be generous and charming. On other occasions he appeared ruthless, hard and even cruel. 'Other uses, master?'

There was a flicker of a smile on Caesar's lips as he responded. 'Where men might be suspected a young boy may well be overlooked. That is when I will need you to be my eyes and ears.' He paused and stroked his chin.

Marcus felt a slight thrill at the implied praise and the confidence that Caesar had in him. Yet this pleasure passed swiftly as he reminded himself of the true meaning of Caesar's words. Marcus was being used as a minor playing piece in the battle between Caesar and his political enemies. But this was no game, Marcus realized. He recalled what Titus, the man he had once thought his father, had told him about the world of politics in Rome. The stakes were high – literally a matter of life and death – and now Marcus would be at the heart of it. It would be dangerous. But if Marcus could make himself valuable and served Caesar well, he could expect to be rewarded. That much he had discovered about the man; he was generous to those who helped him achieve his ambitions. Marcus's pulse quickened as he stared Caesar directly in the eye and nodded. 'I am ready.'

Caesar smiled briefly and then looked at Marcus for what felt like a long time before he spoke again. 'You know, there is something of a mystery about you, my boy. You are no common slave. Anyone can see that. You have courage, determination and toughness beyond your years. Your father would be proud of you, wherever he is.'

Marcus thought quickly. Here was his first chance to put the injustice of his situation to Caesar. 'My father is dead,' he said. 'He was murdered, on the orders of a tax collector named Decimus.'

'Oh?' Caesar pursed his lips briefly and then shrugged. 'That's too bad. But the gods have their reasons for the way things turn out.'

Marcus's heart sank at his master's curt dismissal of his miseries.

'And what of your mother?' asked Caesar.

'A slave, master. Though I don't know where she is.' As much as Marcus wanted help to track down his mother, for now he decided it was best to lie. It would be safer if his mother remained hidden from Caesar. If ever his true identity was discovered, then Marcus would be put to death, and so too would anyone who claimed the same blood as him. This man Caesar, for all the gratitude he showed Marcus for saving his niece's life, would kill him on the spot the instant he discovered that Marcus's real father was Spartacus, the gladiator general who had commanded the rebel slave army that defied Caesar and his high-born friends. The gladiator who had almost brought about the destruction of Rome and all that it stood for.

2

Once Caesar had dismissed him Marcus left the yard and made for the slave quarters at the rear of the house. On his arrival at the house, Marcus had been taken to Caesar's steward who explained the rules that would govern his life, and then showed him to the small cell that Marcus would share with two other boys who were also slaves. The younger boy was not far off Marcus's age, and was named Corvus. He was tall and skinny with a hooked nose, and had a gloomy air of resignation. The other boy, Lupus, was nearer sixteen and had a natural flair for letters and numbers. As well as occasionally helping in the kitchen, he served as Caesar's scribe. A scribe was responsible for taking down notes for his master, Lupus explained proudly. Most days he accompanied Caesar on his official business. Lupus, short and slight, with neatly trimmed dark hair, was far more cheerful than his younger companion and had warmly welcomed the new arrival to their humble quarters. Their cell was no more than ten feet long by four feet wide, with a slit high up that let in a dim shaft of light from the street outside. The other boys slept on ragged sleeping rolls, side by side at the end furthest from the door. Marcus was given a similarly worn roll and told he would sleep to one side of the narrow entrance.

Since then, he'd been given plenty of small jobs about the household until the morning Festus had summoned him to appraise his skills as a fighter. Now, as he headed back indoors towards his miserable living quarters, the sounds of the Subura – the district surrounding the house – faded into a dull background drone. One of the older slaves had told Marcus that the Subura had been a respectable neighbour-hood when Caesar's ancestors first built their home here, but the area had gone downhill since then. Now ramshackle tene-ment blocks loomed up all around the houses, filled with dispossessed farming families forced into the city to find work. These had been followed by immigrants from all around the Mediterranean: Greeks, Numidians, Gauls and Jews. All were now crowded into the Subura and the narrow streets were filled with voices crying out in several tongues, while the distinctive wafts of their cooking traditions blended together, powerful enough to overlay the background stench of rotting food and sewage.

Despite being in the capital for nearly ten days, Marcus was still getting used to the stinking streets. The colourful mix of clothing styles and the noise and bustle of the crowded neighbourhood fascinated him. Growing up on an isolated farm on a small Greek island, Marcus had only ever known the limited delights of the local market town where dour farmers met three times a month to trade. The memory tugged at his heart as he recalled walking to the market beside the man he had once believed to be his father. Titus had been tough and often cold – an ex-soldier who had been strict with Marcus for the most part. But once in a while his stern facade had melted and he had playfully wrestled with Marcus in the small yard of the farmhouse, or told him stories of his adventures as a soldier.

Marcus sighed unhappily as he recalled his early childhood, torn between fond memories and the knowledge that he had been lied to. Titus was not his father. That had been revealed to him less than a month ago, when he had left the gladiator school and was on the road to join his new master in Rome.

It was Brixus, once a follower of Spartacus, who had followed him and told him the truth. Marcus reached a hand over his shoulder, his fingers slipping under the neckline of his tunic to trace the outline of the mark with which he had been branded when he was only an infant: the head of a wolf impaled on a sword, the same secret brand that had been shared by Spartacus and his closest followers, including the woman he loved and their child – Marcus. Brixus had told him it was his destiny to complete his true father's work and lead the next slave revolt – the one that would finally overwhelm Rome and free all the slaves who lived under the whip of their cruel Roman masters.

Marcus frowned angrily. His world had been turned over. All that he had known was false and his heart was filled with a turmoil of emotions. He still loved Titus, the tough, proud veteran of the legions. Yet there was not a drop of Roman blood in Marcus's veins. His true heritage lay in the ranks of the millions of downtrodden slaves who lived and died chained together in the mines, or on the farms owned by wealthy Romans, as drudges in their fine villas, or as a source of bloody entertainment in their gladiatorial games. That was Marcus's true identity, what he had always been – nothing but a slave.

The knowledge burned painfully in his heart. He felt bitter

about the deception, and couldn't believe his mother had hidden the truth from him all his life. His anger towards her was immediately followed by intense guilt. She was all he cared about in the world and his one goal in life was to find and set her free.

Marcus's plan had been to track down General Pompeius, the former commander of Titus, and ask him to help save his mother. It was a favour a Roman general might grant one of his former officers, but it would be a death sentence for both Marcus and his mother if Pompeius discovered Marcus was actually the son of the most hated and dangerous slave in all of the Roman Empire. This would be equally true if his new master, Caesar, discovered the name of his real father. Spartacus was the enemy of all Romans.

Marcus sighed again, this time in frustration at his apparently impossible situation. He had to find a way to help his mother that would not risk revealing his real identity. And quickly . . .

'Curse Brixus!' he muttered angrily as he entered the inner atrium of the house, where a colonnade surrounded a small shallow pool. Marcus stared down at the flagstones, deep in thought as he began to make his way round the pool.

'Brixus? Who is this Brixus that upsets my saviour and personal bodyguard so much?'

Marcus stopped and looked round anxiously – he should not have uttered Brixus's name aloud – as a slender figure emerged from behind one of the columns. It was Caesar's niece, Portia – a girl just a few years older than Marcus, with light brown hair tied back in a simple ponytail and the same piercing brown eyes as her uncle. Marcus had been told that Portia's mother had died in childbirth and her father was serving with the legions in Spain, so she had come to live with her uncle in Rome.

He bowed his head. 'Good day to you, Mistress Portia.'

A light frown creased her high forehead. 'Mistress? Must you be so formal?' She waved a hand around the atrium. 'We're alone. You can speak freely to me. There's no one to overhear us.'

Marcus glanced at the entrances to the atrium and saw she spoke the truth. Even so, he lowered his voice as he responded.

'I could be flogged for addressing you disrespectfully.'

'But I don't consider it disrespectful,' Portia countered in a gentle tone. 'I just want you to speak to me as a friend, Marcus. Not as my uncle's slave.'

He stared at her in silence. Since arriving at the house he had spoken to Portia on just a handful of occasions, always with other household members present. Portia had visited him at the gladiator school when he was recovering from wounds received while saving her from the wolves in the school's arena. She'd been full of gratitude and Marcus had expected a warm welcome. But since he'd arrived Portia had seemed as indifferent to him as to all the other slaves in the household. The change in her manner, so disdainful after her earlier gratitude, had confused and hurt him at first.

Then, not long after his arrival, he'd been ordered to mop the floor in Portia's quarters. Struck by the stark contrast between his dismal cell and Portia's comfortable existence, he'd realized how far apart their two lives were. Even as he marvelled at her soft sleeping couch, covered with ornately patterned woven blankets, he understood the social gulf between them was as wide as any ocean of the world, and just as dangerous. Looking at the fine-quality furniture – the table for her scents, an ebony chest for her jewels and a large rack holding scrolls of poetry, histories and letters from her father – he saw clearly that two utterly different worlds existed side by side in the same household.

Marcus was a slave, and his master was free to do with him as he wished. How could Caesar's niece ever be considered the friend of a slave boy? And Caesar was not merely a citizen of Rome. His family was one of the most respected in the city, claiming descent from the goddess Venus herself. As such Caesar would not take kindly to discovering that one of his slaves had spoken to his niece on anything like equal terms. A master could have his slave executed for less.

Only now, Portia seemed to be acting as though that gulf didn't really exist. Marcus opened his mouth as he struggled to reply, then closed it when he couldn't find a safe way to address her.

She saw his discomfort and let out a light laugh.

'Very well, if it would make you feel safer we can talk in the garden. There's a private spot in the far corner. Follow me.' There was an unmistakable tone of command in her words as she led him through the short passage into the modest garden beyond.

The garden was a neatly kept space no more than a hundred feet across. Past generations of Caesar's family, the Julii, had taken great pride in it and it was composed of carefully shaped shrubs and roses and other bright flowers trained by wooden frames. These created shaded avenues that crossed the garden and ran down each side and filled the air with a pleasant fragrance. A small fountain tinkled in the centre of the garden. It was hard to believe that something as beautiful and sweet smelling could exist in what he'd seen of this crowded, filthy and stinking city, Marcus thought.

Portia led him down one of the side paths to the corner where the tall plastered walls met. Here there was a small seating area shielded from view by a hedge. She sat down on one of the two wooden benches lining the angled walls. Behind them, the plaster had been painted with a view from an ivy-clad balcony overlooking rolling hills that led to the sea. Tiny ships with bright sails rode the still waves. *Getting no closer to their destination*, Marcus thought. *Going nowhere. Just like me.*

Portia patted the space beside her. 'Come. Sit down.'

He hesitated, then glanced over his shoulder.

'Marcus,' Portia chuckled, 'no one can see us here. Trust me. Now sit down.'

He sucked in a deep breath and reluctantly lowered himself on to the bench, a good two feet away from Portia and as near to her as he dared sit.

'This is dangerous,' he said, turning his head to look at her.

'You're safe enough. If anyone comes, you can stand up and I shall pretend to have summoned you to fetch me a drink.'

'What if they don't believe you?'

She arched an eyebrow imperiously. 'I am the niece of a consul of Rome. Who is going to question my word, in my own household?'

'Your uncle, for one. I doubt that he'd be happy for his noble niece to be caught having a friendly chat with a slave boy.'

'Pah!' Portia gestured dismissively. 'I can run rings round my uncle if I need to – even if he *is* one of the most powerful men in Rome, next to that old moneybags Crassus and vain General Pompeius – General Pompous more like!' She laughed at her joke and Marcus saw that her teeth were small and bright.

Overhearing the gossip of the other slaves, Marcus had learned that Caesar's only child, his beloved Julia, had been married to General Pompeius shortly before Marcus arrived in Rome. Now it seemed that Caesar had come to regard Portia as a replacement for the daughter who had left his household.

'Anyway,' Portia continued, 'it is quite safe for you to talk to me, Marcus.'

He wanted to believe her, but still felt the need for caution. 'What shall we talk about then?'

Portia looked surprised. 'Why, it's several days since you arrived and I want to know how you're settling in. What do you think of our house?'

'House?' Marcus gestured around the garden. 'I thought this was a palace. Is this how all Roman lords live?'

'This is quite modest by comparison with others.' Portia smiled. 'You should see the great houses of Crassus and

Pompeius. Now those really *are* like palaces. But Uncle Gaius prefers to live here, surrounded by the common people. He says it helps keep the mob on his side. He does have another house, a much grander place than this, close to the Forum. That came with the job when he was elected chief priest a while back. But he only uses it for official purposes. This is our real home.' Portia patted his arm fondly. 'Anyway, Marcus, talk to me. I want to know what you think of Rome. This is the first time you've been here, isn't it?' She reached her hand over and prodded him. 'Isn't it exciting?'

'Exciting?' Marcus was surprised by the question and couldn't help a bitter smile. 'I'm as excited as a slave can be.'

'Come now, you are part of my uncle's household. You're no longer at that grim little gladiator school where he found you. I'd have thought you'd be more grateful at the way things have turned out.'

Marcus didn't like her tone and a burst of indignation flared in his heart. 'And I would have thought your uncle might be grateful that I saved your life.'

Portia winced, then bowed her head and looked down at her hands resting in her lap. She was silent for a moment before she continued humbly.

'I *am* grateful, Marcus. Really I am. And so is my uncle,

though he wouldn't dream of being indebted to a slave. I'm sorry for the way I spoke just then.' She glanced shyly at him. 'I don't want to be your enemy. I want to be your friend. I suppose I'm feeling a bit lonely. I don't really have many friends . . . Please don't hate me.'

'I don't hate you,' Marcus replied stiffly, then stabbed his thumb at the brass plaque hanging from his neck on a thick chain. His name and that of his master were neatly engraved on its shiny surface. 'It's just this that I hate. I shouldn't be a slave. I was born free and lived that way until less than a year ago – until my mother and I were kidnapped by a tax collector and my . . . father . . . was killed. One day I will find her and set her free. And I will have my revenge, and kill that tax collector, Decimus. I swear it.'

Portia looked shocked. 'What happened?'

'My father got into debt. He borrowed money from Decimus and when he couldn't repay it, Decimus sent his thugs in. Their leader, a man called Thermon, killed my father, and took my mother and me away to be sold into slavery to cover the debt.' Marcus's heart filled with sorrow at the memory and he looked away.

Portia was silent, then spoke softly. 'Then you will need to win your liberty, Marcus, so you can search for your mother.'

Or I could escape, thought Marcus. Briefly, he considered the possibility. He would not get far with a slave's collar round his neck. And once caught, he'd be dragged back to Caesar's house where his master would punish him harshly. It would be expected of him, to make sure an example was given to the other slaves in the household, as well as the slaves in all the households across Rome. Marcus sighed. There was little to be gained from escaping right now. It would be far better to follow his original plan and see if he could plead his case directly to General Pompeius, while keeping the secret of his true identity.

Marcus cleared his throat. 'If I serve your uncle well, perhaps he will set me free. Until then, I will protect you with my life.'

Portia smiled. 'Thank you. And, Marcus – maybe I can help you. I'd like to, if I could.'

A brief silence fell between them, then Marcus spoke again. 'Perhaps. But you must know that I can never be a real friend to you. Not while I am a slave and you're the niece of a consul.'

Portia paused before she replied. 'I imagine you think I'm a pampered brat. Just like all those other silly girls riding in litters about the city. Well, perhaps I am in some ways. But my uncle is powerful and that means many men and women want to be counted among his friends. So they toady up to him, and their sons and nieces toady up to me. No one treats me like a normal person. To them I am a means of winning Caesar's favour. I am thirteen years old. By this time next year I may well be married. My uncle will want to use the wedding to further his political ambitions.' She smiled weakly. 'I don't want your sympathy. I have always known that would be my fate, and I accept it. But before it happens I'd like to have had at least one true friend in my life, Marcus. When I fell into that arena I saw my death in the eyes of those wolves. But you saved me. And that means we share a real bond. Doesn't it?'

Marcus recalled that Titus had once told him that when one soldier saved the life of another, they were as brothers. But his feelings for Portia were more than that, though he hardly dared admit it, even to himself. Despite his knowledge of their different lives, he desperately wanted her words to be true. 'I suppose so.'

'Then you can be my secret friend, and I will be yours. I can talk freely to you and you to me. In time, I may even be able to help you win your freedom.'

More than anything, Marcus wanted someone with whom he could speak freely, but there was no question of even hinting at his true identity to Portia. For her, her uncle, and for every Roman, the spectre of Spartacus haunted their dreams. He meant an end to their way of life.

Still, he forced himself to smile. 'Thank you, Mistress Portia.'

She looked hurt. 'Just Portia when we are alone. Please.'

'As you wish, Portia.'

She smiled. 'There! It's settled. We are friends, and we will talk like this whenever we can. I want you to tell me how Festus trains you, what you think about Rome, and I'll tell you all that goes on in the finest houses of the city.'

Marcus forced a smile.

Portia was about to speak again when a shout carried across the garden.

'Marcus! Marcus! Where are you, boy?'

Marcus recognized the harsh tone of Flaccus, the household's steward, and turned to Portia as he rose from the bench.

'I have to go.'

'Yes.' She took his hand again and gave it a gentle squeeze. 'We'll talk again soon, I hope.'

Marcus nodded as Flaccus bellowed his name again and he hurried from the sheltered corner along the path at the side of the garden. Emerging into the shaded colonnade that ran across the end of the house, he caught sight of the steward – a short, overweight man in a green tunic. Flaccus was bald, except for a heavily oiled fringe that ran around his head, and his heavy cheeks wobbled as he turned towards the sound of Marcus's light footsteps.

'Where in Hades have you been?' he scowled.

'Here in the garden, sir,' Marcus replied as he stopped in front of the man.

'Well, don't let me catch you at it again. When you're not needed you stay in the slave quarters until you're called for. Understand?' He shot out a hand and cuffed Marcus's ear.

The blow knocked Marcus's head to one side and his ears filled with a dull ringing. He blinked and glared back at the steward. 'Yes, sir.'

'See that you do, or next time I'll give you a hiding you won't forget.' The steward rested his fat fingers on his hips and stared coldly down at Marcus.

'I know what you did at that gladiator school, and I know the master favours you, but don't think that makes you special. You're no better than the rest of us slaves. I'm the steward here. You answer to me. And if you cross me, you'll regret it. I'll treat you no differently from the kitchen boys. Is that clear?'

'Yes, sir.'

Flaccus stabbed a finger into his chest. 'Now then. The master is heading to the Senate. He's given instructions you're to join his retinue. You're to take a cape from the slop chest and wait for him at the main entrance. Well, what are you waiting for, lad – get moving!'

3

Marcus stood with a party of other slaves and servants in the entrance hall while they waited for their master to appear. The cloak Marcus had chosen from those heaped in the kitchen slop chest was the least rancid one he could find. Even so, it stank of sweat and he'd taken care to push the hood well back, deciding he would only wear that if he absolutely had to. The other men wore a mixture of tunics and cloaks that indicated their status. The slaves were dressed as drably as Marcus, while Festus, a freedman, wore a clean red tunic and brown cape, as did the men he had hired to act as Caesar's personal body-guards. Marcus noted their hard expressions, weathered faces and thick muscled arms and guessed that they must be gladi-ators or former legionaries, like his father.

But he wasn't my father, Marcus reminded himself. He thrust memories of Titus aside, together with the grief in his heart. He must be strong. He must not give in to feelings. He could not be weak if he wanted to save his mother. Only the ruthless training he'd received at Porcino's gladiator school mattered now.

'Here, boy, take this.'

Marcus looked up to see Festus holding out a thick stave. The wooden shaft was tapered from its heavy end and bound with strips of leather to provide a firm grip. Marcus took the club and hefted it experimentally to test its weight. He took a step away from Festus and swung it to and fro, sensing that it was well balanced and would be a useful weapon. Festus looked on approvingly.

'Good to see that you're familiar with the tools of the trade.'

Marcus looked round and noticed the other men had either stuck the clubs in their belts, or were carrying them by the thick end, as if they were walking sticks. He turned back to Festus.

'Why aren't they carrying swords?'

Festus raised his eyebrows. 'Ah, yes. You're a newcomer to Rome. Well, lad, the law says no one is allowed to carry a sword within the city limits. No one pays too much attention to that, but it doesn't look good for anyone in the public eye to break the law. That's why we carry the clubs, and a few other things besides. You used a club before?'

'In training,' said Marcus. 'In the first month before we were allowed to use a real weapon.'

'This *is* a real weapon,' Festus growled as he hefted his own club. 'Almost as good as any sword if it comes to a fight. And not quite so messy. Last thing Caesar and the other great men of Rome want is for blood to flow in the streets. Mind you, break a man's skull open with a club and there's a mess all right.' He paused and narrowed his eyes at Marcus. 'One last thing. You call me "sir" when you speak to me. Got it?'

'Yes . . . sir.'

'That's better. Mind you hold that club like a walking stick, and you keep it that way up unless I give the order to lay into anyone. Understand?'

Marcus nodded and Festus patted him on the shoulder.

'That's the spirit.'

'Master's coming!' a voice called out.

Festus and the others quickly formed up in two lines, each side of the entrance to the house. Marcus joined the end of one and stood beside Festus, staring directly ahead as the others did. The clack of boots on the floor tiles echoed off the walls as Caesar swept into the room, his arm round his niece's shoulder. Behind them came Lupus, the satchel containing his note slates hanging from his shoulder. Marcus risked a quick glimpse and saw that his master was wearing a spotless white tunic with a broad purple stripe running down one edge. His boots were fine red leather with tassels dangling from the tops. His hair was neatly arranged with little ringlets around the fringe. Marcus couldn't help being struck by his ornate appearance. It was as if Caesar was setting out to dazzle his audience. Caesar paused before he reached his retinue and turned to face Portia.

'How do I look, my dear?'

She smiled with delight. 'Every inch a consul, Uncle. I'm proud of you.'

Marcus could see what Portia meant about running rings round her uncle.

'As I am of you.' Caesar beamed and leaned down to kiss her on the forehead. He turned away and at once his expression hardened as he faced the waiting men. 'As you know, I have my enemies, but until now they've had the sense not to lay a finger on a consul of Rome. That may well change. It is my intention to propose a new law before the Senate this morning. It's sure to divide members of the Senate and there may be trouble. Although my enemies might be cowards, I most certainly am not. It's important that the people of Rome see I am not afraid. Therefore you will at all times keep position some ten feet behind me. You will only come to my aid if I call for you. And you will not raise so much as a finger against anyone unless I give the order, no matter how rowdy the crowd gets. Is that clear?'

'Yes, Caesar!' the men chorused, and Marcus joined in.

Caesar strode down each line, examining his men, then stood back and nodded towards the doorway. 'Lead 'em outside, Festus. I'll join you in a minute. You go with them too, Lupus.'

Marcus turned to follow the others when a hand pressed on his shoulder.

'Not you, boy. Wait behind.'

Marcus stepped to the side as the others descended the stairs into the street outside. His heart beat with alarm. What did his master want with him? Caesar watched them file out and when the last of them had gone he turned to his niece. 'Portia, you may go.'

'Yes, Uncle.' She nodded, then shot a quick glance at Marcus and raised an eyebrow before gliding off towards the rear of the house.

Caesar stared at Marcus long enough for him to become

uncomfortable under the penetrating gaze. He looked down as a satisfied smile flickered on the consul's lips.

'As far as anyone apart from you, me and Festus knows, I have brought you to Rome to protect my niece. You will carry out that duty day to day. However, as I have mentioned, I will have other uses for you. That is why I want you to join me at the Senate today, Marcus. It's important that you know the faces of the men who call themselves my friends, as well as those of my enemies.' He paused. 'You have a good mind and think on your feet. You also have raw courage. I have every intention of making a great gladiator out of you at one of my schools in Campania when your work is done here in Rome.'

Marcus couldn't hide his despair. He composed himself quickly, but it was too late. Caesar frowned. 'Does the prospect of such a reward not please you?'

Marcus thought there was nothing he wanted less than to be a gladiator, apart from being a slave for the rest of his life. But realizing the foolishness of offending Caesar, he nodded. 'It would be an honour, master.'

'Of course it would be. But it will be some time yet before you leave my household. For now, I want you to pay close attention to today's proceedings at the Senate. You are to stand with the rest of the public and watch. Put the hood of your cloak up. There are sure to be agents of my enemies watching as we leave. They will have eyes for me, and for some of my retinue. They will surely overlook a young boy, but I will not risk them seeing your face and being able to recognize you at a later date. I say this for your own safety as much as my own interests, so do it now.'

'Yes, master.'

Fighting back his distaste, Marcus pulled the hood over his head, far enough to obscure his face. His nose crinkled at the sour odour that filled his nostrils. Caesar nodded his satisfaction. 'That will do. Let's go.'

Following his master out of the entrance, Marcus hurried to take his place at the rear of the cluster of bodyguards, who were ready to move off. A small crowd had gathered to watch the consul emerge from his home and they raised a cheer as Caesar appeared. He smiled warmly at them and raised a hand in greeting, before setting off down the street at a sedate pace. Like almost every street in the Subura, it was narrow and to Marcus's eye seemed squeezed between the tall tenement blocks that lined the route. Most were two or three storeys, but some towered above them, twice as high. He couldn't help looking at the taller buildings with a tinge of anxiety. Some already had large cracks working their way up and down the walls. It didn't look as if it would take much for them to collapse.

As the consul passed along the street he called out greetings to the owners of the small businesses that lined the route. Lupus fell into step beside Marcus and nodded towards their master.

'He puts on quite a show, doesn't he?'

Marcus saw butchers pause in their work to wave their bloodied cleavers in acknowledgement of Caesar, while fullers stopped treading clothes in their tanks to offer cries of support to him. An acrid stink filled Marcus's nose and his face wrinkled.

'What is that smell?'

'Smell?' Lupus looked round at the fullers. 'Oh, that. It's urine.'

'Urine? They're not standing in urine, surely?'

'Oh, yes. There's nothing better for cleaning clothes,' Lupus explained in a matter-of-fact tone. Marcus shook his head in bewilderment as ahead of them a baker rushed out to offer their master a roundel of bread. Caesar graciously accepted the gift and passed it back to Marcus.

'There. Eat it if you like.'

Marcus bowed his head gratefully and broke it in two, handing half to Lupus. He bit into the loaf, savouring the doughy flavour.

Word that Caesar was on his way to the Senate had filtered through the streets and more and more people began to tag along behind his retinue. Marcus had arrived in Rome after dark several days before and this was his first excursion into the heart of the city. Until recently, the only town he had ever seen was the sleepy fishing port of Nydri, scarcely more than a village. His senses were assaulted from all directions. Apart from the raw stench of the great city, there were the sounds of the street criers and people crowded into the slum dwellings that pressed in on either side. Then there were the sights that fascinated him, and the wide variety of clothing of the different races living crowded together. A short distance from Caesar's house stood a synagogue where a handful of rabbis stood in the doorway, debating in their strange tongue. The shops increased in number the closer the growing procession got to the Forum in the centre of the city. They were filled with goods of every kind – from heaps of fruit and grain to bales of silken cloth and fine jewellery.

There were some sights that appalled Marcus too – the pinched grimy faces of hungry children clutching the rags of their barefoot mothers, and the dead lying in the streets like bundles of discarded rags. Some bodies lay propped against the cracked plaster of the walls where they had died, or had been cast into dingy side alleys to stop them hindering the passage of the living. There they would remain until a work party took the bodies to one of the mass graves outside the city walls.

As he passed a midden heap, piled with rubbish as well as mud and faeces, there came a plaintive wail. Turning towards the sound, Marcus slowed his pace and saw an abandoned baby writhing pitifully amid the filth. He felt sick at the sight and would have stopped but for the press of bodies behind him, forcing him on.

Thankfully, it didn't take long for Caesar and his followers to emerge from the Subura district and into the Forum. Once more Marcus was stunned by the scale of his surroundings. The public buildings of the great city spread out along the length of the Sacred Way, the main route that led into the heart of Rome. On the far side of the Forum rose the Palatine Hill where the houses of the richest families in Rome overlooked the city. To Marcus they looked more like palaces than houses, with their gleaming plaster walls, lofty tiled roofs and terraced gardens.

Caesar turned right, towards the looming mass of the Temple of Jupiter and the cluster of buildings at the foot of the Capitoline Hill. Marcus recalled Titus telling him this was where the Senate met to debate the laws that would govern

Rome. Before them lay the great marketplace where the finest goods from across the empire were sold. Here also were the offices of the bankers and merchants. Marcus wished he could take in the overwhelming scene properly, but he had to move on. He struggled to keep his place in the crowd that was now following Caesar as he made his way towards the Senate's meeting place. Among the throng that filled the Forum, Marcus caught glimpses of other senators dressed in fine togas and followed by their own retinues as they too fought to pass through the packed Forum.

'Sod this!' one of Festus's men grumbled. 'Where are the lictors today? Why aren't they here to clear a way for us?'

'Because Caesar sent them away,' Festus responded sourly. 'Didn't want to upset the mob by having the lictors thrust them aside.'

Marcus edged forward until he was beside Festus. 'What are lictors?'

'The consul's official bodyguards. They carry bundles of sticks strapped round an axe. It's their duty to clear the way for the consuls.'

'So why aren't they doing their job?' the other man continued. 'You can be sure the other consul will have his lictors clear the way for him!'

'And that's why he's not the darling of the mob,' Festus explained. 'Not like Caesar. Our master knows his way to the people's hearts. He can play them like a lyre. Now shut your mouth and quit complaining.' Festus raised his voice so the rest of his men could hear him above the din of the crowd. 'All of you, keep your eyes open for trouble!'

Marcus tried to do as he was told but he was too small to see much beyond those people immediately surrounding him.

A dense crowd had formed outside the Senate House and the officials were struggling to keep the steps clear for the senators. As some of them climbed the steps the crowd raised a cheer. Others were greeted with silence, or a scattering of boos.

'What's going on?' Marcus asked Lupus.

'Well, there are two types of senators. Those who want to keep power and wealth in the hands of the aristocrats, and the men like Caesar who want to help the common people. That's who the mob is cheering.'

Marcus couldn't help wondering about his new master's desire to stand up for the poor people of Rome. If he was prepared to help them, then why not slaves too?

They pressed on towards the Senate House, and then at last the way ahead was clear as they reached the foot of the stairs.

Caesar climbed the first few steps and turned towards the crowd. He was greeted with a roar of approval as he raised his right hand and smiled, basking in their cheers, before descending towards Festus. Leaning close to his servant, he issued his orders.

'You and your men stay here. Lupus and Marcus, follow me to the entrance, then find a good viewing point to watch the debate. Lupus, make sure you explain the proceedings to Marcus. I want him to know precisely who's who in the cast of villains.' Caesar glanced down and winked at Marcus. Then he turned and climbed the steps to the entrance of the Senate House. Lupus waited a moment before gesturing to Marcus to follow, and they moved to the edge of the staircase. One of the officials stopped them.

'And where do you think you're going?'

'We're with the consul. I'm his scribe. He wants us to watch the debate.'

The official leaned forward to inspect the brass plate around Lupus's neck, checking who owned him, then jerked his thumb up the stairs. 'You go as far as the public gallery and no further. Got that?'

Lupus nodded and steered Marcus ahead as they climbed the stairs to the colonnade that surrounded the debating chamber. The shutters in the tall windows had been opened and shafts

41

of light illuminated the ranks of stone benches facing the two ornate chairs where the consuls sat. One of the chairs was already occupied by a large man with a round face and wispy dark hair.

'Ah.' Lupus's lips lifted in amusement. 'Consul Bibulus is already here. Waiting impatiently, I expect.'

Marcus leaned on the wooden rail and peered down into the chamber. He saw Caesar making his way through the senators, shaking hands and exchanging greetings. But there were many others who regarded Caesar coolly and Marcus guessed these were the enemies he had mentioned – the faces Marcus was supposed to remember. A chill ran down his spine as he reflected that these senators had been the bitter enemies of his true father, Spartacus. These were the same senators who had ordered the crucifixion of the prisoners after the last battle of Spartacus. Six thousand of them, Brixus had told him – lining the Appian Way from Rome to Capua.

Caesar crossed the open floor between the senators' benches and the consuls' chairs, nodding a greeting to Bibulus as he eased himself into his seat. Now that both consuls were in attendance, the rest of the senators took their places. When the last of them had arrived the crowds were finally allowed to enter. Officials formed a line across the doorway to keep the people out as they moved up the stairs and filled the public gallery overlooking the debating chamber.

'What happens now?' asked Marcus as people jostled around him, trying to get a good view of the senators.

'Now?' Lupus glanced at him with a grim smile. 'Now we find out who is for Caesar and who is against him.'

4

Marcus leaned forward and watched intently as the chief clerk of the Senate cleared his throat and began to read from the waxed slate in his hands.

'The first, and only, item on today's agenda is that proposed by Consul Gaius Julius Caesar.' He bowed his head to Caesar and returned to his desk where he took up his stylus to record key comments of the coming debate for the official archive of the Roman Senate.

An expectant silence fell on the house. Marcus gazed down at his master. Caesar was still for a moment, milking the tension in his audience, before he rose slowly and drew a deep breath.

'As every citizen knows, we are living in a time of great prosperity. Peace has returned to Rome, and it is time we honoured the great sacrifices made by our fellow citizens who fought for the glory of Rome. The soldiers of General Pompeius, who have defeated every enemy sent against them . . .'

The men who killed my father, and those who had fought with him for their freedom, Marcus thought. He wasn't sure how he felt, hearing this.

'Now they have returned to Italia with every expectation that Rome would show its gratitude to them.' Caesar gestured to the faces peering down from the windows. 'I am sure there are many here today who are former soldiers of General Pompeius. To them I offer my thanks, on behalf of all the citizens of Rome. To them I say it is only right that Rome should bear the cost of providing them with the land settlement they richly deserve.'

A series of cheers sounded from the public gathered in the colonnade, and then rippled down the stairs into the Forum. Caesar waited for the cries to die down before continuing.

'Yet here today some senators are opposed to the principle of a fair reward for the gallant service given by our soldiers. I will not name them, as you will know them when they speak against my proposal. They will have to answer to our soldiers for their opposition . . .'

Caesar stared around the chamber and then abruptly sat

down. At once, one of the other senators rose to his feet and raised his arm to draw attention to himself.

'I second the consul's motion.'

'No surprises there,' Lupus chuckled.

'Who is he?' asked Marcus. He looked down at the tall, distinguished-looking speaker as he continued his support for the measure to resettle Pompeius's veterans.

'That's Marcus Licinius Crassus. He was the richest man in Rome – made most of his fortune from buying and selling tax-collecting contracts. But then General Pompeius returned from the east loaded down with treasures he had looted from our conquests there. They used to be bitter enemies.'

Marcus frowned. He had pinned his hopes on General Pompeius. If Pompeius had enemies, then Marcus needed to find out more. 'Then why is Crassus supporting Pompeius and his soldiers now?'

Lupus grinned. 'You can be sure he isn't doing it out of the goodness of his heart. No doubt he's stitched up a deal with Pompeius and Caesar. My guess is that he's after the tax-collection contracts in the provinces that Pompeius has created.'

'I see.' Marcus watched a moment longer as Crassus spelled out the reasons why the Senate should vote in favour of the new law. Then he turned to Lupus again.

'Is General Pompeius here?'

'For once. He doesn't usually bother to attend. Turns out he's a rather better soldier than he is a politician. He made a complete mess of his first speech in the Senate and only comes out when it's important for him to be seen in public.'

Marcus felt a surge of hope. He asked excitedly, 'Which one is he?'

Lupus pointed at a well-built man sitting in the front row. He had blond hair, artfully arranged in a neat quiff, and wore gold torcs on his hairy wrists, with another around his thick neck. He sat back, arms folded, and nodded at each point made by Crassus. Around him sat a group of senators watching him closely for cues as they added their gestures of support to his.

Marcus stared at the famous general, his excitement building. This was the man for whom Titus had fought, and whose life he had saved in the final battle against Spartacus and his rebel army. This was the man who could help Marcus free his mother, the man Marcus had hoped to find when he first set out for Rome. Perhaps Portia was right, and he should be grateful for ending up in Caesar's household. He'd never have known how to track down General Pompeius otherwise.

And now he must find some way to get close enough to speak to Pompeius. If only he could do that, Marcus was certain that he would put an end to his mother's suffering. His mind was suddenly filled with images of her chained to other slaves. He knew she was being forced to work on the farm estate owned by Decimus, the tax collector responsible for inflicting all the suffering that Marcus had endured since the day his men had turned up at Titus's farm. In his mind's eye, Marcus saw Titus die at the hands of Decimus's henchman, Thermon. Then he saw his mother's face, weary and tear-stained. He felt his throat tighten and his eyes sting as his own tears began to well up.

He cuffed them away before Lupus noticed, angry with himself. He had to be strong, or there would be no chance of saving his mother and himself. He had to remember his gladiator training which had taught him to withstand suffering, to bear pain and injustice without complaint. With an effort, he pushed the images of his mother aside and concentrated on the debate. He needed to think about how it could help his own cause.

Crassus had finished his speech, to mild applause from most of the senators, and loud cheers from the public. One of the senators close to Pompeius stood up to offer his support, before entering into a lengthy speech in praise of Pompeius. The great general accepted this with a modest nod of his head. When the senator had resumed his seat another figure rose to his feet. A complete contrast to the other senators, the tall, thin man was dressed in a simple beige toga over a brown tunic. He wore plain sandals and his hair looked unkempt. The muttering of the watching public died away.

'Here comes trouble,' said Lupus. 'That's Cato. One of our master's bitterest enemies. And, incidentally, the father-in-law of the other consul, Bibulus.'

The senator glared round at the other senators and the watching public, before finally fixing his dark, piercing eyes on Caesar.

'This measure,' he began in an icy, contemptuous tone, 'is little more than a brazen attempt to win the support of the mob for the personal political glory of Caesar and his puppet master, Gnaeus Pompeius. The fact that Senator Crassus has performed an about-turn to add his support to theirs smacks of a conspiracy aimed against the members of this house and the people of Rome!'

'Ouch,' Lupus muttered. 'Caesar's not going to like that.'

Marcus turned his gaze towards his master and saw that he sat as still as a statue, his face fixed in a calm expression of concentration. If he was hurt or angered by the accusation, no onlooker would have guessed it. Marcus felt a growing admiration for his master.

'The land owned by the Republic is there for all the people!' Cato thundered. 'It is not the personal property of a general to distribute to his soldiers, however deserving they *may* be.'

His sarcastic tone was not lost on the onlookers and there were angry shouts from the crowd pressing round the windows.

'Aristocratic scum!' a voice close to Marcus yelled.

'They want the land for themselves!' yelled another.

Cato folded his arms and waited for the shouting to stop before he continued. 'Whatever the merits of rewarding our soldiers, this measure is a dagger aimed at the heart of Rome. Caesar and his allies intend to tighten their grip on power. It is up to us, fathers of the nation.' Cato swept his arms wide to indicate his fellow senators. 'It is up to us to make a stand against these men, these powerful figures conspiring against us from the shadows.'

An older man at his side clapped his hands together in loud applause and other senators joined in.

'That's Cicero,' Lupus explained. 'He's one of the wiliest jackals in Rome. He'll argue black is white and have you believe it too, until the moment you trip over the truth and fall flat on your face. Cicero's a man to keep an eye on – any devious back-room deal negotiated in Rome, you can be sure he'll be in on it.'

As Cato resumed his address, Marcus couldn't help wondering at the bitter rivalry between the members of the Senate. He had never really thought about politics before – Rome had seemed so far away from his old life. Titus had always regarded politicians with contempt and said that man for man they could never be a match for the general who had marched his armies across much of the known world. From what little Marcus had gleaned from Titus as he was growing up, and others he had encountered since being brought to Italia as a slave, the Senate was supposed to be where the finest minds of the Republic met to discuss and pass new laws. Yet now that he stood in front of these senators, Marcus was struck mostly by the fact that they seemed to hate one another.

Cato continued to talk and talk and talk, as the first hour of debate dragged on into the second, and on past noon. He piled one accusation and insult on top of another and then went on into a rambling account of the long history of resisting tyranny that stretched back over hundreds of years to the age in which the Roman people rose up against their last king, Tarquin the

Proud, and first became a republic. At length some of the people gathered at the windows began to drift away. Marcus felt his feet begin to ache and he eased himself forward, resting his weight on the wooden rail. He had stopped listening to Cato and was bored. He was not the only one. Down on the senators' benches, several older members had dozed off, heads slumped forwards. The snores of one spindly old man, slumped against the back of his bench, were clearly audible as Cato droned on. Marcus noticed that Caesar's earlier patience had begun to crumble. Now he was openly scowling at Cato.

'It's as the master anticipated,' said Lupus. 'Cato means to talk out the proposal.'

'What does that mean?' asked Marcus.

'It means that if he keeps talking until sunset, then the clerk has to postpone the debate until the next day. If he does it tomorrow the measure will be put back again.'

'Is he allowed to do that?'

'It's in the rules,' Lupus shrugged. 'That's politics for you.'

'Surely our master won't allow him to get away with it.'

'No. He won't. But equally he doesn't want to be seen breaking the rules to push the measure through. Not if he can help it.'

Marcus looked down towards the two consuls sitting in their

special chairs. Caesar was frowning as his fingers drummed on the arm of his chair. Bibulus sat beside him – a faint smile on his face as he folded his hands together contentedly.

An hour after noon Cato paused momentarily to sit down and send a clerk to fetch him a drink. At once Caesar was on his feet.

'I thank Senator Cato for his contribution to the debate. I'm sure we've all enjoyed the history lesson.'

Several of the senators laughed. Cato rose up, shaking his head as he raised his arms to draw attention to himself. 'I have not concluded my speech!'

'But you have,' Caesar insisted with a smile. 'When you took your seat again.'

'I was merely pausing. I have not finished.'

'You have said more than enough already, and tested our patience to the limit,' Caesar responded firmly.

'I will not yield my right to speak until I am ready to,' Cato countered.

'You have abused your right,' argued Caesar. 'You have made your opposition to my measure clear to all. Now it is the turn of someone else.'

'That is for me to decide! I will not stand down.'

'Then you are refusing to respect the rules of the Senate.'

Caesar sat down and clicked his fingers towards the lictors standing behind the consuls' chairs. 'Remove that man from the Senate House!'

A series of gasps and mutterings came from the senators. After a brief hesitation the leader of the lictors gestured to his men and they strode up between the stone benches and surrounded Cato, who folded his arms and stood his ground defiantly. When he refused to budge, two of the lictors took him by the arms and dragged him towards the aisle.

'You can't do this!' Bibulus protested loudly. 'This is an outrage!'

'And Cato's actions are against the rules,' Caesar responded. 'He has made his point and now he is obstructing a free and fair debate. We shall continue without him.'

Marcus watched in astonishment as Cato was dragged out of the chamber and pushed a short distance down the steps outside. He made an attempt to re-enter but the lictors firmly barred his way. Inside the chamber Bibulus had risen to his feet, his face almost purple with rage.

'This is a scandal! An outrage! This is tyranny!'

'No, it isn't,' Caesar replied calmly. 'If it was, then no doubt you would already be dead.'

'You dare to threaten me? A consul of Rome?'

'Calm yourself, dear Bibulus, before you do yourself some mischief. Let us continue the debate.'

'No! I refuse.' Bibulus struggled to raise his ponderous bulk from his chair. His head held high, he strode towards the entrance of the chamber. 'I will not go along with this attempt to abuse the power of the Senate. Furthermore, I will veto any attempt to vote on the measure.' He paused to look round at the other senators. 'I urge any of you who value your honour to join me, and Senator Cato.'

There was a short pause as the senators looked at each other self-consciously, then Cicero stood up and made his way over to Bibulus. Another senator joined him, then another, then more, until Marcus estimated that nearly a third of them had taken sides against Caesar. As they made their way out of the chamber, Caesar stood up.

'Today's business is adjourned. The debate will be resumed tomorrow, in the Forum, when I will set the matter before the people to decide.' As he concluded, he glanced up towards where Marcus and Lupus were watching events. He nodded at Lupus, then turned away to lead the rest of the senators out of the chamber.

'Come on!' Lupus grabbed Marcus's arm.

'What is it?'

'A little surprise for our friend Bibulus that Caesar planned earlier. It's richly deserved . . .'

They pushed their way through the remaining crowd and hurried down the steps at the front of the Senate House to where Festus was waiting with Caesar's bodyguard. Above them, the senators of both factions were mingling on the stairs. Marcus could see Cato and Bibulus protesting indignantly as they rallied their supporters.

Lupus stood in front of Festus. 'The master is ready to spring his surprise.'

'Oh, good!' Festus rubbed his hands together and turned to one of his men. 'Everything ready?'

'Yes, sir.' The man chuckled as he nodded towards something behind him that Marcus couldn't quite see. 'He'll get the shock of his life.'

'Right then, we'll strike the moment Bibulus heads down the steps. You boys stay close to me and watch yourselves. Could get rough.'

'Yes, sir,' Marcus replied. 'But don't worry, I can look after myself.'

'So I've seen. Then keep an eye on Lupus for me.'

They waited a moment until there was a cry from the crowd in the Forum.

'Here he comes!'

Caesar emerged into the afternoon light, flanked by Pompeius and Crassus. He pointed an accusing finger at Cato and called out loudly, 'You have defied the people's will today, my friend, but you cannot deny them their due reward forever.'

'We'll see!' Cato shouted back. 'Come, Bibulus, the air here is too foul for us to linger.'

Swinging round, Cato began to descend the stairs, as Bibulus and the rest of their faction hurried after him.

'Here we go, lads!' Festus waved his arm towards them.

The men surged forward, shouting threats and insults as they stormed up the steps. Marcus did his best to stay close to Lupus while keeping up with the men, clutching the shaft of his club tightly. The scribe's eyes were wide with fear and he clutched his satchel to his side as they were buffeted by the crowd. Ahead, Marcus could see Cato. Fear momentarily flickered across his face. But then he stopped, drew himself up and glared scornfully at the band of men. Bibulus and the others stumbled to a halt.

'Down with Cato!' Festus bellowed. 'Down with Bibulus!'

Caesar's men closed in on the senators and jostled them. The lictors assigned to protect Bibulus rushed forward to break up the struggle.

'Now!' Festus called out.

Marcus saw the man he had been speaking to press forward with a large bucket in his hands. He pushed his way through until he was standing beside Bibulus and then tipped the contents over the consul's head. A lumpy slurry of sewage poured over him, covering his face and streaking down his white toga. The air was filled with a foul stench and the crowd around Bibulus sprang back.

Festus and his men roared with laughter as they retreated and so did the crowd in the Forum as they caught sight of the hapless consul. Even Lupus had forgotten his fear and was grinning as they watched Bibulus stand in numbed shock before attempting to wipe the excrement from his eyes.

'Oh dear, oh dear,' Caesar called out as he made his way down the stairs. 'You seem to be up to your neck in something unmentionable, my dear fellow.'

Bibulus turned towards him, thrusting out his finger. 'This is monstrous! This is an outrage! And you are behind it, tyrant!'

'Me?' Caesar touched his chest and did his best to look innocent. 'I would never even think of doing anything so dishonourable to one of Rome's most outstanding figures, and your figure is certainly outstanding.' Caesar nodded at Bibulus's huge belly.

The senators at his back joined in the laughter of the crowd. Burning with rage at his humiliation, Bibulus stormed down the stairs, accompanied by Cato and the others. The crowd scurried out of their way and jeered as they passed through the Forum.

'That's that then.' Caesar nodded with satisfaction as he exchanged smiles with Pompeius, Crassus and their friends.

Marcus had enjoyed the humiliating spectacle as much as the rest of Caesar's men, but his smile froze on his lips as his gaze fixed on one of the men standing close to Crassus – a tall, bald man with a thin face. He was smiling widely as he offered his congratulations to Caesar. Marcus recognized him at once, even though they had met only briefly on a single occasion. His heart filled with icy hatred and he tightened his grip on the handle of the club.

As Caesar turned his attention to another of his supporters the man stepped back and glanced round the crowd. His eyes passed over Marcus and then he looked away again, his attention drawn by something Crassus was saying.

Marcus continued to stare at him, his body rigid with tension as he recalled their last meeting. When he and his mother stood in a slave pen in a small Greek town, the night before they were due to be auctioned, this man had come to gloat over their miserable fate. That same man, the tax collector Decimus, was the cause of all their suffering. A short distance behind him stood another familiar face, and Marcus caught his breath. Thermon. The man who had killed Titus.

5

Marcus hardly slept that night, but lay on his bedroll staring up at a thin shaft of moonlight shining through the slit window high up on the wall. Lupus was lying on his back, snoring. The other boy, Corvus, lay curled up under his worn blanket, muttering to himself as he dreamed. So far they had exchanged only a few words about their backgrounds. Returning from the Forum, Lupus had told Marcus that he'd been born into Caesar's household and been a slave his entire life. And he'd heard from Corvus how he'd been sold as an infant to a gladiator trainer by his poverty-stricken parents. But the trainer's hopes of teaching Corvus disappeared when the boy broke his leg and was left with a limp. The lanista duly sold him to a slave dealer who had brought the boy to Rome, where he'd been bought as a kitchen slave by Flaccus.

Marcus's thoughts turned away from them. Since seeing Decimus and Thermon outside the Senate House, his mind had been in turmoil. For a while, his original plan to appeal to Pompeius for help were replaced by a burning desire for revenge with far-fetched plans to track down and kill Decimus.

Gradually his rage faded and Marcus began to think about the implications of the tax collector's presence in Rome. If he was a supporter of Crassus, who in turn was an ally of Caesar and General Pompeius, then the situation was more complicated than before. How could Marcus appeal to Pompeius for help in freeing his mother and bringing Decimus to justice for kidnapping them, if the tax collector was a close associate of Pompeius's key ally? Pompeius would never side with Marcus against a man as powerful as Crassus.

Even while he felt despair at this new turn of events, Marcus realized it also gave him an opportunity to discover where his mother was held. If he knew the location of Decimus's farming estates in Greece, he might find out where his mother had been sent. Then he was struck by the cold reality of his situation. Marcus was only a slave. How did it help to know where she was if he couldn't free her? And Pompeius clearly had more important matters to think about – why should he help Marcus?

The confrontation at the Senate House had shown Marcus how divided the powerful families of Rome were. From all he'd heard and seen today, the Senate was riven by politicians jostling for power and the affection of the mob. What struck Marcus most was the way Caesar had abused his power, deliberately offending his opponents. Clearly, he enjoyed taking risks. Although Marcus understood little of Roman politics, it seemed to him that such men were a danger to themselves, and to those who followed them.

Marcus shuffled on to his side and closed his eyes. For a moment his mind wandered, and then he found himself thinking of Portia. She was the closest he'd had to a friend for a long time. At first fearful of the consequences of speaking to her alone, he'd begun looking forward to more time with her once he assumed his duty as her bodyguard. But first he had to complete his training and wondered if this would be as hard and dangerous as that of Porcino's gladiator school. One thing was clear: Marcus would be in as much danger on the streets of the capital as he had been facing wild wolves in the arena.

It was hours later, after his mind had turned over the situation with Crassus, Pompeius and Decimus a hundred times and he was still no closer to coming up with an answer, that Marcus's weary mind finally began to embrace sleep.

'Wake up, Marcus, you dozy fool!' Festus shouted at him, whipping his cane out and flicking the end on to his shoulder. There was a burning pain and Marcus grimaced as he jumped back and held his club out in front of him, ready to parry the next blow. Marcus did not resent his hard treatment. After all, Festus was training him to survive, and he knew he'd been slow this morning, finding it difficult to concentrate after his miserable night. But he had reached a decision – he would bide his time and find out how Decimus fitted into Caesar's world. Then he could decide how best to act. He focused himself once more on the fight, knowing these skills were needed to protect Portia.

'That's it.' Festus nodded with satisfaction. 'Much better, Marcus. Now stay alert. You can't afford to react slowly in the streets. You could face an attack from any direction, at any time. And unless your eyes and ears are razor sharp it'll be too late to do anything.' Before he had completed his sentence his cane was lashing out again. This time he aimed it in a wide arc

64

towards Marcus's other shoulder. It was an obvious move and Marcus instinctively moved to block it. As soon as he did so Festus flicked the cane up and brought it down towards Marcus's head, hissing through the air. Marcus dropped down on one knee and threw his club up so that the cane cracked against the shaft instead.

'Good lad,' Festus grunted approvingly as he stepped back and lowered the cane. Once again they were in the small yard at the side of the house where Festus trained and exercised his men. 'When you're outside the house that club will be the first weapon you can use in a fight. Any blades you carry will be tucked in your belt or hidden under your tunic. They'll be no use if you're suddenly attacked. They're only for when you have time to draw them out. Or when it's you that's making the attack, or setting an ambush. Got that?'

'Yes, sir.'

'Of course, there's more than one way to use the club,' Festus continued as he swept his cane above his head. 'Only an idiot or an untrained fighter, which comes to the same thing on the streets, just swings the thing around.'

He lowered the cane and thrust the tip forward, pulling back the blow at the last moment so the point gently tapped Marcus on the chest. Marcus did not flinch, or even blink, just as he'd been taught. Taurus had once said that a fight between gladiators was half won the moment one of the combatants stared out his opponent.

Festus chuckled approvingly. 'Perhaps the master was right. There's a natural warrior inside you. With the right training and provided you live long enough, you might be a fine gladiator one day.'

Marcus felt his blood chill at the thought. The last thing he wanted was to be forced to fight another person to the death just to entertain a bloodthirsty mob – two slaves turned on each other for the pleasure of their masters.

Suddenly he had the unnerving sensation of another person standing at his shoulder, watching over him. He glanced round briefly but saw only the plain weathered plaster on the wall of the yard. Nevertheless, he had felt the presence of something, or someone, and a chill rippled down his spine. Perhaps it was the shade of his father – his real father, Spartacus. What would he think of his son working for one of the most powerful men in Rome, someone who represented everything his father had fought against?

Marcus realized a brief silence had fallen and saw Festus looking at him irritably. He quickly recalled the last words spoken to him and hurriedly cleared his throat.

'Yes, sir. I hope so. A champion that Caesar will be proud to own.'

Festus's expression relaxed into a smile. 'That's the spirit, boy. You have ambition. I like that. Still, ambition is only a small part of the struggle towards greatness. A gladiator needs strength, self-discipline and skill, and these only come through absolute dedication and training. Is that clear? There are no short cuts.'

Marcus nodded, and Festus continued. 'Now back to the lesson. It's vital that you are adept with the club before you guard Mistress Portia. If you fail to protect her, you can be certain the master will make you pay for it with your life. In that case, what have you to lose? If you are forced to fight to save her, you must be prepared to die.'

'Yes, master.' Marcus nodded solemnly. He had a brief vision of rescuing Portia again, saving her from some faceless attackers. He pushed the image aside. 'I understand.'

'Of course, fighting is a last resort,' Festus told him. 'Escape is always the first and best option. A bodyguard must not think like a soldier. If there is a choice between fight or flight, then you must always get the person you are protecting out of danger. But if it comes to a fight, remember you can use the point of the club as well as slashing with it.' He stabbed the tip of his cane savagely into the wall beside Marcus's shoulder, cracking the surface and sending chips of plaster flying through the air.

'See there.'

Marcus turned and saw the depression in the wall with the spidery lines leading out from the impact point. He could easily visualize the damage that blow could have done to flesh and blood.

'Imagine that was a man's face, or his chest,' said Festus. 'If you were lucky enough to strike him in the eye it would blind him, and perhaps kill him. Either way he would be out of the fight. A slashing blow from a club bruises muscles and might break bones, but it is a crude and clumsy technique and not as effective. Always look to end a fight as quickly as you can. There is no audience to please, no glory to be won. Just get it over with and get Mistress Portia to safety as soon as possible.'

They practised with the club for the rest of the day and Festus did not spare Marcus much pain as they sparred. Marcus gritted his teeth and continued, gradually refining his technique until he could block almost every blow, and anticipate his trainer's moves. Towards the end of the afternoon he even began to land his own strikes on Festus, making little effort to take the sting out of his cuts, or the power out of his thrusts with the end of the club.

Finally, Festus ended the lesson, rubbing his wrist where Marcus had just landed a sharp blow. He nodded grudgingly. 'You learn fast. Tomorrow we move on to the stave. Off to the kitchen with you. And get a good night's sleep. We'll start at first light.'

6

Dusk had closed over Rome by the time Marcus felt his way into the slave cell and dropped on his bedroll, exhausted. He touched the sore spots on his arms and chest where Festus had struck him during training and winced. There would be many more bruises in the days ahead. He lay on his back and shut his eyes. How he wished for his comfortable bed on the farm, with his mother and Titus asleep in the next room. Free to roam his father's land and play with Cerberus. He even missed helping the shepherd round up the goats and then sitting and watching over them as Aristides hummed a tune from the shade of an olive tree. At the time he'd found it boring, but how peaceful it had been – he hadn't even realized his own happiness.

The sound of shuffling steps and low muttering disturbed

his sleep and his eyes flickered open. Sitting up with a start, he saw two shadows heading past his bedroll towards the far end of the cell.

'Sorry,' Lupus muttered. 'Didn't mean to wake you.'

Marcus eased himself back on to one elbow and twisted round towards them as the two boys slumped on to their bedrolls. 'You're late to bed. What's up?'

'Flaccus, that's what,' Corvus growled. 'He had the two of us scouring the storeroom floor. Rats had left droppings every-where. Took forever to clean the place.'

'That's why I was roped in,' Lupus added.

'But not you, Marcus, eh?' Corvus complained. 'Seems you're special. You're in the master's good books. Lucky you.'

Marcus ignored the sneering tone. 'I'm still a slave, like you.'

'Well, there are slaves and there are slaves,' Corvus contin-ued. 'Kitchen boys like me, and scribes like Lupus here, and others like you.'

'How am I different?' asked Marcus.

'You're training to be Mistress Portia's protector, right?'

'Yes, so?'

'So you get better food than us, and you're favoured by the master. It's different for the likes of us. We work in the kitchen from before first light until nightfall, later if the master has

71

guests. I doubt he even knows I exist, so there's never a small reward or a tip for me. That's how we're different.'

'From what I heard,' Lupus interrupted, 'Caesar has you marked down to be one of his gladiators when you're old enough.'

'I'm already a gladiator,' Marcus replied.

'You?' Corvus laughed. 'You're still a boy. How can you be a gladiator?'

'I was trained at a school near Capua.'

'Have you ever been in a fight?' asked Lupus, sitting up and hugging his knees. 'You know, in the arena?'

'Once.'

'What was it like?'

Marcus was silent for a moment as he recalled the moment he had entered Porcino's small arena and walked across the sand to present himself to the wealthy Romans who had paid for a private show: four pairs of men and two boys, chosen to fight to the death. The memory filled his mind so vividly that he could recall the terror in his limbs, the sick feeling in his clenched stomach and the clammy sweat on his brow, even though the day had been chilly. Up above, in the box, the Romans laughed, snacked and placed their bets. He recalled that Caesar was busy chatting to a companion and had acknowledged the salute of Marcus and his opponent, Ferax, with a disdainful wave of his hand. Portia had been there too, though unlike the others, there seemed some pity in her eyes as she watched the spectacle. Then came the moment when Marcus turned to face Ferax and he recalled the fierce, cruel gleam in the young Gaul's eyes as he announced, in a low contemptuous growl, that he would kill Marcus. That had been the worst moment of all. Even now he shuddered.

'What was it like? I have never been more afraid of anything in my life.' Marcus spoke softly. 'There are no words to describe it. Just be grateful you have never had to live through it for yourself.'

There was a brief silence before Corvus snorted. 'Gladiators are supposed to be tough!'

'Be quiet,' Lupus said irritably. 'Marcus has faced death. He knows.'

'Then lucky him. If Fortuna smiles on him he'll be dead before he's twenty or he'll have won his freedom. Not like us, my friend. We were born into slavery and we'll be nothing more than common slaves until the day we die, or the master throws us out in the street to find our own graves. Ours is a living death. Your mate over there will never know what that means.'

Marcus listened to the exchange with a growing sense of bitterness. Unlike the other boys, he had been born free and lived free for the first ten years of his life. He knew what had been taken from him and felt that loss keenly, every day. He rolled on to his front and propped himself on his elbows, so he could face the others more directly.

'Do you not hope for freedom? Don't you even dream about it?'

'Why bother?' Corvus sniffed. 'I can never buy my freedom. There's no chance of coming to the master's attention through hard work or loyal service. Nothing I do can change things. This cell, the kitchen and slaves like you are all I will ever know. The only thing that matters is keeping your head down to avoid being beaten.'

'What about you, Lupus?' Marcus asked. 'Do you have no hope?'

The scribe was silent for a moment as he collected his thoughts. 'There's always hope. I've a plan. I can read, write and add up. If I work hard as Caesar's scribe, then he might reward me one day. I know others in my position have managed to save enough to buy their freedom. If they can do it, then so can I.'

'And then what?' sneered Corvus. 'After a lifetime slaving

74

for Caesar, and having paid him for the privilege, then what will you do?'

'I don't know exactly. Perhaps I'll also try to save enough to buy myself a small inn, close to the Great Circus. There're always hungry mouths at the races. I can make a decent living and buy a few slaves of my own.'

What hope was there that slavery might end if the slaves themselves looked forward to being masters? Marcus sighed inwardly, but said nothing. He knew many slaves were like Corvus, unlikely to stir themselves if it meant adding to their existing hardship. Then there were the others, in vast chain-gangs, worked until they dropped and too exhausted to think beyond surviving the next day. He couldn't bear to think of his mother enduring that. Perhaps Brixus had been right after all, he thought. Of all the evils in the world, slavery was the worst. To end it was the one cause worth fighting for, and dying for, if it came to that. He turned his attention back on his companions.

'If you both hate slavery so much, then why don't you do something about it?'

'What?' Corvus laughed. 'Has all that fighting knocked the wits out of you? We're just household slaves. There's nothing we can do but endure it.'

'You could fight it,' Marcus suggested softly, in case he was overheard by anyone in the corridor outside. 'You wouldn't be the first slaves to defy their master. It's been done before.'

There was a nervous pause before Lupus spoke up. 'You're talking about Spartacus, aren't you?'

'Of course.'

'You should be careful what you say,' Lupus hissed. 'If Flaccus heard you he'd have you beaten. The gods know what Caesar would do if he found out. It was his friend, that Crassus, who crucified the slave rebels along the Appian Way. Is that what you want for yourself, Marcus?'

Marcus had heard of the terrible punishment imposed by Crassus, a man who was now the ally of Caesar, and apparently of Decimus too. Much as he'd come to admire his new master, Marcus was wary of his ambitions, and of those men Caesar called his friends. He was silent for a moment before he continued.

'But what if Spartacus had won? You'd be free to do as you wanted, both of you. Isn't that something worth fighting for?'

'Maybe. But Corvus is right, there's nothing we can do about it.'

'Not alone,' Marcus replied. 'But there are slave bands in the hills and mountains, survivors of the rebellion, and those who escaped to join them. What's to stop us doing the same?'

'What's the point?' asked Corvus. 'Why run away and live the rest of your life in some damp cave, always living in fear of the day you're caught and punished? If that's what you mean by freedom you can keep it.'

'But what if there was a new leader to unite those bands of slaves?' Marcus suggested. 'A man like Spartacus? Someone who could train them how to fight the Roman legions, as he did?'

'Spartacus is dead,' Corvus said bluntly. 'There is no one to replace him. The bands of slaves will be hunted down and destroyed one by one. That's the truth of it, my gladiator friend. But if you're so keen, why don't you become the new Spartacus, eh? Take up the challenge. Be the champion of the downtrodden, and put an end to the greatest empire in the world while you're at it.' He laughed again, a hollow unpleasant laugh. 'I'm tired. So is Lupus. We need to sleep. Keep your fancy dreams to yourself, Marcus.'

Corvus settled down and curled into a ball under his blanket. Lupus stayed sitting for a moment before he whispered, 'Could it be done? Another revolt? Could we win next time?'

Marcus took a deep breath and sighed. 'I really don't know . . .'

'A pity,' Lupus muttered. 'I'd have liked to know what it is to be free.'

He lowered himself down and began to breathe deeply, then started to snore. Once again, Marcus felt sleep wouldn't be so easy for him. He turned on to his back and stared up at the ceiling, deep in thought.

7

As the days of early spring passed, Marcus learned to use all the weapons that Festus required him to master before he could be entrusted with Portia's safety. He'd had no further opportunity to see Pompeius or to learn more about Decimus's involvement in Caesar's political circle. Marcus was sure his influence couldn't be good, but he could no more prove that to his master than he could hope to escape and find his mother on his own. For now, he resigned himself to doing well at his task and hoping that Caesar might reward him in a way that would help his cause.

Festus had taken Marcus into the streets on a few occasions to teach him to blend in with a crowd and watch for signs he was being followed, or for any ambushes. He was also taught the layout of the heart of Rome and districts that surrounded it. There was one place Festus didn't take him, an area on the side of the Aventine Hill known as 'The Pit', where some of the hardest street gangs in Rome were to be found.

'Trust me, Marcus, you never want to go anywhere near The Pit. The men that live there are animals . . .'

Besides the club and staff Marcus learned how to use knives, and how to throw them. Festus had hurled a blade across the yard so that it landed a short distance from the centre, handle canted up at a slight angle.

'A good strike will usually bring a man down if it hits him close to the spine, or in the back of a knee. But that would be a lucky throw. You're more likely to just slow him down and make him bleed a bit before you can close the distance and finish him off. That's if you're good enough to hit him in the first place.'

Festus pulled out another knife from the holsters at the back of his broad belt. 'Here. You have a go.'

Marcus took the knife and felt its weight. The blade was no more than six inches long but broad in proportion, with a deadly tapered point. The handle was thin and covered in an abrasive material – shark skin, according to Festus. He stood side on to the target and spread his feet wide to balance his body when he threw the knife. Then he held the blade between

80

thumb and forefinger as he'd seen Festus do a moment before. Drawing his arm back behind his shoulder, Marcus squinted at the straw archery butt and hurled his arm forward, releasing his grip on the blade at the last moment. The knife whirled end over end across the yard, deflecting off the corner of the target before striking the wall beyond with a dull clang.

'Not bad for a first effort,' Festus conceded, handing Marcus another knife. 'Try thinking of a pipe between your eye and the target, then concentrate on throwing it down the line right through the centre of the pipe.'

Marcus did as he was told and this time his aim was better. But he had concentrated on accuracy rather than power and the blade fell short of the target. But after a few more attempts he began to hit the target and he felt a thrill of pride each time.

'That's good,' Festus said, nodding. 'A few more like that and you'll be able to kill at a distance. That'll save you the risk of taking 'em on hand to hand.'

Marcus felt his pride turn to guilt as he recalled the grim purpose behind the new skills Festus was teaching him. Even so, he continued his training, grimly determined to master the weapons of his trade. He knew that one day Portia's life might depend on it.

After the knives, Festus moved him on to the sling, bolass and knuckledusters. Landing blows with the latter was a painful business, but Festus drove him for an hour at a time. Marcus threw his weight into the blows, landing on a tough, leather-covered post in the yard. Each time Festus would call out the targets in a monotonous tone. 'Head . . . Gut . . . Head . . . Gut . . . Head . . .' Marcus found the training brutal and relentless, but at least it forced him to forget his problems.

It was late one afternoon and they had nearly completed training for the day when the sound of a commotion in the street outside carried over the wall of the yard. There were desperate shouts amid the baying and jeering of a mob and the crash of stalls being overturned. The sounds quickly passed along the side of the house and were followed by a hammering at the front door.

'Come on!' Festus commanded and they ran back into the house and down the short corridor to the entrance hall. Caesar had just returned from his duties at the official residence in the Forum and was already standing by the door as a handful of his bodyguards spilled out of their quarters, armed with swords and clubs. He looked round as Festus and Marcus joined him.

'Better prepare for a fight!'

Festus drew a knife from his belt and nodded as Marcus

clenched his fist tightly round the grip of the knuckledusters, lowering himself into a crouch.

The hammering on the door increased in intensity and someone cried out, 'For pity's sake, open up!'

'By the gods, I know that voice!' Caesar exclaimed. He stepped up to the door and shot open the viewing slot, peering cautiously through it. 'Crassus!'

He grabbed the locking bar, shoved it into the receiver and raised the latch. At once the door pressed inwards and Senator Crassus stumbled into the entrance hall, swiftly followed by a handful of men and the slaves who'd been carrying his litter. All of them were bruised and blood oozed from cuts on their arms and heads. Crassus had lost his toga and his finely patterned purple tunic was torn in several places. Behind them came three of the senator's bodyguards, burly ex-gladiators, fighting off the mob outside with thick staves that they thrust into the shouting faces of their pursuers.

'Help me shut the door!' Festus ordered as he braced his shoulder against the heavy studded timbers. Some of the body-guards hurried to his side and braced their feet on the tiled floor. Festus shifted to the side and raised his knife. Marcus joined him.

Together they swung home the heavy timbers and the door

closed with a deep thud. At once Caesar snatched at the locking bar and wrenched it across into the bracket. For a moment the other men continued to press against the door, as if they feared it might suddenly lurch open, but the pounding on the far side and the angry shouts came to nothing as the door held firm.

Caesar hurried to help Crassus up from the floor. 'My dear friend, are you all right?'

'I am now.' Crassus smiled weakly. 'But that was close. I'm sure they would have killed me if they could.'

Caesar shook his head. 'They wouldn't dare.'

'Really?' Crassus cocked an eyebrow and nodded towards his men. 'I've lost five of my bodyguards, and most of the litter bearers.'

'What happened?'

'I was on my way to confer with Pompeius. We had just crossed the Forum and were by the edge of the Subura when a crowd blocked the route ahead. Before we could react, another group had blocked the street behind us. That's when they started throwing the rocks. There was nothing my litter bearers could do to protect themselves. They had to set the litter down. As soon as I got out I could see we were trapped. There was only one way out, an alley leading into the Subura.

Your house was the closest safe shelter I could think of, and here we are – what's left of us.'

Crassus was trembling as Caesar took his arm and steered him gently away from the front door.

'We need to talk. Come to my study. Festus!'

'Yes, master?'

'See to these men. Have their wounds treated.'

'Yes, master.' Festus bowed his head then turned towards Marcus. 'You can help me, Marcus. It's time you learned how to treat wounds as well as inflict them. Better take those knuckledusters off first, though, or you'll do more harm than good.'

8

Later that evening, after Crassus had left the house under the protection of every man that Caesar could spare, Marcus went to the benches in the corner of the garden to think. He was deeply frustrated by his situation, and Crassus's impromptu visit had reminded him he was failing in his goal to free his mother. Once he had thought his quest would be over the moment he reached Rome. He just had to find General Pompeius's house and explain what had happened, and it would all be sorted out. He and his mother would be freed and Decimus punished. But now? He was no closer to finding a way to put his case to Pompeius. Worse still, Decimus was a friend of Crassus, and Crassus was an ally of Caesar and Pompeius. He realized he'd been stupid and naive. This world was far more complicated than he'd thought – how could he ever hope to use it to his advantage? He let out a bitter sigh and cursed the fates that had brought him so close to the end of his quest, only to withhold the final prize.

'I thought I saw you come in here.'

He looked up and saw Portia standing in the gap in the hedge that screened the benches. She smiled at him and came and sat down. 'We haven't spoken for days. I had begun to wonder if you were avoiding me.'

'Festus has kept me busy,' Marcus explained. 'He wants me ready to protect you as soon as possible. There's been no let-up. Now I see why.'

'That attack on Crassus, you mean?'

Marcus nodded. 'If that can happen to a man so powerful, then it can happen to anyone. I had no idea the mob could be so dangerous. Crassus said it looked like a trap.'

Portia nodded. 'I was in the library. It's separated from Uncle's study by a curtain, so I heard him and Uncle Gaius talking. At first I meant to creep out and leave them to it. But then I decided to stay and listen. Uncle rarely tells me much about his plans, so I couldn't resist eavesdropping. I don't see why I should be treated like a child. I'm old enough to under-stand what is going on.' She frowned. 'Just because I am a girl they treat me like a fool. Something to be patted on the head and kept amused while a suitable husband is found for me. All I want is a bit of freedom to make my own choices. It's not fair . . .'

Marcus saw her lip begin to tremble and felt a pang of sympathy for Portia. They were alike in more ways than he had thought.

She bit her lip and forced a smile. 'You remember the trouble over the law that Uncle Gaius is trying to pass? The one to provide land for Pompeius's veterans?'

'I could hardly forget.' Marcus recalled the confrontation between Bibulus and Caesar, and the excrement on the head of the unfortunate Bibulus. He could not help smiling at the memory. 'A messy business, for the other consul.'

Portia laughed briefly. 'Well, apparently, after that Bibulus went back to his house and has refused to come out since. He issued a proclamation that it isn't safe for a consul to be seen in public while Caesar's thugs rule the streets. He's also said that he will refuse to recognize any laws passed in his absence – which makes no difference to my uncle. He's carried on with things at the Senate House without Bibulus, even though Cato's done everything to throw obstacles in the way. But that's not all. There have been attacks on several senators who support Uncle, just like what happened to Crassus. He thinks there's more to this than the usual clashes between supporters of the political factions.'

Portia's information was interesting. It was difficult for Marcus to piece together the events of Caesar's world, and he nodded thoughtfully as he recalled his earlier conversations with his master. Caesar had known he would be facing dangerous opponents, men prepared to use violence to get their way. So far it seemed Caesar had been restrained, but Marcus knew his master would be forced to match the tactics of his enemies, if only to preserve his own life and that of his family.

Marcus looked up at Portia. 'Sounds as if Cato and his friends have been stirring up the mob.'

'That's what Uncle thinks. He's heard someone is spreading a rumour that he has a secret plan to take control of Rome together with General Pompeius and Crassus.'

'That's the kind of rumour you'd expect his enemies to put about.'

Portia's eyes widened as she leaned closer to Marcus. 'That's just it. There actually is a secret plan. I heard Uncle and Crassus talking about it. Until a few months ago Pompeius and Crassus were bitter enemies. Then Uncle persuaded them they could have more power if they worked together instead of obstructing each other. He reminded Crassus of it this evening. In exchange for supporting each other in the Senate they'll each have command of a big army and a chance to win more glory and loot.'

'Loot?' Marcus asked, even though he knew the answer already.

'The usual kind. Gold, silver and slaves.'

Slaves, he reflected bitterly. Even more misery to add to that endured by the millions Rome already kept in bondage. The idea sickened him. Much as he'd come to admire his master, Marcus reminded himself that Caesar was Roman to the core and would always be an enemy of all that Spartacus stood for.

'Anyway,' Portia continued, 'that's not the most interesting part. Uncle Gaius and Crassus were planning the best way to make sure their deal with Pompeius continues to work. Uncle suggested it might be best to bind Pompeius more closely to him by arranging another marriage.' Portia paused and her expression darkened. 'My uncle is going to suggest to Pompeius that I should marry his nephew to cement their arrangement . . .'

'Married? You?' Marcus stared at her in shock. 'But you're only thirteen, just two years older than me.'

'I'm nearly fourteen,' Portia replied dejectedly. 'More than old enough to be offered in marriage. Many girls are married at my age, some even younger. That is the way in Rome. Sometimes it's for love, but mostly to create alliances between families with influence.'

Marcus digested the news with a sense of distaste. What was marriage without affection, he wondered. He remembered his mother and Titus. Despite the way they had first met there was genuine fondness between them, until the end. As Portia's news sank in he felt a pang of despair at the thought of losing his friend so soon.

'How do you feel about being married?' Marcus asked.

Portia clasped her fingers together as she considered her reply. 'I'm not really sure. It's so sudden. Uncle never mentioned the possibility to me. I always knew that I would be married one day and forced to leave my family and home behind. I just hoped I'd be lucky enough to marry someone I liked.' She was silent for a moment before she continued bravely. 'I suppose I should consider it an honour to marry into a family as famous as Pompeius's.'

Marcus watched her face as she contemplated the possibility and saw the sadness in her eyes. He shared her mood. He would miss her. Then a further thought struck him. If Portia married Pompeius's nephew, maybe she could use her influence to allow

Marcus to put his case before Titus's former commander. Before he could think this through, Portia spoke again.

'There is a problem, though,' she said. 'Crassus is not keen on the idea. He told Uncle Gaius that I should marry a relative of his as a way of repaying him for all the money Uncle has borrowed.'

Marcus's brain was whirring. He needed to think. If Caesar was indebted to Crassus and Crassus was in league with Decimus, what did that mean, for Caesar, and for Marcus? 'What did your uncle say to that?' Marcus asked her.

'He said he knew how much he was indebted to Crassus, and that he'd always be his loyal friend. But Pompeius does not share that bond, and it would be useful to make sure he didn't break away from their secret alliance. Crassus didn't sound convinced.' She frowned briefly and they both sat silent again. Marcus thought how both their lives were at the mercy of the ambitious manoeuvring of supposedly 'great' men. And for whose benefit? Then Portia sighed and her forced smile returned. 'There's no use moping. I suppose I should be pleased at the idea.'

'Yes, I suppose so.' He forced a smile in return.

Her forehead creased into a faint frown. 'The news saddens you too?'

'Yes . . . Yes, it does,' he replied truthfully. 'You're the first friendly face I have known for a long time. I had looked forward to being your protector. That won't be possible now.'

'Maybe it will be. Perhaps I can take you with me if I marry. I'll ask Uncle to sell you to Pompeius.'

Marcus winced at her words. Sold again. *Like a mule.* At least it would take him closer to Pompeius, he supposed.

Portia continued in a flat tone. 'Anyway, it'll take a while to make any arrangement, so there's time to sort something out. I promise I'll do what I can to persuade Uncle to let you remain at my side.' She yawned and patted her mouth. 'I'm tired. It's been a long day and I need to sleep. I just wanted to share the news with you first, Marcus.'

She stood up and Marcus followed suit.

'Goodnight then,' she said.

Marcus bowed his head. 'Goodnight, mistress.'

He watched as she made her way out of the enclosed area and the sound of her footsteps faded away along the garden path.

9

Marcus resumed his training in the morning and did not see
Portia again until Flaccus summoned him the following week,
late in spring, and announced that Marcus was to escort his
mistress to the Forum next day. The master was holding a
small dinner at the house to announce his niece's betrothal and
she was to buy material for a new gown. It had been decided
to hold the marriage ceremony during the summer.

'Do you think I'm ready to protect her, sir?' Marcus asked
Festus when he found him sitting in the yard afterwards, drinking some wine. 'There's been trouble on the streets.'

'Not for a few days now,' Festus countered. 'Besides, it's a
political struggle between the master and his enemies.
Hopefully, no one will pay much attention to his niece and
the only thing you have to worry about is cutpurses and

footpads. You'll do fine, boy. I've trained you well. If there's any trouble you'll know how to react. Just remember to have the hood of your cloak up. It will help you keep an eye on your surroundings without making it obvious that's what you're doing.' Festus took a sip from his cup. 'Look out for any sign of trouble between Cato's supporters and our own. If anything kicks off, then get the mistress back to the house straight away. Don't stop for anything until she's safely indoors. Other than that, make sure you're tooled up. Club and throwing knives should be sufficient. You might want to take a felt cap with you.'

Summer was fast approaching and Marcus was confused by this suggestion. 'I think I'll be warm enough without it, thanks.'

'It isn't for warmth,' Festus explained. He put his cup down on the ground beside him and rummaged inside his tunic, then took out a small bundle of felt. 'See?'

He opened the cap out and Marcus saw it was bulkier than a usual cap.

'I've sewn some thick strips of cork into it. If you take a blow to the head, it'll absorb some of the impact. Here, take it. It'll be loose, so put some stitches in tonight to be sure it fits properly.' He shrugged. 'You never know, it might save your life.'

Marcus took the proffered cap, his heart warmed by this act of generosity from the crusty Festus. 'Thank you, sir.'

Festus drained his cup and patted Marcus on the shoulder. 'Best get some sleep, my lad. You'll need to be alert tomorrow.'

'Yes, sir.' Marcus turned and started walking in the direction of the slave quarters. Then he paused and looked back, holding the cap up. 'And thanks for this.'

'Look after it.' Festus smiled. 'I'll want it back, undamaged.'

Early next morning the small party emerged from Caesar's house and stepped down into the street. Besides Portia and Marcus there were the two kitchen boys. The cook had drawn up a list of the meats and fruits required for the feast and Lupus and Corvus were to carry these home once their mistress had paid for them. They set off towards the Forum, Portia leading the way, followed by the kitchen boys. Marcus walked a few paces behind them, where he could watch for danger and be ready to rush forward and protect her. Portia was wearing a plain cloak over her long tunic and her purse was out of sight. There was nothing to distinguish her from any other girl from a well-to-do household, out on a shopping expedition.

The street was already filled with people and the traders were setting out their wares on stalls lining the pavement on each side of the street. Passers-by were forced to pick their way through the piles of rubbish and human and animal waste that collected amid the cobbles until the next rainfall, when they would be washed away. Marcus barely noticed the stench, tensing as he concentrated on every side alley and looked for anyone suspicious, or any unusual movement. Every so often he would look back quickly to see if anyone might be following them. Immediately ahead of him, Corvus and Lupus chatted away, enjoying the escape from their regular duties. Marcus wondered if they would still enjoy the experience when they struggled back to the house, laden down by purchases. He smiled at the thought. Marcus had settled in with the other boys in his sleeping cell now they'd grown used to each other, with good-natured teasing and joking each night before they fell asleep, and he looked forward to ribbing them for being Portia's pack mules.

They reached the Forum without incident and merged with the crowds in the markets. As well as customers, the usual gangs of youths hung around the public fountains, talking loudly about the most recent chariot race and abusing other gangs who supported different teams. The beggars lining the side of the Sacred Way, or propped up in arches beside the temples, endlessly repeated their requests, their arms outstretched. Portia, moved by their plight, stopped to instruct Lupus, who was carrying her purse, to hand out a few small coins. Marcus casually wandered to the other side of the road and pretended to examine the fruit on a nearby stall as he scanned the street both ways.

Just then, a gap in the crowd opened up and Marcus noticed two men some fifty paces behind him. They had also stopped, and they stared up the street for a moment towards him before turning to each other, as if in conversation. They wore plain brown tunics, like most people in Rome, but their hair was cropped short and they looked tough. A certain tension in the way they held themselves caused Marcus to be suspicious. He kept watching them out of the corner of his eye while he stood in front of the fruit stall.

'You going to buy something, or just waiting to steal it?'

Marcus glanced up at the stallholder, a large woman with thick arms and a hard face. He shook his head and moved to the next stall. Further down the street, the two men had moved towards a stall where a dark-skinned trader was selling belts. Marcus watched them a moment longer, until Portia had tucked her purse away and was ready to continue. They entered the open area in front of the Senate House and turned towards the basilica, where the luxury items were sold. Marcus carefully looked back and scanned the crowd, but saw no sign of the two men. He wondered if he was jumping at shadows, but remembered Festus's stern advice – having an over-developed sense of suspicion was part of the job. Marcus glanced round the crowd again and still couldn't see them, so he hurried a few paces to catch up with Portia.

After the daylight in the street it seemed gloomy inside the basilica and it took a moment for Marcus's eyes to adjust. As he looked round, he was astonished by the variety and quality of the goods on sale: fine rolls of bright cloth and the shimmer of silk, baskets of dried fruits from across the seas, racks filled with jars of the best wines, sets of finely carved figurines of Roman soldiers, barbarians and gladiators – all at prices far beyond the means of the vast majority of Rome's inhabitants. Marcus had never seen such riches all in one place.

'We'll leave the cook's purchases till last, since they will be the heaviest,' Portia decided, smiling at Lupus and Corvus. 'No point in you being loaded down while I look for some cloth and scents.'

'Thank you, mistress.' They bowed their heads in gratitude.

'Well, come on then,' Portia chuckled. 'No dawdling.'

They slowly made their way between the shop counters laden with rolls of cloth and Portia stopped every so often to examine any material that caught her eye. Eventually she paid for a length of shimmering emerald-green cloth and instructed Marcus to carry it for her.

Marcus shook his head. 'It wouldn't be wise, mistress.'

'Oh?' Her nose lifted indignantly. 'And why is that?'

'For two reasons. It would make me stand out, and it would also encumber me if I had to act swiftly. Festus was quite clear on the need to avoid attention and being ready to fight.'

'Well, Festus isn't here, is he? Besides, it's all nonsense, Marcus. Who would be stupid enough to attack me in the heart of the Forum? And how could you not draw attention to yourself, the way you're skulking along behind me!'

Before Marcus could protest any further she turned and made off towards the scent shops, leaving him with the roll of material. He hissed through his teeth in frustration. Then he turned to the two boys. Corvus instantly held up a hand.

'No use looking at us, mate. We'll have our hands full as it is.'

'I'm serious.' Marcus held out the cloth. 'Take it. I have to protect her.'

'No way – she told you to carry it and we're not going to risk a flogging for disobeying her orders.' Corvus tugged the other boy's arm and they hurried after Portia.

Marcus muttered a violent curse under his breath as he tucked the material under his arm and took another look round before he followed them.

Portia went from shop to shop along the row of scent traders, sniffing from the fine glassware containers that she sampled. At length, she made a selection and reached for her purse as the shopkeeper beckoned her inside to choose a fine jar and stopper to take a measure of the scent away with her.

'Wait here,' she instructed. 'Once I'm done we'll head to the spice shops.'

She disappeared through the narrow doorway and Marcus glanced after her. Beyond the door the shop opened into a deep room with another door opening on to the street outside the basilica. There, another stall was manned by a young assistant who tried to tempt passing customers. The shopkeeper ushered Portia to a counter holding a selection of ornate scent bottles.

'By Jupiter,' Lupus muttered. 'I thought she'd never make up her mind.'

'And did you see the price of it?' asked Corvus with a shake of his head. 'Ten denarii! Unbelievable . . . Just to smell nice if anyone gets close to her at the dinner.'

'You might try some one day,' Lupus sniffed. 'You stink of fish.'

'That's because the bloody cook had me marinading stuff in garum first thing this morning. You try it and see if you come up smelling any better.'

Marcus moved away from their wrangling and looked up and down the row of shops, but there was no sign of the two men he'd seen earlier and he decided he must have been worrying about nothing. Just to make sure, he wandered a short distance to the end of another row of traders' stalls before returning to his position outside the scent shop. His thoughts returned to Portia's news from the week before. Having thought the matter over, Marcus saw how it offered him precisely the chance he needed to appeal to General Pompeius for help. But the presence of Decimus in Rome, and his closeness to Crassus, didn't look good and Marcus's mind clouded with doubt.

Marcus's thoughts were interrupted by a cry from inside the shop. He thrust the roll of cloth on to the table of scent jars and raced for the entrance.

Corvus looked startled. 'What's going on? Marcus?'

Marcus ignored him and ran into the shop, club held tightly in his clenched fist. The shopkeeper was lying on the floor, blood pulsing from a wound on his head. His eyes flickered as his assistant knelt beside him and pressed his hand over the wound to try to stop the bleeding. Marcus took in the scene in an instant.

'Where is she?' he asked.

The assistant glanced up with a dazed expression but did not reply.

'WHERE IS SHE?' Marcus shouted.

The assistant flinched, then thrust a quavering finger towards the door on the other side of the shop. 'They took her.'

A cold, sick feeling filled Marcus's guts. He heard footsteps as Corvus and Lupus entered the shop. Marcus ran towards the other door, shouting back over his shoulder.

'Follow me!'

10

His heart pounding with dread, Marcus burst into the street on the far side of the basilica, narrowly avoiding a chain gang of slaves carrying bundles of animal pelts. Lupus and Corvus scrambled after him. Even though the street was wide, it was filled with people and Marcus couldn't see far in either direction. He clambered on to a table, knocking a large jar off the edge to shatter on the flagstones below. At once the air was filled with a sweet, flowery fragrance.

'Oi!' a man at the counter of the neighbouring shop shouted. 'What's your game, lad? You'll have to pay for that!'

Marcus ignored him as he searched the street to his right desperately. The crowds stretched away in the shadow of the tall wall of the basilica, but there was no sign of anything out of place. He turned the other way as some of the passers-by stopped to stare. Marcus strained his eyes and then saw them – the two men he had spotted earlier, fifty paces away, and thrusting through the crowd while Portia's fists pounded the broad back of the man holding her. Several people who had been knocked aside shouted angrily in their wake.

Marcus cupped a hand to his mouth and thrust the shaft of his club after the men. 'Stop them!'

His voice was shrill with alarm and carried clearly down the street. One of the men glanced back, pulling at his companion's arm, and they turned into a side alley, out of sight. Marcus jumped from the table and chased after them, weaving through the throng as Corvus and Lupus did their best to keep up. As he ran, Marcus's mind was already racing ahead of him. He couldn't lose Portia. How could he live with himself if he let something happen to her? Not only that, but Caesar would exact a terrible price from the person entrusted with guarding his niece. No excuse would be accepted. He forced himself on as fast as his feet would carry him.

Faces in the crowd passed in a whirl and he ignored the cries of surprise and angry protest as he and the other boys dashed along the street. A short distance ahead, Marcus saw the entrance of the alley and pointed it out to the others.

'In there!'

He turned round the corner, half expecting to see the two men waiting for him, knives drawn. Instead, he met the sight of a gloomy passage winding up a gentle slope between closely packed tenement blocks. The ground was covered with packed-down refuse and at irregular intervals small heaps of rubbish were piled against the walls. The air was thick with the stink of sewage and an unpleasant trickle of dark liquid ran down the centre of the alley. There was a handful of people – a young mother leading a toddler by the hand, a struggling infant strapped to her chest and, further on, an old crone sitting on the steps beside the entrance to a tenement block, unpicking the stitching from a heap of old clothes.

Up ahead, two dark shapes, one burdened by Portia, were hurrying away. Marcus steeled himself to close on them as quickly as he could. Behind him, he heard the slap of the other boys' feet and the gasp of their breath as they struggled to keep up.

Ahead, the alley turned a corner and Portia and her kidnappers were lost from view. Marcus forced himself on, and as he reached the bend he saw them again, realizing with a surge of hope that he had closed the distance. They hurried on a short distance before turning into another alley. By the time Marcus reached it and raced round the corner, they were lost from view again. He scrabbled to a halt, blood pounding in his ears. Ahead, an even smaller alley snaked into the slum area, so narrow that two men side by side could barely make their way along it. There was no sign of them. More side alleys led off on either side for as far as Marcus could discern in the gloom. He started forward and looked down the first one to his right, but there was no sign of movement. Nor was there anyone in the next one on the left. A stab of despair pierced his heart. *If I've lost her, then Caesar will have me killed, or sent to the mines . . .*

Behind him there was a scramble of boots as Corvus and Lupus caught up.

'Where . . . are . . . they?' Lupus gasped, leaning forward to rest his hands on his thighs.

Marcus shook his head. 'Don't know. Must be close.'

Then ahead of him he saw an old man hunched up in a doorway – he hadn't noticed him at first. Marcus ran over.

'Have you seen two men pass just now?'

The man looked up and stared across the alley with a pair of milky-white eyes. With a sinking feeling, Marcus realized the man was blind. He began to turn away when the man gave a hoarse laugh.

'Seen 'em? No. Heard 'em. And the child that was crying.'

'They passed here? Which way did they go?'

The old man extended a hand up the alley. 'There, and then there was a crash of a pot before they continued.'

'Thank you.' Marcus patted him on the shoulder and waved the other two boys to follow him. After a short distance another alley, even darker, led off to the right. A pile of broken storage jars nearly filled the entrance, and Marcus turned into the winding passage, gesturing to his companions. 'This way.'

The alley led between the rear of two rows of tenement blocks and there were few doors or openings along its length. Marcus and the others had only gone a little way when the passage bent sharply and they could see the end, where it opened out on to a busy street. There was no sign of the two kidnappers. Marcus drew up.

'Where have . . . they got . . . to?' gasped Lupus.

'They must be along here somewhere,' Marcus reasoned swiftly. 'We must find them before they get away. We'll split up. You two go back and try every door we passed, every possible way they might have left the alley. I'll go on from here.'

Corvus looked at him. 'And what do we do if we find 'em?'

Marcus had little doubt the two men he'd seen were more

than a match for the two boys. He shrugged. 'Shout for help and pray to the gods that it comes.'

'Very useful,' Corvus grumbled.

Lupus pushed him back down the alley. 'Come on. There's no time to waste.'

Once they had gone, Marcus walked slowly forwards, ears straining for any sound that might lead him to the men who had taken Portia. The steady hubbub of the Forum had faded to a faint hum, with just an occasional voice from the apartments overhead and the dripping from a drain that emptied above the alley. The first few doors on either side were securely bolted from within and rattled when he tried them. An opening to the right further on led into a small courtyard, dimly lit by a small opening high above. Several women sat beside a communal fountain chatting. They looked up and fell silent as Marcus cautiously entered the courtyard. Glancing round, he raised a finger to his lips.

'Whacha want?' asked an older woman in a grating voice.

'I'm looking for some men.'

'Ain't we all, dearie?' said another woman, and her companions let out a shrill chorus of cackles.

'They had a girl with them,' Marcus persisted. 'Did they come this way?'

'A girl? Then we're out of luck, ladies. Seems the men are already taken.'

Marcus frowned angrily and left the courtyard, continuing his search further along the alley. He had tried two more doors when he heard a muffled cry a short distance ahead. He froze, ears straining as he held his breath. Then he heard it again, followed by a low growl. Marcus crept towards the sounds. There was a door ahead to the left and he edged towards it. The door was slightly ajar and looked as if it had been kicked in. There were sounds of a struggle before he heard a blow landing followed by a shrill cry of pain. Marcus reached the door and paused. He glanced back up the alley but there was no sign of the other boys. He dared not call out to them and alert the kidnappers, if they were the men beyond the door. Swallowing nervously, Marcus held his club ready while he eased the door back with the other hand. Slowly it began to open, revealing a large storeroom lined with shattered furniture and boxes, broken up for firewood. The two men stood a short distance inside the room, side on to Marcus. The one on the right held Portia, pinning her arms behind her back while his other hand was clamped over her mouth.

'You try to bite me again, you little witch, and I'll snap yer neck. Understand?' He tugged her arms up painfully and Portia let out a brief whimper before she nodded.

'That's better,' said the other man. 'You need to be taught some manners. Who'd have thought such a well-brought-up lady would be so vicious? Well, it's time you had a lesson. Something you'll never forget. Nor that uncle of yours.' He pulled out a knife from his belt and held it up to her cheek. 'When he sees what's happened to you, he'll know the price for making enemies in the Senate. Not that he'll be around long enough to grieve. Caesar will join you in the underworld soon enough, my lady,' he concluded with a sneer.

Portia's eyes widened in terror. Marcus swapped his club into his left hand and felt for the handle of one of the four throwing knives hidden in his belt. Kicking the door open, he stepped into the dimly lit storeroom.

'Let go of her!' he shouted.

The man grasping the folds of Portia's tunic turned angrily. But when he saw Marcus his mouth opened in a bark of laughter. Then his expression instantly switched to irritation. 'Get lost, boy! Or else . . .'

Marcus's throwing arm snapped forward and his fingers released the knife. The dull blade gleamed as it tumbled end over end across the room. With a loud whack, it struck the

111

man's shoulder, the lethal point punching deep into his flesh. He let out a howl of pain and surprise as Marcus snatched out another knife and hurled it towards the man's face. This time the man threw up his arm to protect himself and the blade pierced the palm of his hand. But Marcus had lost the advantage of surprise and the other man released his grip on Portia, thrusting her to one side. She stumbled across the room, crashing on to a pile of kindling. Her captor snatched a dagger from under his cloak, long-bladed with a deadly point. Lowering himself into a balanced crouch, he moved towards Marcus. His friend growled like an enraged animal as he tried to pull the knife from his hand.

Marcus drew his club back as he focused his attention on the man coming at him.

'You'll pay for that, boy,' the man snarled through gritted teeth. 'I'll cut you up good before I finish you.'

11

Marcus fought back his terror at taking on two men, far bigger than him. He knew that if fear took over, both he and Portia would surely be killed. An icy calm took hold of him as he assessed his hulking opponent – seeing the powerful build of his upper body, the scars on his face and forearm, and the way he favoured his right leg. The man feinted with the dagger, stabbing towards Marcus's face. He dodged to one side and swung his club, striking the man close to the elbow with a sharp thud.

The kidnapper grimaced and rushed forwards, trying to catch Marcus against the wall beside the door. Marcus held his ground until the last instant, then dived to one side and rolled back on to his feet. At once he swung the club again, aiming at his attacker's right knee. It struck a solid blow and the man let out a cry of agony as he crumpled to the floor. Festus's training was fresh in Marcus's head. When your opponent went down, you had to strike quickly while the initiative was yours. Marcus swung his club again, hitting the man's knife arm. It was a numbing blow and the man's fingers opened up, his dagger dropping to the floor. Marcus shifted his aim and struck his opponent's shoulder, and again on the head, a glancing blow. The kidnapper threw up his left arm trying to ward off the attack as he groped for the handle of his dagger.

'Marcus! Look out!' Portia's voice cut through the damp air.

He turned to see the man he'd wounded with the knives rushing towards him, a small studded club in his uninjured hand. Blood stained the cloth around the tear on his shoulder. Bellowing, with rage-filled eyes, he charged at Marcus. With no time to dodge, Marcus hunched down just before the man bowled into him, knocking him to the ground. The impact drove the breath from Marcus's lungs. Gasping for air, he scrambled to the side of the room as the man's impetus carried him forward a short distance. He turned and came at Marcus again, studded club swishing through the air as he swung at Marcus's head. Despite his quick reflexes, Marcus knew it was only a matter of time before he was struck and the greater power of the man's blows would shatter Marcus's bones like the kindling that lay heaped around the room.

He ducked one blow, and dodged the next, forced to give ground until he was caught against the far wall, close to Portia. He held up his club, ready to parry the man's vicious slashes, even as the knowledge that he would lose this fight filled his mind. He felt ashamed at his failure to protect Portia, and then fury that he was not strong enough to do the job properly. Despite his training, despite his toughness, the odds were over-whelming. The man towered over him, then raised up his club and swung it directly towards Marcus's head. Marcus grasped the shaft of his club in both hands and pressed it up to block the blow. There was a sharp crack as wood struck wood and the savage energy of the impact shot down his arms painfully. The man struck again and this time there was a splintering snap as the shaft of Marcus's club gave way.

'Hah!' The kidnapper roared with triumph, raising his club high to strike a crippling blow.

'No!' Portia cried out and there was a dark blur as a lump of wood struck the man on the side of the skull. He shook his head and whirled round towards her with a guttural snarl. 'You'll pay for that, girl!'

Marcus had to stop him. Still holding the two splintered ends of his club, he thrust them into the kidnapper's stomach with all his strength. The sharp splintered points ripped through material, then flesh and on into the man's guts and vital organs. The man groaned, arms dropping as he doubled forward, his face only inches from Marcus's. His jaw sagged and Marcus caught a waft of warm garlic breath. Marcus yanked the ends of the club back and thrust again, working them around in the kidnapper's stomach, doing further damage to the man's insides. He felt the warm gush of the man's blood on his hands.

With a tortured groan, the man tried to escape his tormentor, stumbling backwards, pulling the ends of the club out of Marcus's hands. He stared down in shock at the two lengths of wood protruding from his guts as he backed away. Marcus was still fighting to draw breath after his winding. Breathing heavily, he rose to his knees and glanced at his mistress.

'Are . . . you all . . . right, Portia?' he managed to wheeze.

She closed her eyes and shuddered as she nodded. Marcus had to get her to safety as swiftly as possible. As he stepped towards her, his ankle was grabbed in a powerful vicelike grip.

'Little swine!' the other kidnapper growled.

Marcus looked down to see the man grasping his ankle in one hand while the other held the dagger he had retrieved. He wrenched Marcus's ankle and Marcus fell heavily on to his back. Portia screamed. Instinctively Marcus lashed out with his spare foot and felt his studded sole strike the man's skull. He kicked again and again, desperately, but the man held on to his other foot, keeping him down, and then punched Marcus in the face with his dagger hand. A bright, numbing light burst inside his head and Marcus slumped back. The kidnapper thrust him aside and crawled towards Portia. She was trapped against the corner of the storeroom and stared in panic as the man shuffled forwards to loom over her, pinning her down with one hand. He raised his dagger, angling the point towards Portia's heart.

'This time you *will* die,' he muttered savagely.

'No . . .' Marcus stretched out a hand as his vision began to clear.

Two shapes blocked the light in a blur of movement behind him. The man paused to glance over his shoulder. Corvus reacted first, snatching a length of wood from a pile near the door. Springing forwards, he struck the man on the back of the head, forcing him to release Portia. As he turned on the two slave boys, Corvus struck again and the man lashed out with his dagger. The point caught the boy in the side, the impact driving the air from his lungs as he toppled against the wall. Lupus sprang past him with another length of wood and battered the man's head again and again, as hard as he could. The sound of the blows echoed around the storeroom and this time the kidnapper collapsed to the ground, unconscious.

In the stillness that followed, Marcus stared at the fallen kidnapper, and Lupus looked round the room, aghast. The only sounds were the gasped breaths from Corvus, then a long groan of agony. Marcus scrambled over to where the kitchen boy lay on his back, his mouth slowly working as he stared up, eyes wide with shock.

'I . . . can't . . . breathe,' Corvus mumbled thickly, a bead of blood trickling from the corner of his lips.

Marcus looked down and saw the tear in his tunic. It was already saturated with blood and when Marcus gently prised the cloth back he saw the wound in the kitchen boy's side through which the blood pulsed. Despite Festus's training, there was nothing Marcus could do to save him. He folded the bottom of Corvus's tunic over the injury and pressed on it, trying to stem the blood. Corvus groaned and squirmed under the pressure.

118

'Lie still or you'll make it worse,' Marcus ordered. 'Be brave, Corvus.'

The other boy looked up at him and nodded faintly. Then he licked his lips and whispered, 'Is she safe? Mistress Portia?'

'Yes.'

Portia heard her name and crossed the room to kneel beside Marcus. Quietly, she took Corvus's hand. His eyes flickered towards her and he smiled.

'You see, I live.' Portia forced a smile. 'Thanks to you.'

There was a brief silence before Portia squeezed his hand and continued. 'I owe you my life. I'll see that you are rewarded handsomely. I promise. There are few slaves who would be so loyal.'

Corvus frowned and his breathing was laboured as he struggled to reply. 'Didn't do it . . . because you're . . . my mistress. Did it . . . because you were in . . . danger.'

Abruptly he convulsed and tore free from Marcus's grip as a great rush of blood spilled from his wound.

'Marcus, *do* something!' Portia cried out, clinging to the kitchen boy's hand.

Marcus held Corvus down with one hand, trying to apply pressure on the wound with the other. Corvus began to shudder, his eyes blinking violently. Then he let out a long, deep sigh and his body slumped against the ground, lifeless. Marcus held his hand on the wound a moment longer, as if there was a chance that Corvus was still alive. Portia continued to hold his hand, her bottom lip trembling.

No one spoke for a moment and the only sound was the distant hubbub of the crowd in the Forum.

'He's gone, hasn't he?' said Lupus as he stood over them. 'Corvus . . .'

Marcus looked round and saw that Lupus's face was clouded with grief. He tried to offer some comfort. 'He's passed into the shades. He's free now, Lupus.'

'He's dead,' the boy replied bitterly. 'A handful of years as a slave and now he's dead.'

Lupus lowered himself to the ground and took Corvus's other hand. Marcus saw the tears glimmering in his eyes as Lupus stared down.

'He was like a brother to me. All the family I ever had.'

Portia looked at him, across the body. 'I – I had no idea.'

'Why should you? As far as you're concerned, we're just part of the furniture of your uncle's household. Now . . . he'll just have to buy himself a new kitchen boy.'

Marcus gently placed his hand on the other's shoulder. 'We

can grieve later, Lupus. Right now we must get Mistress Portia out of here.'

Portia shook her head. 'We can't just leave him here. It's – it's not right.'

'We'll send someone to fetch him once we reach home,' Marcus countered. 'Then Corvus can be given a proper burial.'

'Yes.' Portia nodded. 'I'll see to it myself.'

She allowed herself to be raised to her feet, and Marcus was pulling Lupus away from the body when a low chuckle came from the across the room.

'How touching.' The man with the shafts of wood protruding from his stomach gave a dry laugh and then winced. 'You'll all be joining the boy there soon enough. You, Caesar and the rest of them.'

Lupus snatched up the club he had used to knock the other man out and Marcus grabbed his arm to restrain him. 'Wait.'

'What?' Lupus snapped angrily. 'Let me kill 'em both.'

'He's finished.' Marcus nodded at the sneering man. 'His friend will be too, when his master discovers he has failed.'

'Then what difference does it make?' Lupus insisted.

'The difference between us and them, and that means everything. Besides, we have to get out of here. Now.'

Lupus stared at Marcus in confusion, then nodded slowly

and lowered the club. He turned towards the man at his feet and spat on him before he paced towards the door. Marcus gently took Portia's arm and steered her after Lupus. But before they reached the door, the man called after them.

'You're dead! You know that? Dead. You think this is the end? We'll never rest until you and that precious uncle of yours bleed to death in the streets!'

Marcus felt Portia shudder. Then she spoke in a quiet, numbed tone. 'Take me away from here, Marcus. Take me home.'

12

'This is an outrage,' Caesar said quietly when Marcus had finished his account of Portia's abduction.

The consul was sitting on a chair in his private study with General Pompeius when Marcus, Portia and Lupus returned, dishevelled and bruised. As soon as Marcus explained to Festus what had happened, Festus led a party of men to retrieve the bodies of Corvus and the two kidnappers. Meanwhile, the two boys and their mistress were taken to Caesar's study to describe the event in full.

'An outrage indeed,' Pompeius said, nodding. 'And not an isolated incident either. First Crassus was attacked and now your niece. And from what your slave boy here says, your enemies intend to threaten your life too. It seems our political opponents have increased the stakes, my dear Caesar. And they will pay dearly for their folly. I simply have to say the word and my veterans will scour the streets until we find the men behind this cowardly attack.'

Caesar shook his head. 'That is exactly what they hope for. The moment your followers start roughing people up, you can be sure that Cato, Cicero and their noble friends in the Senate will scream from the rooftops that tyranny has returned to the streets of Rome. If that view takes hold, then we will be undone, General – you, me and Crassus. We'll be called to account on whatever made-up charges they care to bring against us and you can be sure the jury will be stuffed with our enemies. It'll be exile for the three of us, and they'll confiscate all our property.'

'What can we do then?' Pompeius threw his hands up. 'Let them get away with it?'

'Not that, certainly.' Caesar shook his head. 'But whatever we do, it must not antagonize our supporters in the Senate. We'll deal with it later. In the meantime . . .'

He paused and held out his hand to Portia. 'Come here, my sweet.'

Portia stepped lightly forward and took his hand. Caesar looked up at a slight angle into her face, and then cupped her cheek with his hand. 'Are you sure they didn't hurt you?'

'I'm fine, Uncle – shaken, but no real harm done. Thanks to Marcus, Lupus and Corvus.'

'Ah yes, the kitchen boy who was killed in the fight. He can be replaced. But you can't be.'

'Corvus gave his life to save me, Uncle,' Portia said with deliberation. 'It was brave and noble of him.'

'Of course it was.' Caesar lowered his hand and patted her arm.

'And Marcus too. He fought like a lion and put one of the men down before he was overwhelmed.'

'He shall have his reward,' Caesar said soothingly, then nodded towards Lupus. 'The other boy too. Never let it be said that Caesar is ungrateful.'

Pompeius snorted. 'Reward the slave? Why? It was thanks to this young fool that she was taken in broad daylight in the first place.' He leaned forward in his chair and stabbed a finger towards Marcus. 'It was your duty to protect Caesar's niece. What kind of a bodyguard do you call yourself, eh? You are supposed to keep a watch on her at all times and yet Portia was snatched right from under your nose. I don't think you should be rewarded at all. In fact, if you were my slave, I would have you scourged, or nailed up as a warning to my other slaves of the price of failing in their duties.'

Marcus endured the tirade in silence. There was nothing else he could do. He was a slave and it was not his place to speak up for himself. The very act of doing so would place him in far greater danger. His mind still reeled with shame that he had failed Portia, and he seethed with anger at the way Pompeius was talking to him. Even worse, this was the very man he had hoped could help him find and free his mother – and now he regarded Marcus with open contempt and hostility. Why would the general ever want to help him?

'It's not Marcus's fault,' Portia intervened.

Pompeius turned to her, composing his angry expression into a kindly look of concern. 'I think that it is, my dear. I would be angry enough if he simply failed in his duty. The fact that he did so with respect to the young woman who is soon to be a member of my household is unforgivable.'

'No. It was my fault those men could take me without Marcus knowing. I ordered him and the other two to wait outside the shop. He was only doing as he was told. I don't blame him for that. Nor should you.'

Pompeius smiled at her. 'You have a good heart, child. But you do not understand that a man, no matter how young, has no excuse when he fails in his duty. For that he should be punished.'

Caesar shook his head. 'There will be no punishment for Marcus. I am in his debt for saving my niece once already, and today has only increased that debt. Look at him. See the bruises and cuts? I don't doubt that he risked his life to save my niece. Marcus, again, I offer you my thanks.'

Marcus was grateful his master didn't take the same view as Pompeius. He bowed his head and replied as steadily as he could. 'Yes, Caesar.'

'There shall be a reward for you, in due course.'

Before Marcus could respond there was a sharp rap at the door and Caesar straightened up in his chair. 'Come!'

The door opened and Festus stepped into the room, flushed from hurrying back from the slum. He closed the door behind him, strode up to Caesar and bowed briefly.

'Well?' asked Caesar. 'What did you find?'

'We have the boy's body, master.'

'What about the two men?'

'There were no other bodies in the storeroom. However, there was a smear of blood leading outside. We followed the trace a short distance before we found a man's body lying in a nearby alley. I had the men bring that back as well.'

'And the other attacker?'

'There was no sign of him, master.'

'A pity. It would have been useful to question him. We need to know who gave them orders to target my niece.' He turned to Marcus. 'While your memory is fresh, what can you remember about these men?'

Marcus collected his thoughts. 'They didn't look like ordinary men, master. They were solidly built. Close-cropped hair, like soldiers, or gladiators. They moved like professional fighters.'

'Gladiators?' Pompeius raised his eyebrows. 'Do you think our opponents are resorting to using gladiators against us?'

'Why not?' Caesar responded. 'It makes perfect sense. If Cato and the others are taking our conflict on to the streets, then why not employ men who know how to fight? In fact, I wish I'd thought of it first. I own several gladiator schools in Campania.'

'You're joking, of course,' said Pompeius. 'Think how it would look to the mob if a consul unleashed packs of gladiators upon them. It would be a scandal. Worse than a scandal, it would be a mistake.'

Caesar reflected a moment and flashed a smile. 'You are right – I am joking. Nevertheless, I will send for some of my best gladiators and have them billeted close to Rome, just in case.'

Pompeius sucked in a quick breath. 'It's your funeral, Caesar.

Just don't let it be mine as well, or that of our dear friend Crassus.'

Marcus was reminded of his conversation with Portia in the garden – it definitely appeared that whatever alliance existed between the three powerful aristocrats, it was an uneasy one, founded on mutual suspicion rather than any affection. And yet Caesar had let this man's nephew marry his only niece – a move that spoke more of his ambition than his love for his own flesh and blood. Caesar may have spared Marcus from any punishment this time, but Marcus mustn't forget a slave meant nothing to him, and he hardened his feelings.

Caesar was gently stroking his jaw as he considered the situation. 'If the other side has decided to use gangs to undermine us, then we must meet force with force. The trick of it will be to find an intermediary who has connections with the street gangs of Rome. Someone who can be persuaded to use his influence to serve our ends.' He looked up and fixed his eyes on Pompeius. 'There is such a man.'

Pompeius thought briefly, then his eyes widened in alarm. 'Not him. Not Clodius. Please not Clodius. The man is a thug, little better than a common criminal. We can't use him.'

'Why not? He could well be the answer to our difficulties.'

'Or he could just be adding to them, or making them worse.'

'Then let's sound him out. Get him in here and talk to him.'

'On what pretext?'

Caesar thought for a moment and then smiled. 'So that he can help us identify the body of the man who attacked my niece. After that, we change the subject and see where he stands. What do you think?'

Pompeius shook his head. 'I think you are mad. But . . . you are right – there's no one better connected with the criminals of Rome than Clodius.'

Caesar nodded. 'Clodius it is then. He's at his villa in Baiae at present. I'll send for him at once.'

In the silence that followed, Portia glanced at Marcus before addressing her uncle. 'First we must provide for Corvus.'

'What's that?'

'The kitchen boy who saved my life,' Portia reminded him. 'I promised I'd see that he was given a proper funeral.'

Caesar waved a hand dismissively. 'It's not necessary.'

'I gave my word, Uncle.'

He frowned at her and Marcus wondered if he would refuse. Then he shrugged, and nodded his assent. 'Very well, you can use one of the carts. Do it at first light tomorrow and return here as soon as it's over.'

'Yes, Uncle.'

Caesar clicked his fingers at Festus. 'And you go with them. Take two of your best men with you.'

'Yes, master.'

'Now I need to be alone with General Pompeius. The rest of you, leave us.'

They filed from the room and Marcus glanced back at the two men as they began speaking in low tones. He focused his attention on Pompeius, heavily built, ornately robed in a purple tunic and cloak, and enslaved by his self-regard. Marcus was determined to show Pompeius he was wrong in his accusation that Marcus had failed to protect Portia. He must prove himself and somehow win the man over. Only then could he claim the one reward he would ever want from Pompeius or Caesar – freedom for himself and his mother, and, one day, revenge on Decimus and his henchman, Thermon.

13

The sun had not yet risen as the cart trundled through the quiet, cold streets of the capital. The cockerels kept within the city's walls had yet to crow and the numberless people crowded into tenement blocks and houses still slumbered. Festus and his men led the small procession of cloaked figures. Led by a mule, a two-wheeled cart came next, carrying a simple bier on which the body of Corvus had been laid, wrapped in a plain white sheet. Marcus held the mule's bridle, Portia following the cart with Lupus a short distance behind her. The body lay atop the faggots of firewood to be used for the pyre, with an axe to cut down any further lumber required. No one spoke as they made their way to the city gate and were passed through by the sleepy sentries nearing the end of their watch.

Outside, a thin mist covered the ground as the cart clattered along the road leading south towards Campania. A short distance from the gate they passed a large open grave where the bodies of the unknown and uncared for were dumped and sprinkled with lime. Low mounds on either side of the road marked the position of earlier mass graves. Further along the road the first of the tombs loomed up. It seemed from a distance to be floating on the slow swirl of the mist. Marcus could not help a nervous tremor at the sight of further tombs stretching far ahead and spilling out on either side.

'What is this place?' he asked in awe.

'The Necropolis – the city of the dead,' Festus explained in a quiet voice. 'This is where the remains of generations of Romans have been laid to rest. The laws of the city forbid the cremation or burial of the dead within the city boundary for all but the most honoured of citizens.'

Marcus nodded as he glanced warily at the dim outlines of the tombs on either side. They continued in silence a while longer before Festus halted.

'Up there.' Festus pointed to a bare hillock a short distance away. Marcus nodded and steered the mule off the paved surface and on to the uneven ground. The cart jolted as it rumbled between the silent tombs before emerging on to open ground. The route to the hillock was well travelled and two ruts led to the crest, where Festus gave the order to halt. As he tethered the mule to the withered stump of a tree, Marcus saw that the ground was marked with the scorch marks of previous cremations.

Festus gestured to Lupus and Marcus. 'It's customary for those closest to the dead to make the pyre, but would you prefer that my men and I did it?'

Marcus glanced at Lupus but saw from his trembling lips that the scribe was not ready to speak. He cleared his throat. 'Lupus and I can do it.'

'And me,' Portia added.

For a moment it seemed as if Festus would protest, but then he nodded. 'As you wish, mistress.'

While Lupus and Marcus lifted the bier from the cart and carried it a short distance away, Portia, having taken one of the faggots, followed them and laid it beside the body.

'No, that's not the way to do it,' Festus said gently. 'Let me show you.'

He returned to the wagon and fetched the two trestles he had packed in with the faggots. With the help of his two men, he raised the bier up and supported it at each end, so that it was waist high. 'The faggots go underneath,' he explained.

Once the two boys and Portia had packed the last of the

faggots and kindling tightly together under the bier, Festus took a tinderbox from his haversack and struck sparks into the fine sheets of charred linen. As soon as he had coaxed a small flame to life he set fire to the bundle of dried moss at the foot of the bier. The flames spread rapidly with a light crackling noise, working their way through the faggots then licking up around the shrouded corpse.

Marcus watched for a moment before his attention was caught by a distant glimmer a mile away, on the other side of the tomb-lined road. He was puzzled briefly by the ghostly flames wavering in the mist before he realized he was watching a second cremation take place. As he stared he noticed yet another flicker, then one more on the far side of the Tiber, beyond the tiled roofs and columned temples of Rome. Marcus realized there were other people out there, mourning the loss of a friend or member of the family, death being the one thing that made everyone equal in the end.

No, he corrected himself. Not everyone. Of all the pyres burning this morning, it was almost certain this was the only one to honour the death of a slave. He turned his gaze back to the flames consuming the body of Corvus. Death was a tragedy only for those who were free. For the slaves it was a release, Marcus realized.

The flames roared up around Corvus's corpse, charring the white shroud and burning through its folds until they began to scorch the dead flesh. The aroma of burning meat filled the air and Marcus felt his stomach tighten in disgust and horror. The bier and the trestles eventually burned through and the body crashed down into the heart of the blaze, sending sparks whirling into the dawn. As the sun crested the line of hills to the east, filling the sky with a pink hue, the fire began to die down. The small party stood in silence until the last flames flickered feebly and then faded to nothing but thin trails of smoke rising up from the ashes and charred remains.

Festus brought a spade and a small urn from the wagon, then broke up the larger chunks of blackened material with the edge of the spade before he swept them into the urn. He pressed the stopper back into the wax-lined top and held out the urn.

'Who will bury this?'

Portia shook her head, then Marcus gestured to Lupus. 'He was your friend.'

Lupus nodded, tears running down his face as he took the urn and held it to his chest.

Marcus touched his shoulder. 'I swear by all the gods that

we will avenge Corvus. We will find those responsible for his death, and they will pay for it with their lives.'

Marcus had no idea how he would do it, but he made a promise to himself and to Corvus's memory that he'd do everything in his power to see this through.

14

After the funeral, Caesar decided it was too dangerous for Portia to venture into the streets again while the struggle between the political factions was so bitter. He instructed her to remain within the house. Besides, Portia had told Marcus somewhat bitterly, she had been promised to General Pompeius's nephew and it was the custom for ladies of the nobility to be removed from temptation's way during preparations for the marriage – in case they ran off with a new admirer. That left Marcus without a role to play, so Festus had ordered him to continue with his training.

Each morning Marcus made his way into the yard to practise against the post with his sword and club, before moving on to knife-throwing and slingshot. During the morning Festus would emerge from the house to oversee his efforts, snapping sharp rebukes when Marcus failed to perform to the desired standard, and sometimes offering advice or teaching him a new technique for street fighting. At noon Festus allowed Marcus to stop for a break while he went for a drink with his men. Marcus was left with a small jar of heavily diluted wine that Lupus had brought from the kitchen, together with bread and olive oil for them to share.

Six days after the attack, while Marcus sat on the cart during one of these breaks, he asked the question that had been gnawing at him for days. 'When Mistress Portia marries, she will be leaving the house, I suppose?'

Lupus dunked his bread in the olive oil as he nodded. 'Of course she will.' He tore a chunk of bread off and chewed vigorously. 'Why do you ask?'

'Because she still needs protecting. That's my job. It's my duty.'

'Not when she's married it won't be. Pompeius's nephew will look after her. I'm sure he has plenty of slaves to protect her.' Lupus paused as he held the next chunk of bread in mid-air. 'It's funny, the mistress asked exactly the same question the other day. I heard her talking with Caesar. She was adamant that you stayed at her side.'

Marcus felt his hopes rise. He had been dropping hints to

Portia to ask that he might go with her to her new home. There might still be a way he could get close enough to Pompeius to ask for his help. He finished his mouthful and cleared his throat before he asked, 'What did Caesar say to that?'

'He said you were too valuable to give away.' Lupus jabbed a finger at Marcus. 'But don't let that go to your head.'

'Valuable? Me?' Marcus was confused. 'Why am I valuable?'

'You may be assigned the job of protecting Mistress Portia at present, but it's clear you have potential to make a name for yourself in the arena and add to the reputation of your master.' Lupus stared at Marcus, sizing him up. 'I heard the master say he has never seen a boy so suited to the life of a gladiator. You have mastered every weapon Festus has introduced to you. Festus reckons you already have a strong body and in time will be as tough as any man who ever set foot in an arena. But there's more than that, he says. You are quick-witted and decisive.'

'He said that?' Marcus felt a surge of pride.

Lupus nodded. 'He said it's as if you were born a fighter, that you must have inherited it from your father. A warrior of some kind I imagine, eh?'

Marcus nodded slowly as he prepared his lie. 'He was a centurion. He served General Pompeius in the east.'

Lupus frowned. 'Then how did you come to be a slave?'

Marcus told him the tale of Titus's death at the hands of a tax collector's henchmen and how he and his mother were taken to be sold as slaves. He deliberately left out the fact he had escaped from his original owner before being seized by Porcino for his gladiator school. He also left out the name of Decimus. He liked Lupus and thought he could trust him, but until he knew why Decimus was in Rome, and how close a friend he was to Crassus, it would be best to say nothing.

'Quite a tale,' Lupus responded. 'The gods have played their games with you. Now I see why you're keen to join Pompeius's household.'

'Oh?'

'I wasn't born yesterday.' Lupus chuckled. 'You want to get in the general's good books, then tell him your story and trust he'll use his influence to help rescue your mother. Am I right?'

Marcus was taken aback. He hadn't realized his motives were so obvious. There was no point denying it. He nodded warily.

'Well, even if you stayed with Mistress Portia, I think you'd be disappointed. Pompeius traded in his sword for a seat in the Senate. I doubt he'd be too concerned about the wife of a junior officer who left his service a decade earlier. He probably wouldn't even remember your father.'

'I doubt he will ever forget my father . . .' Marcus replied, thinking of Spartacus momentarily. But then he remembered he was talking about Titus, the man who had adopted him. 'Not after he saved the general's life, I mean.'

'Perhaps.' Lupus shrugged. 'But don't place too much hope on that. Also, be honest, it's not as if Pompeius is your biggest fan . . . Anyway, as far as I could tell, Caesar intends keeping you for a career in the arena.'

Marcus's heart sank. He hated not having control over his own destiny – how could he ever free his mother while he was a slave, his fate always decided by his owner? And the prospect of a life spent fighting other slaves on bloodsoaked sands while his ears filled with the baying cries of a cruel audience made him sick.

'Marcus!'

They turned to look across the yard and saw Flaccus beckoning. 'The master wants you in his study at once.'

Lupus and Marcus exchanged a look. Then Marcus lowered his cup and eased himself on to his feet. 'I'll see you later.'

Caesar and Festus were in the company of another man when they reached the study. A tall, slim figure in a heavily patterned tunic, he wore rings on every finger and a thick gold chain around his neck, from which hung a large emerald in a gold setting. His hair was light brown and painstakingly arranged in little curls that ran along his hairline. His face was fine-featured, almost feminine, and two sharp eyes regarded Marcus closely as he entered the room.

'This is the boy?' he asked.

'It is,' Caesar replied. 'And you will not find a more promising trainee in the whole of Italia, let alone Rome, my dear Clodius.'

The other man leaned forward in his chair and inspected Marcus closely. 'Hmmm. I'm not so sure. He looks a bit scrawny. Come closer, boy.'

Marcus did as he was told and stopped just beyond arm's reach of Clodius, recalling the earlier conversation between Caesar and Pompeius about the dubious character of the man. Clodius's brow creased in irritation.

'Closer.'

Marcus moved nearer, though the sweetness of the man's scent was so overpowering it made him feel slightly sick.

Clodius turned to Caesar. 'May I?'

Caesar smiled indulgently. 'Be my guest.'

Clodius reached out and squeezed Marcus's shoulder hard.

Marcus flinched slightly, but stood still, staring stonily into the man's eyes.

'Oh, you don't like that, do you? You have some spirit then.' Clodius laughed, and then let his hand slip down to Marcus's bicep where he squeezed again, gently. 'He has good muscle tone, Caesar. Sinewy and hard. You may be right. Are you training him with a net and trident as a retiarius perhaps?'

'That was my first thought. But with the right diet and exercise he could be bulky enough to train as a heavy fighter.' Caesar took a deep breath. 'But enough of that. We're not here to talk about Marcus's future. We've got other fish to fry. As I was telling you, Marcus was the boy who saved my niece's life, twice now.'

'I can't deny that I'm surprised,' Clodius remarked. 'I had expected to see someone a bit . . . older.'

'He's old enough for our purposes,' Caesar replied. Then he stood up and gestured towards the door. 'Come, let's see what you make of our, er, find. Festus, lead the way.'

'Yes, master.' Festus bowed his head and indicated that Marcus should follow him as he turned towards the door. They headed into the corridor and crossed the garden to the slave quarters. Beyond the kitchen, a narrow flight of stairs led down into a cellar where perishable foods were kept. There were two large chambers with a light well in each that pierced the gloom just enough for the contents of the shelves to be clearly seen. As they turned into the narrow archway connecting the two rooms, an appalling smell met them. Marcus wrinkled his nose in disgust.

'Good grief, Caesar,' Clodius exclaimed. 'Your meat store is off.'

Caesar smiled grimly as he led the small party through a narrow arch into the second chamber. 'There's the meat.'

A large table stood against the far wall, and upon it lay the body of one of the men who had attacked Portia. The man's skin was pale and mottled with livid blue patches. His jaw hung slackly and his eyes were wide open as they stared up at the bare bricks of the low vaulted ceiling. Close up, the cloying sweet smell was unbearable and Marcus had to clench his nostrils tightly to keep out the stench. Beside him, Festus also seemed to be struggling to control his stomach. Clodius had pulled up the hem of his cloak and pressed it over his mouth and nose. Only Caesar seemed unaffected as he stared coldly at the body for a moment. He turned to Clodius.

'Well? Do you recognize him?'

Clodius leaned over the body and examined the face. 'No. Can't say I do. The fellow has a distastefully common look to him. Just another street thug, it would appear . . .' He rolled up the tunic sleeve on the corpse, working it on to the shoulder. 'But see here.'

Marcus and the others leaned forward for a closer look. There was tattoo on the dead man's shoulder. Two crossed daggers.

Clodius straightened up, nodding in recognition. 'That's the mark of the Blades, one of the gangs from the Aventine district. Nasty bunch. Normally, they run protection rackets and, for the right fee, will bump off anyone in Rome, right up to the rank of senator. Of course, these days they are run by Milo, who has been hired by Bibulus, Cato and Cicero to use against your followers, though you could never prove it. Bibulus might be a fool, but he's not so stupid as to leave any evidence of connections to Rome's most notorious gangs in his wake. And if he's prepared to deal with the Blades, then you and your friends are in danger, Caesar.' He turned to Marcus with a curious look. 'If you took on this man, and one of his fellow gang members, then you are brave indeed, young Marcus. And also very foolish. These men would not have hesitated to kill you. In fact, I'm sure they would have enjoyed doing so, and made it last as long as possible.' He licked his lips at the thought.

Marcus fought the urge to shudder before he replied, 'I did not doubt that at the time, master. But Mistress Portia was in danger. What else could I do?'

'If it had been me, I would have gone for help.'

'And my niece would be dead,' Caesar cut in coldly. 'None of us is safe now. Our enemies are more determined, and dangerous, than I thought.'

Clodius pursed his lips and nodded. 'You're right. So what are you going to do about it, Caesar? Strikes me that you could use some help.'

Marcus saw Caesar's eyes narrow as he stared directly at Clodius.

'I know. That's why we sent for you.'

Clodius smiled faintly. 'And what would you ask of me?'

'If our enemies are using street gangs to intimidate and harm our supporters, then we must meet violence with violence. We know you have connections with some of the gangs and we want you to organize support for our side.'

Clodius considered this a moment before he replied. 'I can do it. But there will be a price. These gangs are quite deadly, Caesar. They will go to any lengths to control their districts.

Anyone who stands in their way is killed, often butchered in broad daylight to make sure everyone gets the message. If I am to take them on, then I'll need to hire gangs of my own. And they won't come cheap.' His eyes glinted.

Caesar shrugged. 'Whatever the price is, Crassus can afford the services of the scum in these street gangs of yours.'

'I'm sure he can afford to pay them. But I'm talking about my price, Caesar.'

'Your price? How much do you want?'

'Nothing you can't afford. I don't want your gold or silver.'

'Then what do you want?' Caesar asked impatiently.

There was a pause.

'I rather fancy the notion of becoming a tribune.'

Marcus remembered what Lupus had told him about the post of tribune, a position for those who were supposed to stand up for the rights of the common people.

Caesar's eyes widened in surprise. He shook his head. 'Impossible! That would give you power over the mob. Besides, you are a senator and the post of tribune is only open to people of common rank.'

'I've thought of that. There is a way round that obstacle. I can be adopted by a commoner, a plebian, and you have the power to authorize my adoption. Once that's done I am free to stand for the office of tribune. And then, when I *am* a tribune, I can make sure the mob stays on your side.'

While Caesar considered the proposal, Festus and Marcus stood in silence. Marcus couldn't help wondering how these two powerful men could make their devious plans in front of their slaves, as if they were not present – as if they were just part of the furniture.

'Very well, we are agreed.' Caesar nodded, holding his hand out to Clodius.

After shaking hands, Clodius nodded towards the corpse. 'Now the business is concluded, might we move away from our malodorous companion? A cup of wine should be enough to remove the rather nasty taste that death tends to leave in one's mouth.'

'Yes . . . Yes, of course. Festus, we no longer have need of the body. You and the boy can dispose of it.'

Caesar put his hand on the shoulder of his guest and guided him back to the stairs into the more wholesome air of the house. As the steps faded Festus turned towards the body and puffed out his cheeks.

'Right then, Marcus, I'll take him under the shoulders, and you take his feet.'

Marcus did not move. He stared down at the corpse with a

sick feeling. This was not the first body he had seen close up, but he had never handled a corpse and the idea revolted him. And more than that, Marcus was responsible for the man's death. Flashes of the terrifying fight in the storeroom filled Marcus's mind and made him feel sick in the pit of his stomach.

'He won't bite, lad,' Festus said gently. 'Just try not to think of it as a person. It's just a lump of rancid meat we're disposing of. That's all.'

Marcus turned his gaze away from the body. 'Rancid meat? Thanks, that makes it so much easier.'

Festus chuckled harshly and stood at the end of the table. He slipped his hands under the corpse's shoulders and heaved the body on to the floor. It landed with a soft thud and he dragged it into the other room towards the steps. Marcus followed reluctantly. As they reached the stairs, Festus nodded. 'Take his feet.'

Marcus gritted his teeth and fought down his nausea as he picked up the man's cold calf, just above the boot. The skin was cold and clammy and he flinched, forcing himself to grip firmly.

With much grunting and cursing from Festus, they heaved the body up the stairs, then dragged it down the short corridor that led to the yard.

'On to the cart with him,' Festus ordered.

Once the body had been heaved into the small cart, Festus covered it with a length of old sacking. 'It's daylight, so we can't hitch up the mule. No animal-drawn carts are allowed on the streets during the day. If we pull it ourselves we should get round the regulations.'

'Where are we taking it . . . him?' asked Marcus. 'Out to where we held Corvus's funeral?'

'No chance. We'll drop him into the first sewer opening we come across. There's one at the end of the street. Just need to wait until we're alone before we do the deed.'

With one of them pulling each of the yokes, the cart trundled into the narrow street outside. Few people paid much attention other than to grumble as they moved aside to let the cart pass. Festus steered the cart into a dead-end alley leading off a small square and stopped beside an iron grating two feet across. They set the yokes down and waited for a break in the steady flow of human traffic through the square.

Festus glanced from side to side, then pulled the sacking off. 'Quickly – shift the grating!'

The iron grille was heavy and Marcus strained his muscles to raise it, letting it fall on the cobbles with a clatter. They eased the body into the drain, hearing it splash as it dropped into the sewage.

Festus let out a weary sigh. 'Dangerous times ahead of us, Marcus . . . It's bad enough that Milo's lot are stirring up trouble. If Clodius and his thugs are unleashed on the streets there'll be plenty of fighting, and deaths. The streets will run with blood, I tell you.'

'You really think so?' Marcus said. 'Isn't it better that the gangs fight each other? Might mean they leave the rest of us alone . . .'

'Oh, the gangs will fight, to be sure. But the rest of the time they'll be on to the common people – breaking up meetings and doing their best to intimidate the other side into silence. It's bullies' work, and I wouldn't thank you for it. Slave or not, we're part of Caesar's household, so we're targets too. Same's true for Bibulus and his cronies once Clodius intervenes. We're in for a bad time. You'd better watch your back, Marcus.'

'I will,' said Marcus as he stared down at the grille. If Festus was right, the man they'd just disposed of would be the first of many. It seemed as if Caesar and his enemies were embarking on a war that would rage through the streets of Rome. And Marcus might be fighting for his life just as he had in the arena at Porcino's gladiator school. Only then, his enemy had faced him. Now enemies could strike without warning in a crowded street. Never mind the problem of escaping his situation or saving his mother; it seemed he would need all his wits, and every skill Festus had taught him, if he was to survive in the streets of Rome.

15

Spring had given way to summer and the temperature in the city was climbing. The cold clammy air that filled the narrow alleys and streets was replaced by a smothering heat that steadily increased the stench of rubbish and sewage. The rains of spring had passed and few torrents gushed down the streets to wash away the filth. Flies and mosquitoes swirled in the still air and added to the discomfort of Rome's inhabitants.

At the same time the temperature of the people was also rising. Since Caesar's meeting with Clodius, hardly a day had passed without news of a clash between Milo's and Clodius's gangs, often escalating into full-scale riots in the district surrounding the Forum and spilling over into the very heart of the Forum itself. Hundreds had been beaten or stabbed and many had died, each death provoking further rage and revenge attacks. Marcus had witnessed a few riots when he escorted Caesar and his men to the Senate House. In normal times, Festus explained to Marcus, the procession was to display the influence of the politician at its head. Now a small band of tough men walked in front of Caesar, clearing the way and looking for danger, while the rest of his followers were there for protection.

Marcus wore his thick leather skullcap to protect his head. It was uncomfortable and made his head sweat in the close heat of the city's streets, but Festus insisted he keep it on, joking that it was there to protect 'Caesar's investment'. He also carried a dagger tucked into the wide belt under his cloak, and a stout club slipped up his sleeve, ready to drop into his hand the instant it was needed. So far no one had dared attack the consul or his entourage. But Marcus didn't think that would last much longer. As the procession crossed the Forum, insults were hurled at Caesar from the safety of the crowd. Soon, Marcus feared, the insults would be accompanied by lumps of filth, or rotten vegetables, then stones and bricks, before order disintegrated into a bloody struggle amid the screams of those running away.

On this particular day, an ominous mood permeated the Senate House as Marcus and Lupus watched Caesar take his seat. A group of senators clustered about Cato, muttering in low tones as they waited for proceedings to begin. Not until the benches of the Senate were almost filled did Caesar nod to the chief clerk. The man stepped forward, cracking his staff on the flagstone floor to command silence.

'In the name of the consul, Gaius Julius Caesar, the daily proceedings of the Senate are declared open. The consul invites the first item of business for the day.'

At once Cato was on his feet, his arm raised, a scroll held high. 'I have a Bill to present!'

Cato saw the weary look in Caesar's face as he gestured towards Cato. 'Proceed.'

Cato nodded, then paused to stare around the chamber, building up a tense air of expectation. Before he could speak, Caesar coughed and addressed the house first.

'If you don't mind, my dear Cato, we don't have all day for your theatrical tricks. Please spit it out.'

At the ripple of light laughter around the Senate, Marcus turned to Lupus with a questioning look. 'What's so funny?'

'Our master has ruffled Cato's feathers,' Lupus smiled. 'Actors are the lowest of the low in Rome. For a snob like Cato that's a painful comparison. Look at him! The man's furious.'

Marcus saw that Cato's brows had knitted together in a deep

frown as he glared at the consul. He waited until the last of the laughter had died away before speaking in a bitter tone.

'I shall come to the point. Caesar has requested that he shall be given command over our Celtic provinces this side of the Alps when his consulship comes to an end. It would be a fair reward for a consul as obviously capable as Caesar. He has already proved himself as a fine commander in Spain and I am certain he would be most effective in countering the threats to our interests in Gaul. However . . .' Cato paused and waited for complete silence before he continued. 'However, we have more pressing need of Caesar's military skills. You all know of the continuing raids on isolated villas and farming estates by large bands of brigands hiding in the hills and mountains down the spine of Italia. Many of these bands comprise the remnants of the rebel army of Spartacus – runaway slaves who continue to terrorize their masters, and defy the authority of Rome. While they live, the spirit of Spartacus himself lives on!' Cato jabbed a finger into the air. 'Even now, there are reports that a new leader has emerged. Some scoundrel by the name of Brixus . . .'

Marcus felt an icy shiver ripple down his spine. Could this be the same Brixus he had known at the gladiator school? He had told Marcus he'd fight slavery until his dying breath, and urged

Marcus to join him. 'Until the last supporters of Spartacus are eliminated, we face the very real prospect of a new revolt flaring up in our faces!' Cato exclaimed. 'The consequences of this will be even more dire than was the case in the previous uprising. To that end, I move that the Senate reassign Caesar to hunt down and eliminate every last rebel and brigand operating in Italia. Only then can decent Romans afford to sleep at night, untroubled by fears of being murdered in their beds by those who still follow in the footsteps of Spartacus.'

Cato sat down abruptly and folded his arms as his followers cheered loudly. Marcus saw the smirk on Cato's face and turned his gaze to Caesar who was sitting quite still on his ornate chair, glaring at his political opponent. Despite his stillness, Marcus could see that the blood had drained from his master's face and the tightly clenched jaw confirmed the rage seething within. Marcus undersood his master's anger. Far from letting him continue to build his military reputation, Cato was attempting to divert Caesar into policing the troubled countryside. If Caesar's enemies didn't succeed through the Senate, what would they resort to? Marcus and Lupus had heard the threats from Portia's kidnappers – Caesar's life was in danger, and Cato had just upped the stakes.

The clerk rapped his staff for silence. Caesar paused a moment before standing to reply.

'Senator Cato's proposal comes as something of a surprise, since the area of my responsibilities when I step down as consul has already been defined. I shall have to consult with the clerks to see if there is a precedent for such a change. The house will adjourn while I investigate the matter.'

Cato was instantly on his feet again. 'There is a precedent. I checked. All that remains is to put it to the vote.'

His supporters shouted their support until the clerk rapped his rod again, and turned to Caesar.

'I will look into it myself, and the Senate will resume its consideration of the motion this afternoon.'

The consul's words were greeted with howls of protest from Cato and his supporters, but he ignored them as the clerks packed up their writing materials. Caesar left the chamber and climbed the stairs to join Lupus and Marcus, watching from the public gallery. When he reached them, his words were harsh and clipped. Marcus hadn't seen his master this serious before. He almost didn't recognize the emotion on his face. But then he realized – Caesar was afraid.

'Lupus, go outside and find Festus. Tell him to ready his men and wait outside the Senate House. He is to do what he can to delay any senators from slipping away before I can teach Cato a lesson. Then get yourself home, before the trouble starts.'

'Yes, master!' Lupus bowed his head and scurried away as Caesar turned to Marcus. 'I want you to find Clodius. He's most likely to be at the Blue Dolphin Inn, at the far end of the Forum. Do you know it?'

'Yes, master. I went there once with Festus.'

'Good. Then tell Clodius to have his men gather outside the Senate as soon as possible. I want Cato and every one of his supporters to know they have stepped over the line. I'll make sure I leave before Clodius's thugs arrive. Tell Clodius to keep an eye out for Milo's gangs. There are bound to be some nearby, waiting for an order to come to Cato's aid.'

Marcus glanced round to make sure they weren't overheard, then lowered his voice. 'What do you want Clodius to do, master?'

Caesar closed his eyes an instant as he replied, 'Tell him to go in hard. They can do anything, short of killing anyone. Understood?'

'Yes, master.'

'Then go.' Caesar turned swiftly and made his way back down the stairs to join the huddle of senators who supported him, as well as Pompeius and Crassus. Marcus saw that they looked anxious. But Caesar approached them with a wide smile and open arms, exuding calm and confidence.

Marcus pushed through the crowd in the gallery and left the Senate. He hurried through the Forum towards the edge of the Subura district. When he reached the inns lining the road to the Forum, he saw groups of tough-looking men sitting on the benches outside, while others squatted against the cracked plaster of the walls. Marcus made to enter the courtyard of the largest inn, the Blue Dolphin, but a huge man with a thick stave barred his way.

'What's your business here?' he growled.

'I'm on Caesar's business. I need to speak to Clodius.'

The man eyed him warily, then nodded. 'Follow me.'

He led the way down a narrow passage into the courtyard. Marcus instantly recognized Clodius at the head of a long table with burly-looking men on either side. They were dressed somewhat more finely than the men in the street and many had gold bracelets and chains round their necks. Some were scarred, and they had the broken noses of men brought up to use their fists. Marcus realized these must be the leaders of the street gangs that Clodius had recruited.

'This one claims he's been sent by Caesar.' The man jerked his thumb at Marcus.

Clodius looked up and nodded. 'It's all right, I know him.'

The guard nodded and turned away. Marcus took a deep breath and moistened his lips.

'My master needs you and your men at once.'

'Where?'

'At the Forum. Cato is trying to force Caesar to campaign against the brigands next year. Caesar's furious. He wants you to rough up Cato's supporters. Make sure they understand what will happen if they vote with Cato when the Senate is reconvened later today.'

Clodius nodded. 'Did Caesar give any specific instructions?'

Marcus lowered his voice and spoke deliberately. 'Anything short of murder.'

Clodius raised his eyebrows. 'I see.'

He stood up and looked down the table at the cruel faces of the gang leaders. 'You heard the boy. Gather your men. Make for the Senate and let's show Milo and his political cronies that the gangs from the Subura are the real power in Rome!'

As the men scrambled up from their benches and hurried out into the street to summon their gangs, Clodius turned to Marcus. 'You'd better stay with me until this is over. Might as well have every fighting man I can find at my side. That is, if you have the stomach for it, young Marcus.'

Marcus drew himself up to his full height. 'I'm ready.'

'Courage is one thing. The right tools for the job are quite another. Are you armed?'

Marcus let the club slip down his tunic sleeve, caught it in his hand and held it up.

Clodius smiled. 'Hope you know how to use it.'

'I do, master. Besides, that's not all I have.' Marcus quickly switched the club into his left hand and reached with his right to pull out one of the throwing knives. There was a blur of movement, a sharp crack, and Clodius looked down the table to the chair at the far end. The knife was stuck fast in the chair back, its handle quivering.

He chuckled, then patted Marcus on the shoulder. 'You'll do nicely. Let's go.'

16

It didn't take long to reach the Forum. Fright and panic surged through the crowd as they caught sight of the huge men armed with clubs and staves. Marcus watched as mothers snatched up their children and stallholders packed their wares, hurriedly piling them on to handcarts before trundling away to safety. By the time Clodius and Marcus, near the head of the gangs, had reached the crowd outside the Senate, the Forum was starting to empty.

Scrambling on to a pediment, Marcus saw Festus and his men pressing forward against the entrance of the Senate House, where angry senators were demanding to be let through. As soon as he saw Clodius and the first of his gang members, Festus shouted an order and his men fell back. The senators pressed forward down the steps, a steady stream of clean white togas amid the brown and grey tunics and cloaks of the common people. The faces of senators who supported Caesar were well known and they were allowed to pass unhindered as they glanced nervously at the hordes of fierce-looking fighters surrounding them. The other senators were blocked. Clodius's men pushed them back roughly, jeering and shouting insults into their faces.

Clodius gestured to Marcus to follow him and pushed through his men until he stood in the front rank of those opposing the senators. He scanned the faces before him until he caught sight of the man he wanted, then cupped a hand to his mouth and called out.

'Cato! Hey, Cato! Over here!'

Marcus saw the thin man in his plain toga turn towards the shout and slowly descend the steps until he stood a short distance in front of Clodius. He stopped one step from the bottom so that he could see, and be seen, over the crowd gathered before him.

'Clodius . . .' He spat the word out with contempt. 'I might have guessed you'd be leading this rabble. Are there no depths to which you won't sink? You and your kind make me sick.' He drew himself up proudly. 'Tell your scum to get out of our way. They have no right to block the path of their betters. Move aside!'

There was a shrill catcall from the crowd, and a boo, then more joined in to create a mocking din. Marcus could feel the tension rising, waiting to explode into violence, and he was afraid. This was not like the fear of standing in front of another fighter. It was quite different. The crowd felt like a force of nature, out of control and dangerous – a storm waiting to break.

Clodius stepped forward, raised his hand and shoved Cato back. 'Make me!'

A huge cheer erupted from the crowd at his insolence. Cato was furious. He stepped forward and slapped Clodius across the face. The sharp sound of the blow silenced the tongues of those watching, but Clodius merely reached up to his mouth and touched his lip. His finger came away stained with a small red smear. He smiled.

'It would appear that you have drawn first blood, Cato. Whatever happens now, it is on your head.'

'Don't be ridiculous –' was all Cato managed in reply before Clodius smashed his fist into the other senator's jaw. Cato fell back with a grunt, into the ranks of his followers.

'Now!' Clodius yelled. 'Teach 'em a lesson!'

With a roar, the surrounding men hurled handfuls of filth, rotten vegetables and any other missiles they had gathered.

The white togas of the senators were quickly stained brown and green, and they raised their arms to protect their heads from the stones and bits of wood raining down on them. The senators began to retreat up the steps, towards the entrance of the Senate House.

Marcus had not moved, however – he was frozen before the spectacle. Clodius looked at him in surprise and leaned down to speak to him. 'What are you waiting for, Marcus? An invitation? Join in.'

'I – I can't,' Marcus stammered.

'Why not?'

'Because I'm a slave, master. If I was caught injuring a free citizen . . .'

'You won't be. And why not take advantage of the situation, eh? Surely a slave cannot resist the chance to get his own back? Go on, throw something. Do it on behalf of all the slaves who are owned by senators. Do it for them. Do it for yourself.' He giggled. 'And do it for Spartacus. No one will ever know.'

Caught up by the mob's frenzy and frustrated by his situation, the mention of his father stirred Marcus's heart. A seething whirlpool of indignation, rage and hatred for every wrong he had suffered since being wrenched from his home flowed into his limbs. Before he was aware of it Marcus had snatched a pebble the size of a quail's egg from the flagstones at his feet. His arm swept back, throwing it hard into the writhing mass of men and togas struggling towards the shelter of the Senate House. He did not see where the pebble went, but couldn't have missed at that range. He felt a burst of elation.

Clodius laughed as he too threw a stone. 'Go on, Marcus! Again!'

Marcus was ready to find another missile, or to smash his club on the nearest senator. But looking up, he saw a mad gleam in the man's eyes as his lips curled in cruel pleasure. Clodius was giggling like a child as he stooped and threw, again and again. Marcus felt the fire inside him fade, and a chill took over. There was something frightening about Clodius. He no longer seemed in control of himself.

Marcus's thoughts were interrupted by a cry close at hand. 'Watch out! Milo's here!'

The warning was taken up and Clodius's men looked round. The senators took advantage of the break in the bombardment to stagger into the Senate House. A moment later the doors swung closed with a deep thud. Marcus, shorter than the surrounding men, felt hemmed in. He needed to see what was going on. He ran up the first steps and turned to look over the

Forum. Clodius's men had turned to face the figures spilling into the Forum from the direction of the Aventine Hill. The ground between the two sides was empty, aside from the handful of statues above, casting long shadows over them. Milo's men had come armed with clubs, cleavers, axes, knives and a variety of other deadly-looking weapons.

But he only had a moment to examine the battleground before Clodius called him to his side, then pushed through the mob to the far side, facing the oncoming horde. Pulling his skullcap down tightly over his head, Marcus's blood froze at the line of fighters opposite him. He suddenly felt trapped, young and very small. At least in the arena a fighter had room to move. This was different. Terrifying.

The cries of Clodius's men had died away as Milo's followers approached. A hush descended on the Forum, broken only by the grating rumble of nailed boots. At the head of the rival gangs marched a tall, broad man with a wide leather belt. He wore a plain black tunic and thick leather boots that extended halfway up his thick calves. In his hands he carried a heavy club, studded with the heads of iron nails. His dark hair was cropped short and a livid white scar cut across his brow, nose and cheek.

Clodius smiled as he muttered, 'Milo, magnificent as ever.'

Around him, Clodius's men were brandishing their weapons, ready for use. Marcus let his own club slip down into his left hand.

When Milo was no more than twenty paces away he raised his hand to signal his followers to halt. He nodded at Clodius.

'I got word that you were causing trouble.'

'Trouble?' Clodius pretended to look offended. 'Me? Not a bit of it. Me and the lads here were just speaking up for the people. The trouble is, some of the senators don't want to listen.'

Milo laughed. 'It's hard to listen when you're being stoned by a bunch of low-life, cowardly thugs from the sewers of the Subura.'

A wave of angry muttering swept through the ranks. Clodius cupped a hand to his mouth. 'Quiet! Let the loudmouth speak his mind, what there is of it!'

The grumbles turned to laughter and a scowl twisted Milo's craggy face.

'That's enough!' he bellowed. 'Get your men out of the Forum, Clodius. Before I make you.'

'Pffftt!' Clodius sneered, drawing his cloak aside to pull out a short sword, and raising the tip to point directly at Milo. 'Make me! You don't own the streets any more.' Clodius held

170

his arms wide. 'We do! The streets of Rome belong to Clodius and the gangs of the Subura!'

His men greeted this with a roar of approval.

Milo punched his club into the air and bellowed, 'Get stuck into 'em, lads!'

He charged across the Forum, hordes of his men following. Marcus switched his club to his right hand and raised it ready to strike as he took his stand beside Clodius. His heart was beating wildly, but he didn't have long to feel afraid. The charge struck home with a deafening series of thuds and cracks as weapon met weapon. A tall man with a badly trimmed beard rushed towards Marcus, a thick club raised above his head, feral grin widening as he saw what he took to be easy prey.

Marcus sidestepped as the man's club swished down and struck the cobbles with a loud crash. At once he punched his club into the man's side with all his strength, driving the air from his lungs and cracking a rib. The man slumped down and gasped for air. Marcus heard a wet crunch behind and turned to see that Clodius had buried his sword in the top of the man's skull.

'Nice work, Marcus!' He laughed as he pulled the blade free and kicked the body over, then leapt forward to stab another man in the guts. Marcus was crushed by the bodies pressing in, surrounded by violent tussles. Some men were locked in an embrace as they tried to wrestle for advantage. Others were crushed together tightly, clawing at their opponents' faces or headbutting each other. Marcus lost sight of Clodius and was jostled by the other men from the Suburan gangs as they pressed forward.

He found himself a short distance behind the men locked in combat and paused, wondering what to do. His instinct was to fight, but as he caught his breath, the excitement gave way to clear thought. He was too small for this. He was trained to fight in individual combat, not in a violent mob. The most likely outcome would be that his skull would be smashed in or his bones shattered and then he would be finished, a cripple for the rest of his life, if he survived. Any hope of freeing his mother would die with him. He needed to prove himself to Caesar and Pompeius, but this was not the way.

'Marcus!' A hand grabbed his shoulder and turned him round. He looked up and saw Festus.

'Marcus, we have to leave. It's for Clodius and his gangs. Not us. Come on!' He turned Marcus away, pushing him to the back of the mob, along the Senate steps towards the side of the Forum, well away from the battle around the front of the Senate House. Looking back, Marcus caught one last glimpse of Clodius, standing on a pediment to urge his men on, waving his bloodied blade and laughing like a maniac.

17

'What the hell were you thinking?' Caesar said through clenched teeth as he addressed Clodius, Festus and Marcus in his study later that day. 'Over a hundred men killed, and at least three times that number injured. By Jupiter, the Forum was running with blood by the time you'd finished. You were only supposed to put pressure on the senators, and make them change their mind about supporting Cato.' He shook his head and waved a hand as if trying to brush something aside. 'Not this . . . this bloodbath.'

'Oh, tush! You wanted to step up the conflict, Caesar. Now that both sides are using the street gangs, violence was inevitable. In any case, my instructions were that I could do anything short of murder,' Clodius responded with a shrug. He turned to Marcus who was standing quietly to one side of the study.

'Isn't that right, boy? That's what Caesar told you to tell me?'

Marcus nodded and shot a quick glance at Caesar before he replied, 'Yes, master.'

'See?' Clodius smiled as he turned back to Caesar. 'Besides, only a handful of senators came to any actual harm. Not anyone who would be missed.'

'Twenty of them were injured. One seriously. His skull was shattered when he slipped on the stairs.'

'Not my fault then,' Clodius responded dismissively.

'Whatever *you* might think, the damage is done,' Caesar countered. 'You've caused a bloody battle right outside the Senate House, and now Cato will milk it for all it's worth. He'll be calling me a tyrant in front of everyone when the Senate meets tomorrow. The last thing I need is more people against me – they're voting on whether to send me back to the middle of nowhere. I haven't done all this for Rome just to end up in the mountains fighting slaves.'

While Clodius and Caesar argued, Marcus's mind was turning over an idea. The conflict between Caesar and Bibulus had reached a deadly stage. First the attempt on Portia's life, then the vote to oust Caesar from Rome, and now the street gangs spilling blood in the heart of the city. Caesar's life was in danger, and there was only one way of uncovering any plot against his life, Marcus decided. The real battle wouldn't be won in fist-to-fist combat in the city streets, he was sure of it. A plan was forming in his mind. If it succeeded, then Caesar would be further in Marcus's debt. He couldn't rely on his original plans for Pompeius's help, but this might be a way to prove himself to both of them and obtain the one reward he really wanted.

'He can try it on,' Clodius was replying, 'but since Milo played his part in things, neither side looks good. Besides, enough senators were so badly shaken up that I doubt they'll show their faces in the Senate House until long after the year is over, when you and Bibulus have handed over to the next pair of consuls. Not that anyone will be aware Bibulus was ever consul since he's refused to take his place in the Senate.'

'Very funny.' Caesar frowned. 'But Cato's effort today has made my life more difficult, and today's skirmish, as you describe it, will have strengthened the hand of my opponents in the Senate. Now I'll have to force the Senate back into line and find a way of countering Cato's scheme. I need some legislation that will force the Senate to follow my will. But that will raise the stakes and increase the danger to me and to Portia.'

'Then we must guard against it, Caesar,' said Clodius.

'How can we do that without knowing where or when they intend to strike?'

Marcus had thought quickly as he listened to their exchange. Now he cleared his throat, building up his nerve to intervene. The sound caused Caesar to turn towards him, arching an eyebrow.

'You have something to say, Marcus?'

'Yes, master.'

'Then spit it out, before you choke on it.'

Marcus glanced nervously at the two men. His idea might be far-fetched but it seemed the only way forward.

'Master, there is no question about it. Your enemies intend to kill you. I heard it straight from one of the men sent to kill your niece. I think they will be planning another attempt on her life, and yours. You could stay safe within the walls of your house, like Bibulus, but the people would think you a coward.' A dark look flitted across his master's face and Marcus continued hurriedly. 'Naturally, you will continue as normal and show no fear. But they will still be plotting against you. This gang war isn't helping. You need to discover what their plans are and be ready to act against them.'

Caesar and the others in the room digested Marcus's words. Marcus tried to remain calm, but his heart was beating hard.

How would Caesar react to a mere slave voicing his thoughts like this?

'And how exactly do you propose that I find out? Milo is hardly going to tell me,' Caesar said mockingly.

'Someone has to get inside Milo's gang to find out their plans, master.'

'Don't you imagine I've thought of that?' Clodius sniffed. 'The street gangs are a close-knit bunch. A man has to prove himself over and again before he is allowed to join, and after that he has to work his way up through the ranks to the inner circle of the gang leaders. It takes a long time – years. We haven't got that long. Besides, if a man turns up wanting to join during the middle of a gang war, then he's bound to arouse suspicion. It won't work.'

Marcus had already thought through this and nodded. 'That is true, master. But what if we didn't send a man? What if we sent a boy instead? Someone young enough to be overlooked.'

Clodius and Caesar fixed their attention on Marcus, then Caesar responded, 'You, you mean.'

'Yes, master. Why not? I am observant. I am skilled with weapons and I do not carry the mark of any of the gangs. Few people know me in Rome so I will not be recognized. Even when I've been out, my head has been covered. If I could get close to Milo and his gang I might overhear their plans, or at least give warning when there is trouble, master.' He paused as he saw the doubtful look on Caesar's face.

'It's too dangerous, and what makes you think they will be so foolish as to discuss important matters within earshot of you?'

Marcus couldn't help a slight smile. 'Because that's exactly what you do, master. You speak openly in front of your slaves. Why should Milo be any different?'

Clodius laughed as Caesar looked uncomfortable. 'He has a good point there! Many a powerful Roman has come unstuck once his slaves are tortured for evidence to use against him. You'd think we'd have learned by now, but it seems not. Marcus is right, Caesar. He might succeed where a grown man would not. It's worth a try at least.'

Marcus stared intently at Caesar, trying to guess what was going through the consul's mind. 'Master, I know I can do this,' he said.

Caesar clasped his hands behind his back and paced up and down the study, while Clodius examined the fingernails of his expensively manicured hands. Marcus looked at him, wondering how this could be the same man who had wildly hurled himself into a vicious street fight just hours before.

'All right,' Caesar concluded. 'It's worth a try. I can't say I'm happy about putting a valuable slave in danger, but there is no gain without risk, as my good friend and business associate, Crassus, would say.' He fixed Marcus with a hard stare. 'Naturally you will expect a reward for this service?'

'I would be grateful for one,' Marcus replied, not sure how far he dare push the situation. In his mind's eye he saw his mother, cold, hungry and imploring him to help her.

'I'm sure you would.' Caesar placed his hand on Marcus's shoulder. 'You may be young, but you know the meaning of honour and have the courage to see it through. Rare qualities. If you stay in my service you will be a formidable gladiator one day, Marcus. And I shall be proud of you.'

'And what if he doesn't want to be a gladiator?' Clodius interrupted. 'What if he wants to be freed?'

Marcus tensed his muscles nervously. It was as if Clodius had read his mind. It wouldn't help his cause if Caesar knew how much Marcus hated the idea of being a gladiator. Marcus had learned that Caesar was not a man to accept the views of those who disagreed with him.

'Then I shall reconsider his situation at the appropriate time,' Caesar replied dismissively. 'Until then, Marcus, you will do what you can to save me from my enemies, eh?'

'Yes, master. When should I begin?'

'At once. It wouldn't surprise me if Cato and Bibulus wanted to finish this quickly after the events of today.' He stared Marcus straight in the eye. 'You should be aware of the risks. If Milo discovers who you are, then he will show no mercy.'

Marcus stiffened his spine and stood as tall as he could. 'I understand, master. But I have faced danger before, more than once. I am not afraid and I know what I'm doing.'

Caesar suddenly let out a loud laugh. 'Oh you do, do you? I wish I could say that!'

Festus charged Lupus with the task of preparing Marcus for going undercover. He had found a worn and tattered tunic and some old sandals to give Marcus the appearance of the runaway he would claim to be. The plaque that hung round his neck to mark him as a slave had been removed, and now his skin had to be covered with a mix of soot and ink, to make him suitably grimy for a street urchin, as well as covering the brand from Porcino's gladiator school.

'Take off your tunic,' Lupus said, ready to apply some of the mixture to Marcus's skin.

Marcus hesitated. No one had seen his scar since Brixus had

identified it as the mark of Spartacus. Now here he was, in the house of Spartacus's most powerful enemy. To reveal it here was horribly dangerous.

'Come on,' urged Lupus. 'Or do you want Milo to work out who you are?'

Marcus realized there was no way to avoid it without causing suspicion. He held his breath and pulled off the tunic.

'What's that on your shoulder?' Lupus asked. He tilted his head for a closer inspection. 'It looks like . . . a sword thrusting through the head of a wolf.'

Marcus snatched up the ragged tunic and made to pull it over his head until Lupus stopped him. 'Wait. I'll have to cover this up too. Hold still.'

He was silent as he worked the mixture in uneven streaks on Marcus's back so that the dirt looked natural. 'Where did you get the mark?'

'I don't know,' Marcus lied. He could hardly breathe for fear that his true identity would be exposed. What if Caesar chose this moment to walk in? 'It's always been there. Since before I can remember.'

'Then you must have been branded as an infant.' Lupus shook his head. 'By the gods, who would do such a thing to a baby? I doubt your father would have used such an unpatriotic image – the wolf is a symbol of Rome. What about your mother?'

Marcus shrugged. 'I told you. I don't know anything about it. Can we hurry this up?'

'Well, whoever it was, they were no friend of Rome. Now hold still.'

Lupus finished applying the grime and paused to admire his handiwork before he stepped away from Marcus. 'Put on your tunic.'

Marcus sighed with relief and Lupus looked him over with a grin. 'You look like the lowest-born scum of the gutters. Perfect.'

That night Lupus and Marcus left the house by a small side gate. Lupus had been ordered to lead Marcus to The Pit on the Aventine Hill, the heart of the district controlled by Milo and his gangs. Festus was too well known to guide Marcus and had decided two young boys stood a better chance of making their way unnoticed through the streets.

They crept round the inside of the Servian wall to avoid the heart of the city, where small groups of rival gang members still prowled and clashed in the darkness. Despite the season there was a chill in the air and Marcus shivered as they made their way through the quiet streets. Above, on the towers along the wall, the glare of braziers provided occasional light to show their way. They climbed the Caelian Hill before descending the far side where rickety tenement blocks were packed together, just as they were in the Subura. Lupus slowed the pace and proceeded more cautiously as they entered the Aventine district. They encountered only a handful of shadowy figures, all of whom gave them a wide berth as they passed by. At length Lupus stopped in a small square, beside an old public fountain. He drew out a small dagger and worked away at the mortar of a large brick at the base of the fountain. When it came free he cut away at the brick until it was half as deep, sweeping away the fragments. Then he carefully replaced the brick so that it matched those on either side.

'If you need to send a message, put it behind the brick.' He paused to look at Marcus in the gloom. 'You can write?'

'Of course.'

'Good. I'll check this as often as I can, by night. If you discover anything we need to know urgently, Festus says you're to come straight to the house. Is that clear?'

'Yes.'

Marcus felt Lupus grasp his arms and saw the outline of his head dimly against the starlight.

'Are you sure you want to do this, Marcus?'

Marcus was silent for a moment. He could not deny he was scared. Yet there was no other way to put Caesar in his debt. How else could Marcus ever ask for the help he needed? He knew he was risking his life, but if he didn't take the chance he would remain a slave and be sent to one of Caesar's gladiator schools. Then he would never save his mother. No, he had to see this through. He nodded. 'I'm ready.'

Lupus gently squeezed Marcus's shoulder. 'Good luck then.' He turned to go.

'Wait, Lupus – one last thing. Will you tell Mistress Portia I said goodbye?' Marcus asked.

Lupus released his grip and nodded. He glanced at the silent streets and padded away. Marcus eased himself on to his feet. He was on his own now. He took in his surroundings so that he could find his way back to the fountain. Then, taking up his stick – the only item he had besides his worn-out clothes – he turned towards the heart of the Aventine district, into Milo's territory.

18

Marcus jolted awake as the toe of a boot prodded him roughly. Snatching up his stick, he scrambled until his back hit the solid wood of the door he'd been sleeping beside. A stocky figure was outlined against the light filtering down between the tenement blocks.

'Get out of here, boy! You're in front of my shop.'

Marcus rose to his feet, groggy with sleep. He was in an arch just off one of the main streets that passed through the Aventine district. He remembered finding the shuttered shop just after the midnight trumpet sounded the changing of the watch on the city wall. He had eased himself into the corner by the door and sat hugging his knees, shivering, until sleep finally crept up on him.

'Go on, get out of here!' The man swung his boot and caught

Marcus a sharp blow on his thigh. He cried out in pain, then scurried across the arch into the street. Looking back, he saw the man watching to make sure he'd left before unlocking his shop door. Looking at the sky, Marcus judged the sun had risen less than an hour ago. Once he was a safe distance from the arch, he stopped to take stock of his situation. He wasn't hungry as he had eaten well before setting out with Lupus. He also had twenty sestertii sewn into a fake lining of his belt, so he wouldn't starve. Aside from that, he would have to survive on his wits.

He knew he wasn't far from the heart of the Aventine district, the area known as 'The Pit', where the cheapest inns and chop houses clustered round a natural fold in the side of the hill. That was where Milo and his gangs gathered when they weren't extorting money, or hunting down the supporters of Caesar, Crassus and Pompeius. Marcus crossed the top of the hill and followed the road down the other side until he reached a crossroads. A stooped old woman was washing some rags in a public fountain.

'Could you tell me if I'm near The Pit?' Marcus asked politely.

The woman turned her head. 'You don't want to know, young 'un. Get back to your home.'

'I have no home,' Marcus replied.

'Well, you won't find one in The Pit.' She laughed, revealing a handful of crooked teeth. 'Just a quick beating before you're kicked on your way. What are you, a runaway?'

'I just want to know if I'm heading in the right direction,' Marcus replied.

She sniffed and wiped her nose on the back of her hand before gesturing towards an alley opposite the fountain. 'That's the quickest way. But it's your funeral, boy.'

Marcus thanked her as he made for the alley. The entrance was narrow and dark and the passage beyond was squeezed between crumbling tenement blocks, so close that a hand could reach from a window on one side and touch the grime-stained building opposite. Marcus made his way down the slight incline. It was so narrow he had to step aside for people coming the other way. A hard crust of trodden-down rubbish and rotten food formed an uneven walking surface.

Nor was rubbish the only thing deposited in the alley. The body of an old man lay against the wall of a shallow alcove, stripped of everything but a filthy loincloth. His eyes were closed and his jaw hung open as flies buzzed between his lips and across the bare flesh. Marcus hurried past, his hand over his nose. There were dead animals in the alley too – mostly rats and a couple of dogs, stepped over and ignored by people.

After a short distance Marcus heard the sound of cheering. Turning a corner, he saw daylight ahead and the cheering increased in volume. Steeling himself, Marcus walked out of the alley and found himself at The Pit.

An open area, perhaps two hundred feet across, stretched between the tenement buildings that loomed over it. The bare earth of the ground sloped into a natural basin. Apart from trickles of sewage running from the tenements above into a small stinking pool, the soil was parched. Around the edges of the open area were a number of inns. Some of these were set into the basements of the tenements with one side open, others were made up of old boards, posts and discarded or stolen rooftiles, little more than lean-tos. As Marcus emerged, blinking, into the light, he saw the inns were almost empty. Their customers had crowded around the muddy centre of The Pit to watch two huge men bare-knuckle fighting.

Marcus made his way down the slope and stopped to look over the heads of the crowd lower down. He edged towards the fringes of a nearby group of boys, some his own age, but mostly older. One boy a little bigger than him stood slightly apart from the others.

'What's going on?' asked Marcus.

'The Blades have challenged the Jackals to see who's top

189

dog,' the boy said with a quick glance at Marcus before turning back to the fight. 'Taurus is taking on Heracles and it ain't pretty!'

Marcus looked down at the fight. The two men were slugging away at each other, exchanging punches that slammed into their flesh like great hammers so that the muscles of their torsos shuddered under the impact. Some blows had already been landed on their faces and blood streamed from open cuts. Marcus looked over the crowd – mostly men apart from a handful of shrieking women who had gathered to watch the contest. Milo, tall and heavily built, was easy to spot, standing in the first rank of the crowd. He punched his fist into a cupped hand as he cheered on the fighters. His lips were curled in a savage smile that caused the scar across his face to crinkle. Marcus shuddered as he remembered the bloody battle in the Forum.

'Hey, you!'

Marcus turned and saw one of the larger boys pointing at him. He was shorter than some of his companions, but powerfully built. His head seemed to merge into his shoulders and his hair was cut short, like the men of the gangs. He wore a black tunic and studded leather bracers on his arms. Fists resting on his hips, the boy paced over and stood in front of him.

'I'm talking to you. This is where my gang is standing. You find your own spot. Now get lost.'

'I didn't mean any trouble,' Marcus apologized. 'Just heard the noise and came to see the fight.'

'Yeah? Well, clear off and find somewhere else.' He lunged forward and thrust Marcus back so that he stumbled and fell, the impact winding him. The other boys laughed. Their leader placed the bottom of his boot on Marcus's chest.

'Just so you don't forget. My name's Kasos and this is my gang – the only youth gang in The Pit. You don't come up and speak to us again, unless we speak to you first. Clear?'

'Yes.' Marcus nodded. 'I understand. Sorry.'

Kasos ground down his boot briefly before he removed it and delivered a lazy kick into Marcus's side. 'Now get out of here.'

Marcus rolled away a safe distance before scrambling to his feet and hurrying to the other side of the crowd. It would have been pleasing to wipe that smug expression off Kasos's face, but there was no point in drawing attention to himself. A loud grunt came from The Pit and one of the boxers stumbled back after a savage blow to the face. He stood there, swaying and shaking his head. His opponent stepped forward, raised his fist with a snarl and delivered the final blow, snapping back the other man's head. He dropped out of sight and a cheer rose from most of the audience as the rest let out a disappointed groan. Milo stepped forward and grasped the wrist of the winner, lifting it high.

'Victory to the Blades! The first round of drinks are on the Jackals!'

That brought another cheer as the crowd broke up and hurried towards the bars that ringed The Pit. Marcus watched as Milo patted the winner on the back and then climbed the slope towards the largest of the inns. He sat down at the head of a long table outside the inn and banged his fist on the wooden top.

'Wine! Now!'

A moment later a thin, grey-haired man in an apron came scurrying out with a large jug in one hand and a tray of silver goblets in the other. He set them down on the table and poured the wine, handing the first cup to Milo with a bow of his head. The spaces along the table were quickly filled by other men, and Marcus was reminded of Clodius and his henchmen at the Dolphin. *Same thugs, different sides . . .* he thought.

All around The Pit the other gang members were filling the inns and starting to drink, amid cheers, occasional shouts and trading of insults. Most of the people who had watched the fight were dispersing back into the alleys, apart from some who squatted down to talk or play dice. The giant who had lost the fight was left where he had fallen to sleep it off. Marcus walked over to a mule-tethering post opposite the inn where Milo was drinking and leaned against it while he observed the leader of the Aventine gangs.

The young gang that Marcus had encountered earlier sauntered over towards the inn and leaned against the wall beside it as if they were part of Milo's inner circle. As soon as the first jug of wine was emptied, Kasos went inside for a fresh jug and topped up their drinks, making sure to top up Milo's cup first. Then he rejoined his companions leaning against the wall. As Marcus watched, a plan began to form in his mind and he eased himself down to sit cross-legged on the ground, while he waited for an opportunity.

The day wore on and the sun rose high above the tenement blocks, baking the air trapped inside The Pit. As it became hotter, Kasos and his friends disappeared up one of the alleys to find some water. Marcus stood up, his heart beating fast as he nerved himself to carry out his plan. He casually strolled round the ring of inns and stopped to lean on the wall – taking up the position that Kasos had left shortly before. The men round Milo's table were deep in their cups and some had already fallen asleep, slumped across their arms and snoring loudly. Milo and the others were still going strong, however, and Marcus watched as one of them poured the last of the current jug into his cup and frowned irritably.

At once Marcus pushed himself away from the wall and hurried inside the inn. It was low ceilinged and crudely constructed tables and benches lined the walls. Marcus strode boldly up to the counter and rapped his knuckles on it.

'More wine for Milo!'

The innkeeper emerged from a back room and looked at Marcus suspiciously. 'And who are you, boy? Where's Kasos?'

'He had to go. Milo sent me instead.'

'I've not seen you in here before.'

'You're keeping Milo waiting,' Marcus replied quickly. 'Shall I tell him you won't let me take the wine to him?'

'What?' The innkeeper's eyes widened in alarm. 'No! Stay there, young 'un.'

He turned and hurried into the back room, emerging a moment later with a fresh jar which he thrust into Marcus's hands. 'There. Now take it to him quick as you can. Go!'

Marcus couldn't help being impressed by the fear that Milo inspired in people, and at the same time it made him more aware how dangerous his mission was. What would Milo do to him if the gang leader discovered his identity? Marcus tried to shake off his fear as he stepped outside and approached the table. He tilted the jar to fill Milo's cup. The gang leader didn't look up until he raised the cup to take a sip. Then he frowned.

'Who are you? Where's that toe-rag, Kasos?'

'I'm Junius, sir. Just standing in for Kasos,' Marcus replied, using the name Festus had given him as part of his cover story.

'Junius, eh?' Milo looked him over. 'I've a good memory for faces. I've not seen you in The Pit before, have I?'

'No, sir. I only arrived today.'

'Indeed? And where have you arrived from exactly?'

Marcus paused a moment before replying. 'Campania, sir. I ran away from home.'

'An escaped slave perhaps? There'll be a reward for your capture, if you've escaped.'

'I'm not a slave. I'm an orphan, raised by my uncle on his farm. But he treated me like a slave so I ran away.'

'And you came to Rome to seek your fortune no doubt,' said Milo with an amused expression. 'Like all of the other half-starved runts who fetch up in the slums. But you seem in good shape. Hard work on the farm agreed with you.'

'It agreed with my uncle more, sir.'

Milo laughed. 'Very good . . . Now be on your way, boy.'

'Let me work for you, sir,' Marcus said quickly, in a pleading tone.

'Work for me? What do you think you can do that these men can't, eh?' He gestured to the men lining the table. Those who were still conscious grinned blearily. Milo shook his head. 'I have no use for you.'

'I'm hard-working,' Marcus persisted. 'I can read and write and I can fight.'

'Well, you've certainly got guts stepping into Kasos's shoes, I'll say that for you. Now you best be off before he returns. Oh, too late!' Milo chuckled as he nodded towards the gang of youths emerging from the alley. 'Ho there, Kasos! Where have you been? If it wasn't for this lad here my cup would have run dry.'

Kasos looked about to apologize but he paused as he recognized Marcus. 'You . . . I warned you.'

'You know this boy?' asked Milo.

'He was bothering my lads earlier. I had to teach him a lesson and show him who's boss around here.' Kasos caught himself and bowed his head to Milo. 'Besides you, of course.'

'It seems your lesson has fallen on deaf ears, Kasos. What are you going to do about it?'

'I'll deal with him,' Kasos snarled. 'Once and for all.'

He made straight for Marcus, fists clenched and eyes blazing. Marcus stood his ground, then at the last moment hurled the jar at the older boy's feet. It was still heavy with wine and it crushed Kasos's toes before exploding on the ground, sending sharp fragments of the jug in all directions and splashing red wine all over Kasos. He let out a yell of pain that was quickly cut off as Marcus punched him in the jaw with all his might. Kasos's head snapped to one side and he staggered back a pace. Marcus hit him again and again, throwing his full weight into the punches, which connected hard with the bigger boy's jaw. Kasos wobbled as he struggled to recover from the furious attack, raising his hands to protect his face. Marcus switched his aim, striking low, into the stomach, trying to wind the other boy and put an end to the fight as quickly as he could.

His blows were beginning to tell as Kasos gasped for breath and stumbled back, slipping on to his knees. Marcus hammered him on the side of the head again, until Kasos collapsed on the ground and threw his hands up, trying to protect himself from further blows.

'That's enough!' Milo snapped. 'Let him be.'

Blood rushed through Marcus's head as he took a step back, fists clenched, ready to fight on.

'Quite the little firebrand!' Milo said admiringly. 'You're

the first boy to knock Kasos down in a while. So you're a good fighter, just like you said. I've plenty of those, but I can always use a promising new recruit. I take it you've got no home, so you can stay here at the inn. Tell old Demetrius that I said so.' He nodded in the direction of the inn. 'He's to give you a corner to sleep and food, and you can serve me wine at the table. I may find other uses for you later. Like I thought – you've got guts.'

'Thank you.' Marcus bowed his head.

'A word of advice, though,' Milo continued, lowering his voice as he leaned closer to Marcus. 'Keep clear of Kasos. You may have got the edge on him this time, but he'll be out for revenge.'

'I'll watch out for him.'

Milo raised his cup and held it up. 'Welcome to the Aventine gangs, Junius!'

19

Demetrius accepted his new lodger with as much reluctance as he dared show to Milo. Once he was alone with Marcus he pointed to a corner of the inn by the counter and grunted, 'You sleep there. You'll have gruel at dawn and whatever scraps are left at the end of the day. In between you fetch and carry the wine for the customers and keep the place clean.'

Marcus looked round at the stained plaster on the walls and the remains of food collected round the legs of tables and benches and wondered if the place had ever been clean.

'Most of all,' Demetrius continued, 'you keep Milo happy. If he sits down, you bring him a drink without asking. Him and his men. If they want food, tell me and I'll sort it out. Then you keep topping them up until they leave, or they pass out. Is that clear?'

'Yes.'

Demetrius cuffed him on the head. 'Yes, sir – that's what you say to me.'

'Yes, sir.'

Demetrius put his hands on his hips and stared down at Marcus. 'By Jupiter, I don't know what he sees in you, and I dare say you'll pass out of favour soon enough. If that nasty piece of work Kasos doesn't stick a knife in your back first.'

For a moment there was a glimmer of pity in the old man's face. 'You should never have come to Rome, lad. I've seen many like you. Of every ten that comes to seek their fortune, nine die alone in the gutter, one way or another.'

'I didn't have any choice, sir,' Marcus replied.

'Well, you're here now. Better make the most of it. You can start by sweeping the place out – hasn't been done in a while. The broom is over there in the corner.'

For the rest of the day Marcus was kept busy sweeping the floor and taking food and wine to Milo and his men whenever it looked like they were running out. Finally, late in the after- noon, the gang left to sleep it off. As Marcus came out to collect the cups and what was left of the bread and sausage they'd been eating, Milo beckoned to him.

'Yes, sir?' Marcus stopped beside his chair.

Despite the amount he had drunk that day Milo examined him with a keen eye and spoke without slurring. 'That was neat work earlier, with Kasos. There's more to you than meets the eye.'

Marcus felt his stomach leap in alarm but he kept his expression fixed and said nothing.

'You're too young to join the gangs now, but stick around, young Junius, and there's a promising future for you here in The Pit.'

'Yes, sir. Thank you, sir.'

Milo let out a loud burp and struggled to his feet. 'I'm off to get some sleep. There's work to do tomorrow.' He winked and strolled away, disappearing into one of the alleys that led off The Pit. Marcus watched him a moment, then was distracted by a shout from the opposite direction. He turned and saw Kasos and his companions leaning against the wall of a tenement block a short distance away. Kasos stared at him and pointed his finger menacingly before he slowly drew it across his throat. Then, with a curt wave to his gang, they strode off, thumbs tucked into their belts as women, children and men hurried to clear out of their path. Marcus felt a stab of anger and disgust as he watched the swaggering bullies walk away.

He wasn't happy to have made an enemy of Kasos on his first day in The Pit.

The next morning Marcus was awake at first light. He lay still for a while, taking in his new surroudings. There were already sounds of life from outside, the light chatter of women as they collected water from the fountain, the shrill cries of the children that accompanied them and – from the room behind the counter – the deep snoring of Demetrius. Marcus was pleased he'd found a way to get close to Milo and hoped he would soon overhear useful information for Festus and Caesar. He still worried that his cover story might be seen through, even though it was clear thousands of young boys like him came to Rome. And from what he'd heard, they endured even more suffering than slaves, scraping by on the edge of starvation and with beatings at the hands of bullies. It was ironic, Marcus reflected. At least boys like Lupus and himself had food and shelter. He found himself missing his quarters at Caesar's house.

Marcus stood up and stretched before heading across the dim interior of the inn. He looked outside. The Pit was still in shadow and only the highest roofs of the tenements opposite were bathed in early morning sunlight. Around the edges of The Pit, the first gang members were stiffly making their way out of their lodgings, emerging from the alleys as they made for the inns that were already opening to serve a hot porridge of barley with shreds of whatever non-rancid meat was available.

Demetrius stirred with a choking, grunting sound and a moment later the door to his room opened and he stumbled out, blinking the sleep from his eyes. He pointed a finger at Marcus.

'What are you doing dawdling about? Think this is a public holiday? Get the shutters open. Light the fire and put the porridge on.'

'Yes, sir.'

Marcus reached for the iron bolts that secured the shutters and swung them open, squinting as the light flooded in. Then he fetched wood from the store and arranged it in the stone-lined hearth at the end of the counter. Using Demetrius's tinderbox, Marcus soon had a fire lit and smoke curled up through the cooking grille into the chimney. It was like being back in the kitchens of Porcino's gladiator school, Marcus thought as he fetched water from the fountain to fill the blackened brass cauldron, then added barley and meat with vegetable scraps and stirred the mixture. Even though the smell was not particularly appealing, Marcus found he had a raging appetite and gratefully ladled a small bowl for himself. He wolfed the meal down with a small wooden spoon before Demetrius emerged again, dressed in the same tunic and apron he had worn the day before, and for many days more before that, Marcus suspected.

'Don't gorge yourself, boy! Save some for the bloody customers or I'll tan the hide off the back of yer!'

'Sorry, sir. I was hungry.'

'I don't care. Can't afford to have no street rat eating my profits – what's left of 'em after Milo takes his cut.'

The first of the day's customers began to drift into the inn, mostly workers who had jobs down in the Forum, or the meat market of the Boarium and the wharf alongside the Tiber a short distance beyond, places Marcus had visited when Festus was teaching him to find his way around the city. As they finished eating and paid their handful of small bronze coins at the counter, the early risers among Milo's gangs came in, many clearly suffering from the wine they'd consumed the previous day. They grumpily called out their orders for porridge and watered-down wine, and Demetrius and Marcus hurried to serve them.

Many were wearing sleeveless tunics so that the crossed

dagger emblems on their shoulders were easy to see. These were the Blades, Marcus realized anxiously, the gang to which Portia's two kidnappers had belonged – one of whom had escaped. Marcus looked round cautiously as he moved among the packed benches and tables, but he didn't recognize any faces. Besides, he told himself, the man had been badly wounded and might have died even if he made it back to The Pit.

As he carried a tray of steaming bowls to one of the tables near the front of the inn he heard two of the men talking.

'There's another job on today. Have you heard?' the first man grumbled as he cracked his knuckles.

'Eh? What's that?' asked his friend, sitting opposite.

'Milo's taking the Blades and the Scorpions down to the Forum this morning. Seems that Cato is prosecuting one of Caesar's followers, Calpurnius Piso. Accused of corruption – what else – when he was governor of Sicily. It's a dead cert that Clodius will have some men there to break up the trial. So we've got to keep them away, and shout down any witnesses for the defence.'

'Shouldn't be too much trouble,' his friend said, shrugging. 'Just give 'em a bit of a battering and that'll sort it out.'

'Aye.' The first man nodded and then looked up sharply as Marcus hovered at the table. 'What d'you want? A tip?

How's this: get lost sharpish before I knock your head off.'

'Har, har,' his friend chuckled. 'That's a good 'un.'

Marcus quickly retreated and continued serving the other customers until there was a blast from a horn outside. Milo's voice bellowed, 'Come on, you scum! Stir yourselves! There's work to be done. Blades and Scorpions – on me! The other gangs aren't needed today.'

The men hurriedly abandoned their breakfast and headed outside.

'Hey!' Demetrius shouted after them. 'You haven't paid for that! Stop! Stop . . .'

No one spared him any attention and soon the inn was empty, except for two workmen squeezed into one corner who had risen late and were eating as fast as they could. Demetrius scowled at the gang members as they assembled round Milo. 'Scum . . .'

He glanced round hurriedly in case anyone had overheard and saw Marcus. 'Clear up this mess. Scrape what's left back into the cauldron.'

While Marcus collected the bowls and cups, Demetrius stumped off to the rear of the inn, grumbling to himself. Outside, Milo stood on an upturned tub as he addressed his men.

'I've seen corpses with more life in 'em than you lot! Stand up straight, clear your heads and listen! We're going up against Clodius and his gutter scum from the Subura again.'

There was a ragged cheer from his men and Milo continued. 'Caesar and his cronies mean to command the streets of Rome. If we let him become too powerful, then he'll turn on the gangs and destroy them one at a time until no one stands in his way. Brothers, are we going to allow that to happen?'

'NO!' His men roared back.

'No! By the gods!' Milo shouted back. 'Rome belongs to the gangs and I'll die before I let some upstart aristocrat take the city from us.'

Marcus wished he could warn Festus, but realized that by the time he could reach Caesar's house it would be too late, and if he was missed at the inn it would arouse suspicion. No, he needed to stand his ground. If he could just get closer to Milo, then he was certain he'd discover information that would be even more valuable to Caesar.

Milo continued. 'There are some gangs who have taken Caesar's gold. The Subura gangs have rolled over, like the mangy dogs they are, at the feet of Caesar. The only real men left in Rome are here! Now take up your clubs and your blades and let's show the scum from the Subura who controls the streets. Go in hard. Show no mercy and do not dishonour those tattoos on your shoulders.' He punched his fist into the air. 'Honour to the Blades and the Scorpions! Death to our enemies!'

His men roared with approval and Milo waved them towards an alley leading from The Pit to the heart of the city. He shouted more encouragement before jumping off the tub to head in the opposite direction, towards the top of the Aventine Hill.

Marcus watched them go and continued clearing the tables. He took the bowls and cups to the trough at the back of the inn where he quickly rinsed and stacked them to dry. As he walked past Demetrius the innkeeper muttered, 'Good riddance to 'em.'

Demetrius kept him hard at work, clearing up after the morning meal, then chopping more firewood for the small blaze to keep the cauldron simmering throughout the day. There was no chance for Marcus to leave The Pit and warn his master about Milo's plans to disrupt the trial. But Marcus doubted if a warning would make any difference. The gangs of both sides would clash and Rome would take another step towards chaos. He would have to stay in The Pit until the gangs returned. Then he would wait on Milo and his leaders again, until he discovered their more secret plans to destroy Caesar.

20

At noon, Marcus's chores were finished for a while and he sat down at the long bench overlooking the open ground. The midday heat had driven most people to seek shade indoors, but Marcus closed his eyes and soaked up the warmth, his mind briefly slipping back to the years he had spent growing up on the farm on the island of Leucas. The surrounding hillsides would be covered by blossom now, stirred by the Ionian winds that caressed the islands with their cooling touch. There was a place where he would sit with the shepherd who tended the goats. Together they'd watch the small trading ships enter the bay at Nydri, and those further out, making passage between the beautiful tree-covered islands that dotted the brilliant azure sea. Cerberus, his dog, would sit at his feet, head between his paws as his eyes slowly closed in contentment. Marcus savoured the memory, refusing to dwell on what had come afterwards to ruin it.

'What are you bloody smiling at, runt?'

Marcus opened his eyes to see Kasos and his gang standing a short distance away. A shiver ran up the back of his neck, but he kept calm and tried not to look afraid.

'You've got nothing to smile at,' Kasos continued. 'So wipe it off before I do it for you.'

Marcus stared at him, noting the bruises on his face. 'You talk too much.'

'What?' Kasos narrowed his eyes. 'Is that supposed to be clever?'

Marcus shrugged. 'Statement of fact. Now if you've finished, I'm having a rest and don't want to be disturbed.'

Kasos snarled. 'I *am* disturbing you. I think you owe me an apology.'

'An apology?' Marcus laughed.

'You don't fight fair. You went for me when I wasn't ready. That ain't acceptable. It ain't acceptable by a long way.'

'I didn't know there were rules.'

'Get on your knees and say you're sorry.'

Marcus looked at Kasos and was reminded of Ferax, the Gaulish boy who had made his life a misery at the gladiator

211

training school. Marcus had put up with it for a long time because he lacked the confidence to tackle the bully. Only when they were pitched against each other in the school's arena had that fear finally gone. This time he wouldn't stand for it. He stood up and took a couple of steps towards Kasos and shook his head. 'No.'

Kasos gritted his teeth. 'You'll regret that, gutter boy. No one takes my place at Milo's table and lives.'

'Well, there you're wrong,' Marcus replied coolly, though his heart pounded and he had to will his limbs not to tremble. 'I have, and I'm quite alive. Unless you want me to teach you another lesson, I suggest you take your friends and go.'

'You're going. Not me. Tell you what, if you up and run off now and never come back, I'll let you. Otherwise, you fight me. Fairly this time.'

'Fairly?' Marcus cocked an eyebrow. 'That means just you. Your friends stay out of it.'

Kasos snorted with derision. 'You think I need their help to beat you to a pulp?'

'It looked that way yesterday,' Marcus replied, deliberately winding up his opponent. Anger was the worst enemy of a gladiator, he had been taught. Anger dulled the mind just when it needed to be sharp and alert. He watched with satisfaction as the blood drained from the other boy's face.

'Tell you what,' he continued. 'Let's agree the stakes. If you win, I leave The Pit for good. If I win, then I lead your gang and *you* leave.'

'If I win, you'll leave this world forever,' Kasos snarled.

'What weapons do you want to use?' asked Marcus. 'Fists, clubs, knives, staves?'

Kasos raised his club and swung it through the air. The wood was dark and hard with age. The shaft tapered evenly, shaped with great care, and the heavy end was studded with nails. The club had a loop in the other end, which passed over Kasos's wrist. It looked a formidable weapon, Marcus decided, as he turned to fetch his own from the inn before rejoining the others outside. He lowered himself into a crouch and raised his club.

'Not here,' said Kasos. 'Down there.'

He pointed to the small basin in the middle of The Pit where the men had fought the day before. Marcus could see the basin was filled with churned-up mud, which would hamper his mobility. This wasn't good – Kasos was far bigger and Marcus needed speed to get an advantage over his opponent.

'What's wrong with here?'

'That's where we do all our fighting, boy. Milo's rule. Break the rule and he'll break you.'

That was it then, Marcus realized. There was no choice in the matter. 'All right, down there. You lead the way.'

Kasos turned to descend the slope and Marcus followed a moment later, off to one side where he could keep both Kasos and his gang in sight. There was a foul stink as they approached the mud in the shallow basin. Kasos squelched into the middle and then backed off a few steps, weighing his club in his hand. Marcus took up his position opposite the gang leader, testing the ground under his feet. The surface had dried out and cracked a little, but just beneath the crust deep glutinous mud sucked at his boots. The rest of the gang formed a loose cordon round the basin to make sure there was no escape for Marcus until the fight was over.

'Last chance to go down on your knees and apologize,' said Kasos.

'As I said, you talk too much. You're big, but you're not fit. Best save your breath. You'll need it.'

It was a calculated remark and it struck its target. Kasos let out a bellow of rage and charged across the basin. The foul gunge sprayed up as he ran and then he slithered, stumbled, regained his balance and kept coming. Marcus crouched, club in both hands, ready to strike. Kasos, teeth clenched, stormed up to him and slashed out with his club in a wide arc. Marcus

214

swung his own club round at an angle so that the blow glanced off and up, over Marcus's head. Kasos had put all his strength into a blow that would have knocked a grown man cold if it had struck him, and it unbalanced the youth, who threw out his left hand to stop himself toppling into the mud. Marcus quickly adjusted his grip and made a sharp chop with his club, whacking Kasos hard across the shoulders. The bigger boy let out a gasp of shock and pain and rolled away, coating himself in the stinking filth. But he recovered quickly, before Marcus could close the gap, and stood up, club held ready. He had faster reactions than Marcus had anticipated, but he was still enraged and that would undo him.

'You look like something that crawled out of the sewer,' Marcus said loudly enough for the other boys to hear. Some of them sniggered.

'Shut your mouth!' Kasos blazed, then pointed his stick at one of his gang. 'And you! I'll deal with you after I've smashed this one to pieces, I swear it.'

The gang member's expression froze and he turned pale. Satisfied, Kasos turned his attention back to Marcus. He took his club in both hands again. 'You've got some good moves with that club, but it ain't going to save you.'

Marcus didn't reply, but fixed his eyes on his opponent

and stood quite still. For a moment neither boy moved, then Kasos sneered and paced warily towards Marcus. He thrust the head of the club at Marcus's face and then, as Marcus moved to block it, swung the club to the left and caught Marcus on the upper arm, just below his left shoulder. Marcus fought down the sharp, stinging pain. He stepped back and clenched his teeth, forcing himself not to utter one sound.

A gladiator does not show pain, Marcus told himself, keeping his face without expression. He repeated in his head the mantra of the training ground. *I will not let my opponent see that I am hurt. I will not . . .*

Kasos looked surprised, then disappointed that his blow had no effect. He attacked again, a diagonal strike aimed at Marcus's head. Marcus blocked again, and the next blow, and the next, until Kasos stood off again, breathing heavily.

Attack is the best defence. Marcus heard Festus's voice clearly in his head. *Attack, Marcus.*

Tightening his grip round the handle of the club, he leapt forward, striking towards Kasos's head in a vicious arc. The other boy parried the blow, and Marcus swung again to the side. Again the blow was blocked and Kasos was forced to give ground. Marcus aimed at the head, the same as before, and

216

Kasos instinctively reacted in the same manner, throwing up his club to block the attack. This time Marcus switched direction as the club was moving through its arc. He swished it round the end of Kasos's club and smashed it into the side of his skull. The blow knocked Kasos's head at an angle – his jaw dropped and his eyes briefly closed in agony. Kasos staggered, blinking wildly. Marcus struck him again, on the knuckles of the hand holding the club. The fingers sprang open in a reflex action and the club dropped into the mud with a soft plop. Holding his weapon as tightly as he could, Marcus rammed the head into Kasos's stomach. The boy slumped back, splattering down on his backside as he folded forward gasping for breath. Marcus advanced a step, bracing his feet in the mud as he raised his club, ready to strike the final blow and smash it down on to Kasos's head.

'Give in?' he growled.

Kasos was still too stunned to reply. Marcus waited a moment before the gang leader's eyes seemed to focus on him once again. He was still gasping for breath and one hand clasped the place on the side of his skull where Marcus had hit him. He stared back at Marcus, terrified.

'Do you give in?' Marcus repeated, wondering if he had beaten his opponent senseless.

Kasos nodded desperately, his eyes pleading for mercy.

There was a tense pause as Marcus loomed over his fallen opponent, club raised high, ready to smash in Kasos's skull.

'Say it out loud,' Marcus insisted.

'You win . . .'

Marcus turned to the gang. 'You all heard that. I win. Now go, clear off!' He brandished the club at the nearest boys and they backed away hurriedly, leaving Marcus and their fallen leader alone.

Marcus took a deep breath, letting the reality of Kasos's defeat sink in. He had sagged back on to the ground in relief at being spared. When Marcus spoke again it was in a flat, cold tone. 'As it happens I don't want your gang. I don't need them. You can have them back.'

'What?' Kasos looked at Marcus suspiciously.

'You can have them back, as long as you swear, by almighty Jupiter, that you will leave me alone and stay away from Demetrius's inn. Swear to that, or you can leave The Pit and never return, and I'll let one of your . . ."friends" take over.'

Kasos didn't answer at first, stunned by the offer. Then he said, 'You could have killed me. Why didn't you?'

Marcus didn't answer. He brandished the club. 'Well – what's it going to be?'

Kasos blinked nervously. 'I swear, by almighty Jupiter, to leave you alone.'

Marcus lowered his club and swapped it to his left hand as he helped Kasos to his feet. Briefly, the pair stared at each other. Kasos was the first to look away, shaking his head.

'By the gods, I've never met a fighter like you. A few more years and you'll be a match for Milo himself.' Kasos looked around quickly but there was no one close to overhear. 'Well, not that good, but a first-class street fighter all the same. You could be my second-in-command if you like.'

Marcus forced a smile. 'No thanks.'

'If you're not here to join the gangs, what are you here for?'

'To find a new life,' Marcus replied. 'An honest one.'

'Well, you've come to the wrong place.' Kasos swept his arm to indicate The Pit. 'If you want an honest living, you won't find it here.'

'It will do,' Marcus insisted. 'For now, at least.' He turned to leave.

He had just reached the door of the inn when a shout came from the other side of The Pit. A bloodied man staggered out of the alley, clutching a wound on his head. Another followed, limping, then two more supporting an unconscious body. More spilled out after them. As the members of the

Blade and Scorpion gangs stumbled into the open space, the first man cried out, 'They tricked us! Caught us like rats in a trap . . .'

'Where's Milo?' a voice called out. 'Find him quick. There's going to be hell to pay for this.'

21

'You first, Spurius,' Milo demanded as he faced the two gang leaders at the table outside the inn. It was shortly after the first men had returned to The Pit. Marcus had hurriedly brought out a jug of wine and some bread for the men who arrived at Milo's table and was standing a short distance away.

The leader of the Blades had a hurriedly tied dressing round his head through which blood was seeping. He collected his thoughts before he answered. 'We got to the Forum without trouble, and saw the trial was about to begin. Cato was there, all ready to begin his opening speech. Calpurnius Piso didn't look like he was facing any charges at all. He was clean-shaven and neatly dressed, not playing the usual trick of looking distraught and repentant. He even seemed to be enjoying himself as he sat with his lawyer. Should've guessed there'd be a reason behind it. Anyway, one of Clodius's gangs was already there, barracking Cato. We fetched up behind 'em and started to push 'em out of the way. There was the usual rough stuff, a few punches thrown and so on, but we cleared 'em out and formed a line round the stage so that no one could get in or out without our say-so.'

Spurius drained his cup and held it up for Marcus to refill. Then he continued. 'Clodius's gang had moved off a short distance to shout insults, more loudly than usual, I thought. Then the other gangs arrived. They must've been waiting for a signal because they all arrived at the same time. Hundreds of 'em, pouring out of every road and alley leading into the Forum. I could see at once we were trapped, and knew that if we stayed by the court we'd had it. So I tell the lads to follow me and run for it. We made for the exit leading to the Boarium, but they caught us before we could reach it. It was out with the staves and whatever else my boys were packing. They were all round us and we had to fight every step of the way until we reached the Tiber and split up to return here.' He paused and looked at his chief. 'We lost a lot of the boys back there.'

'How many?'

'Over fifty, between the two gangs. Don't suppose many of them are alive.'

Marcus saw Milo grind his teeth as he digested the news. 'Damn! Where did Clodius get so many men?'

'They wasn't all from the Subura,' the leader of the Scorpions chipped in. 'I recognized the tags of some gangs from the Esquiline, and even some from the Janiculan district.'

'That's bad. Very bad,' Milo reflected. 'Somehow Clodius has persuaded the other districts to settle their differences and fight with the Subura . . . We're outnumbered. Badly.'

'So what do we do now, chief?' asked the second gang leader.

Milo looked down at the table while he concentrated. The other men looked on, but Marcus saw Spurius turn to nod meaningfully at the other man. His companion shook his head and Spurius gestured more insistently, urging him on. With a shrug of resignation, the leader of the Scorpions cleared his throat. Milo continued to stare at the table, his brow furrowed in concentration.

'Er, Chief . . .'

Milo raised his head with an irritated expression. 'What is it?'

The leader of the Scorpions spread his hands on the table as he summoned up his courage.

'Spit it out, Brutus!'

The sharp tone of command made the man flinch and he stammered. 'The th-thing is, the lads have been talking and –'

'The lads?' Milo cocked an eyebrow. 'Who exactly?'

'Me and the other gang leaders.'

'I see.' Milo placed his elbows on the table as he leaned forward. 'Go on then. You've been talking. And?'

Brutus glanced nervously at Spurius, looking for support, but the other gang leader sat in silence and Brutus was forced to speak out on his own. 'The gangs are supposed to run the street rackets. That's what we've always done. Taken our money from protection charges, running the brothels and settling disputes in our own districts, right? As long as we did that, and the other gangs stuck to the boundaries, then we all lived comfortably on the proceeds. But this gang war started. Since then we've lost men and we're too busy to do our normal business . . .'

He dried up under Milo's withering gaze. After a pause, Milo spoke in a low, cold tone. 'So? Things will return to normal once we've seen off Clodius and his friends.'

Brutus puffed his cheeks out. 'That's just it. The lads want things back to how they was. They've had their fill of fighting other gangs. I said I'd ask you to call a truce with Clodius, Chief, and put an end to the gang war.'

'And how do you think that would look?' Milo asked cuttingly. 'The instant things start going against us I scurry to Clodius and beg him to stop fighting. We'd be the laughing stock of Rome. Before long the other gangs would muscle in on our turf and the people in the Aventine wouldn't lift a finger to stop them. Do you know why? Because they wouldn't be afraid of us any more. Or at least, they'd be more afraid of the other gangs. Fear is what keeps us on top here in the Aventine. If we buckle under to Clodius then we're finished. We have to keep fighting and we have to win. There is no other option. Got that?' He paused, then continued in a tone laced with scorn. 'Or didn't you and your friends think it through?'

Marcus saw the gang leader squirm under his chief's fierce glare.

'Milo, at this rate, there won't be enough of us left to run the Aventine. Don't you see? We have to talk to Clodius. We have to stop this – why are we doing some politician's dirty work, anyway?'

Milo suddenly snatched up the half-filled wine jug and swung it down in a short vicious arc on Brutus's head. The jug exploded into fragments as the dark red wine sprayed out across the table, splattering Spurius, Milo and Marcus who stood close by. Brutus's head slammed down on the table and he uttered a deep groan before losing consciousness. A ragged tear in his scalp began to bleed heavily, mingling with the wine splashed across the table. Despite his training, Marcus flinched and took a step back. Everyone at the table stared at the scene with frightened expressions. Others around the edge of The Pit had become aware that something was going on and they looked towards the inn. Milo climbed on to the table and stared down at the faces below. He called out across the open space, his voice echoing from the walls of the tenement buildings.

'I've just been told some of you are questioning my decision to make war on the gangs of that slimy upstart, Clodius. It seems you don't have the stomach for a fight. Is this how far some of you have sunk? Gutless little worms, too afraid to defend what we've spent so long fighting for? It doesn't matter how this gang war started now. The fact is we're all in it and we have no choice. We must fight and win. That's the Aventine way.' He thrust his finger down towards Brutus. 'This worthless coward told me we should turn our backs on everything we've achieved, beg Clodius to end the gang war and give us peace . . . Some peace! The instant the other gangs in Rome hear about it they'll have no respect for us. They'll take every chance to prove the Aventine gangs are pathetic pushovers, like the vermin at my feet.' Milo lifted his boot and viciously kicked the unconscious Brutus so that he crashed off the bench on to the ground, right beside Marcus. 'That's what will happen to anyone who hasn't the guts to see this war through. I want men, real men, at my back to fight that scumbag Clodius, not weaklings who run to their mothers at the first setback.' His eyes alighted on Marcus and he beckoned to him as he spoke quietly. 'Up here, lad.'

Marcus clambered up beside Milo. The man placed a heavy hand on his shoulder as he addressed his audience again. 'Even this boy is more of a man than Brutus. At least he has the courage to stand against greater odds when he needs to, and win. If this boy can stand up for himself, so can any man here.'

Marcus felt every pair of eyes turned towards him, and couldn't help feeling nervous at the attention. He was supposed to be a spy, not a public example. What if someone recognized him from the battle with Clodius?

'I will cut the throat of the next man who wants to talk peace with Clodius. We shall have peace, one day, I swear it. The same day that Clodius, and the last of his men, lie dead at my feet. Until then we fight on, without rest, without pity and without any doubt that the gods are on the side of the Aventine.'

Milo punched his fist into the air and let out a cheer. Most of his men joined him in a ragged chorus, but Marcus could see many were half-hearted, and some did not cheer at all. Milo kept it up for a moment before he prodded Spurius with the toe of his boot and jerked his thumb towards Brutus, who was lying sprawled on the ground, his head in a small puddle of blood. 'Get that coward out of here. When he comes to, you tell him he's finished as far as the Aventine gangs are concerned. If he ever shows his face here again, I'll carve it from his skull with the bluntest blade I can find.'

Spurius winced at the threat and nodded. 'Yes, Milo. I'll see to it.'

'We don't need the likes of Brutus,' Milo continued thoughtfully. 'The time has come for more direct steps . . .'

He suddenly looked at Marcus. 'What are you still standing there for? Clean this mess up and bring me a fresh jug of wine.'

'Yes, sir.' Marcus bowed his head quickly. With a sigh of relief he jumped down from the table. He trotted past Spurius as he dragged Brutus towards the nearest alley out of The Pit. At the back of the inn Demetrius thrust a broom into Marcus's hands, then picked up a fresh jug of wine for Milo.

'That's a shame,' Demetrius sighed. 'Brutus was one of my better customers – he even paid for his drinks some of the time.'

Milo was waiting for them as they stepped out of the inn. He gestured towards Marcus.

'You can leave the cleaning for now. I need you to find Kasos. There's an important errand I want him to run . . .'

It was late in the evening when Kasos returned to The Pit. He was not alone. Two men were with him, each one wrapped in a cloak with their hoods raised to conceal their features. One of Milo's men had been keeping watch in an alley leading to the gang's lair and escorted them through the other men guarding the approaches to the open space.

It had been a quiet night at the inn. Most of the customers had been subdued – especially the gang members, who had fallen to muttering among themselves, occasionally glancing round to make sure no one was listening. As the inn began to empty, Milo appeared and told Demetrius to get rid of his remaining customers and close the shutters.

'But they haven't finished drinking,' Demetrius protested.

'I don't care. Get rid of them. Now. I'll wait outside. Let me know when the last of 'em is out.'

Demetrius saw the dangerous glare in the gang leader's eyes and turned to Marcus.

'Come on, lad, you heard. Let's clear the place.'

They moved from bench to bench, passing on the instruction. Some customers started to argue, but when told who had given the order they instantly fell silent, downed their drinks and left. One last man had passed out across a table at the back. Demetrius called Marcus and they dragged him outside, dumping him a short distance down the slope. That was when Marcus caught sight of Kasos and the two hooded men making their way across the open space to the inn.

'Come here, Demetrius,' Milo commanded. 'I have a couple of guests I need to speak to in private. We'll use your inn. I take it you won't mind if I help myself to a jar of your good stuff?'

'N-no, Milo.' The innkeeper bowed his head and forced a smile. 'Of course not. Be my guest. Make yourself at home.'

'I'll also need some bread, dried sausage and olives.'

Demetrius flapped a hand. 'I have bread. But no sausage, no olives.'

'Then go and buy some. Enough to feed me and two friends.'

'Of course, I'll send the boy and —'

'No. You go. The boy can stay and serve us with wine.'

Demetrius swallowed his pride and nodded as he took off his apron. 'I'll be as quick as I can.'

'Quicker would be best for all concerned,' Milo responded darkly. 'I'm not in a patient mood.'

'At once then.' Demetrius nodded and hurried to his back room, emerging with his purse. He paused at the door and looked at Marcus. 'Go down to the cellar. That's where I keep the best wine. There's a jar of Arretian, my last.' He fought down a choke at losing his prized wine. 'Use that.'

'You're too kind.' Milo smiled as he patted the innkeeper on the shoulder. 'And use the side door when you come back. We don't want to be disturbed.'

Demetrius muttered a surly reply and disappeared into the darkness. Once he had gone Milo turned to Marcus. 'Fetch the wine, boy.'

'At once,' Marcus said, and made his way to the rear of the inn. As he reached the threshold of the back room, he heard voices and paused to look round. Milo was framed by the entrance as he spoke to someone outside. 'Here's a denarius for you, Kasos. You've done well. Just make sure you don't breathe a word of this to anyone. Now be on your way.'

Then Milo stood aside and ushered two men inside. Marcus edged into the back room and peered cautiously round the door frame to keep the men in view. His heart was pounding in his chest and his skin tingled with excitement. Who were these visitors to The Pit? Perhaps this was the moment when he'd discover something to tip the balance in Caesar's favour.

He looked them over. One man wore fine leather boots and a richly embroidered tunic. His companion was more plainly dressed and wore heavy soldier's boots. A fiery red ruby glinted on the ring he wore on one hand. Milo closed the door behind them and indicated a table close to the counter.

'I appreciate your coming. No doubt you've heard my men were given a good kicking today.'

'We know,' one of the cloaked figures replied. It was impossible for Marcus to know which had spoken from the deep hoods of their cloaks. 'And we're not pleased, Milo. You're supposed to be in control of the streets. That's what you promised us. That's what we paid you a very large sum of money to achieve.'

'Unfortunately, Clodius's backers have rather deeper pockets than you,' Milo replied tersely. 'That's why he's been able to buy the support of the other gangs. If you had paid me as much, there would be no doubt about the outcome of the fight for control of the streets. The time has come to change our strategy.'

'We agree,' said the man in the cloak as he and his companion followed Milo to the table and sat down. 'A more direct course of action is required, and that is why I have brought my friend here.'

'You can drop the hoods,' said Milo. 'We're alone.'

'Since we know each other, that's fair enough for me. But my companion's identity must remain a secret, even from you.' The man reached up with his hands and drew his hood back.

Marcus felt his pulse quicken as he recognized the man and his name almost soundlessly escaped from his lips. 'Bibulus . . .'

If Caesar's bitterest rival had dared come here to talk to Milo in person then it was clear that Bibulus and his friends were planning something so secret they dare not trust to a go-between. Marcus felt his pulse quicken. This was why he had volunteered for this perilous task. At last he might discover some priceless information for Caesar. Something that would help win this struggle for Caesar once and for all.

22

'Where's that wine?' Milo called out. 'Boy?'

Marcus edged further into the room and half covered his mouth with a hand to muffle his reply. 'Coming, sir!'

Ahead of him, to the side of the room where Demetrius lived, slept, cooked and counted his money was the narrow staircase leading down to the cellar. Next to it was the door to the alley outside, which Demetrius kept locked. Marcus took a lamp from the small desk where the innkeeper stored his ledger and shielded the flame as he hurried down the stone stairs. The air was chilly and there was barely enough headroom for Marcus to stand upright. The cellar was lined with jars, some empty, and fine strands of cobwebs gleamed in the amber hue cast by the oil lamp. Marcus found the jar bearing the crudely painted label of the Arretian vineyard and tucked it carefully under his arm before he climbed out of the cellar and placed the lamp back on the small desk. The men talked in low voices as Marcus went into the bar and picked up three cups, then made his way over to their table. His heart was pounding with excitement and fear. This was the opportunity he had been waiting for. He had to be alert, and careful.

'I've got the man for the job,' Milo was saying. 'The name's Lamina. He's done this kind of thing before. Of course, I'll need to find a way of getting him close to his target.'

'How do we know he's any better than those two incompetents you sent to take care of Caesar's niece?' Bibulus asked scathingly. 'No, I think we'll use our own man. My friend here has someone who suits our purpose. Your men have another part to play.'

Milo was about to reply when he became aware of Marcus. 'The boy's here with the wine. We'll talk more after he's gone,' he announced to his companions.

Marcus set down the cups and pulled the stopper out of the wine jar, releasing a rich fruity odour into the air, then filled each cup. The man still wearing his hood was leaning forward on his elbows, only the outline of his jaw visible. He did not look up.

'That will be all,' Milo nodded. 'Leave us alone. Get into the back room and close the door behind you.'

Marcus nodded and returned to the doorway behind the counter. All the time his heart was beating wildly. He needed to hear what passed between the three men. In an instant he decided on his plan. As he passed through the door he dropped to his knees and crawled stealthily back through, hidden by the counter. He pulled the door shut, with enough force to ensure that the latch clicked.

The silence was broken by Bibulus. 'Is there any danger he can still hear us?'

'No,' Milo replied confidently. 'The door's solid and the boy's keen to get on here. He won't risk his position. We're safe. You were telling me about your man. The one who will do the job.'

'Ah, yes. I know you've handled this sort of thing for us before, but this is different. We can't afford to have your men connected with this. It's vital that I am not seen to be involved in any way. My friend here assures me his man is good. He'll carry out the task and disappear. Your part is to provide a distraction and keep Caesar's bodyguards busy.'

'I see,' Milo replied. 'Then I shall want paying, and paying well.'

'We can afford it,' Bibulus replied. 'Isn't that right?'

The hooded man replied in a low voice. 'Money is no object.'

'Just as well,' Milo chuckled. 'Caesar is not an easy target.'

Marcus's blood went cold. These were the details of the plot against Caesar's life. It was vital he heard as much as he could, then quietly leave the following morning to report to Festus. Holding his breath, he inched forward along the base of the counter. He needed to be close to the three men so that he missed nothing. There was a hole in the counter where a knot in the wood had fallen out and Marcus eased himself towards it. He looked out at an angle – Milo and Bibulus were in view, but all he could see of the hooded man was his back.

'So let's talk about the plan,' Milo continued. 'It would be best to strike when he is alone in a room in his house, I'd have thought.'

'No.' The hooded man intervened. 'It's to be done in public. Caesar is planning to push through an amendment to the Land Bill two days from now. In it he will demand that every sena-tor swears an oath not to repeal the Act after it is passed. If they refuse to take the oath then they are to be deemed guilty of treason. Let Caesar announce his amendment before our man strikes. I will sit close to Bibulus and give the signal for the killer to strike by taking out a red cloth and wiping my brow. Caesar will fall as he leaves the Senate and passes through the Forum.'

'That's a suicide mission,' Milo countered. 'It's impossible.'

'Not if your gangs cause a disturbance to cover the killer's escape.'

Marcus saw Milo scratch his jaw thoughtfully. 'It's risky, though it could work. But why not take the easier route and kill him in his home?'

'Because then it would be murder,' Bibulus said, as if explaining something to a child. 'It is better that Caesar is killed after he announces something that can be presented as a gross infringement of the rights of the senators. That way it can be seen as the rightful killing of a tyrant. Do you understand? The last thing Rome needs right now is for Caesar to be portrayed as a victim of those who oppose distributing to the poor.'

They were interrupted by a rattle from the alley as a key was fitted to the lock of the back room.

'Here comes our food,' Milo announced.

Marcus felt his heart leap in his chest. Demetrius had returned sooner than he'd anticipated. If he discovered Marcus hiding behind the counter then he would be exposed as a spy. He would be tortured for information before they killed him. Marcus desperately tried to think of a way that he could get out of this.

The lock clicked and there was a grating sound as the door swung in on its hinges. As it shut the lock rattled again. Then Demetrius called out, 'Junius! In here, boy! I need you to slice the sausage . . . Junius!'

Milo spoke into the silence at the table. 'Strange. I thought the boy was in there. If he's slipped off to amuse himself then Demetrius will take a belt to him.'

'Junius!' Demetrius called out again, then the door to the back room opened and he stepped into the inn, stopping abruptly as he saw the three men. 'I'm sorry, gentlemen. Have you seen the boy?'

Marcus pressed himself into the side of the counter and dared not breathe as he looked to where Demetrius stood poised by the door. The innkeeper had not seen him yet.

'The boy went into the back room,' said Milo. 'Perhaps he's gone out.'

Demetrius frowned. 'No. That's not possible. I keep the door locked and only I have the key.'

'Then where is he?' Milo demanded.

'I'll try the cellar,' said Demetrius. 'If he's helping himself to anything down there, then I'll beat him to within an inch of his life.'

He turned and stopped as his eyes fell on Marcus. 'There he is! Asleep on the floor.'

Marcus shut his eyes, hoping to play along with the innkeeper's point of view, but an instant later a bench scraped on the flagstones of the floor and Bibulus growled, 'Asleep? I saw him go into the room. He closed the door . . . He's been spying on us . . .'

More benches scraped as the other men stood, and Milo cursed. 'He's a spy. Grab him!'

Marcus sprang up and raced for the door to the back room. Ahead of him Demetrius was slow to react. His face was fixed in open-mouthed surprise as Marcus braced his neck and headbutted the innkeeper in the stomach. Demetrius folded up, staggered back a pace and slumped heavily to the floor. Marcus sprinted into the back room and with a surge of relief saw the key still in the door leading to the alley. Behind him, footsteps pounded across the flagstones as Milo and the others ran after him. Marcus reached the door, grabbed the key and turned it quickly before pulling it out. As he jumped through the door, he saw Milo at the other end of the room. Then he slammed the door shut, rammed the key home and turned it – an instant before the studded timbers heaved as the gang leader crashed into it.

'The other way!' Milo yelled. 'Out the front!'

Marcus turned away from The Pit and sprinted up the alley. It was pitch black – few of those living here could afford to keep lights burning. He kept to the middle of the alley, trusting it would be free of rubbish. Behind him he heard shouts, and Milo's voice bellowing across The Pit as he raised the alarm.

'There he is!'

Marcus looked back and saw Bibulus in the entrance to the alley, pointing at him. He ran on, then saw another alley to his left and turned into that, continuing until he passed two openings to his right and then chose the second. Marcus was desperate for his pursuers to lose his trail, even if it meant risking the loss of his own bearings. As far as he could tell, he was heading roughly towards the centre of Rome, and the safety of Caesar's house. Already the sounds of pursuit were muffled, but there were more voices now, men shouting to each other, orders being given.

He ran until the shouts of his pursuers had almost faded before stopping to rest briefly. He leaned his back against a wall and gasped for breath as he thought. It was vital he escaped to warn Caesar. If they caught him, then both Marcus and Caesar were as good as dead.

23

Marcus knew he had to keep running. He followed the alley, hoping it led to the Forum. But no alleys led off on either side and soon it ended abruptly against a towering wall of brick and stone. With a shock Marcus realized it was the city wall. He'd been heading in the wrong direction. With a muttered curse he turned and ran back, towards the junction where he'd chosen the dead end. As he reached it he caught the flicker of a torch in the alley to his right. Just fifty paces away, the flaring glow illuminated a party of eight or ten men.

Marcus turned in the opposite direction. Hugging the side of the alley, he prayed he wouldn't crash into anything. His pursuers stopped at each junction to peer down the alleys. It gave Marcus a small lead while they considered which route to take.

But in looking back he hadn't see the body lying at the side. He tripped and pitched forward, gashing his left knee on a broken brick. The body wriggled away and an old man's shrill voice cut through the air. 'Oi! Watch where you're bleedin' going!'

Now the men were looking at him. Their leader beckoned and they ran towards Marcus and the old man. Overcome with panic, Marcus scrambled to his feet, but a claw-like hand fastened round his ankle.

'Not so fast! Let's see if you've anything worth taking.'

Another hand on his calf groped up towards his belt. Marcus kicked out with his other leg, glancing off the man. He adjusted his aim and kicked again. The man shrieked and he loosened his grip just long enough for Marcus to tear free and run on.

One of the pursuers called out, 'That's him!'

There was a burning pain in his knee, and Marcus felt the warm flow of blood down his shin. From his training he knew that a fast-bleeding wound could weaken a fighter quickly. He needed cover so he could put a dressing over the cut to stem the flow. Once again he darted left into the first alley he came across, followed by another right. But the men were close behind and saw the change in direction. He tried the tactic a few more times without success and then he was running along a wider street, the pounding of boots behind him as the men called out to their companions to join the chase. Every nerve in his body screamed with terror and desperation. He saw a corner ahead, a sharp left round the wall of a shrine. Diving round it, he saw a small square on the far side, where several alleys branched off. There was also a low wall beside the shrine and darkness beyond. It was an instant decision – Marcus rolled himself over the wall and dropped down on the far side. He dropped for another ten feet before landing on a steeply sloped pile of rubbish that flowed down a natural gully in the hillside. The stench filled his nostrils as he half slithered and half rolled down. The men entered the square and he heard shouting before the torch flickered above the wall.

A voice called, 'Over the wall!'

'Not on your life,' a man replied. 'There's an alley over here – this way!'

Marcus reached the bottom with a thud, winded by the impact. He squatted on his heels, one hand braced on the ground as he breathed hard and looked around. The gully had ended in a rubbish dump on a small patch of open ground. He searched for something he could use as a bandage and grabbed a nearby piece of worn sacking. Ripping off a strip, he wound it tightly round his knee. Then he was on his feet again. He headed for the nearest alley but the men were descending the hill. He took the first opening that led away from them but there were shouts from other directions now, and the only safe route seemed to be straight ahead. Marcus took it and ran as hard as he could. Then he slithered to a halt as the way opened up and he saw the wharf running along the Tiber. A hundred paces to his right stood a group of men beneath a torch. The way to the left seemed open, so Marcus turned and ran, once again forced away from the heat of the city. To his right were barges and smaller craft, and to his left the warehouses, all securely locked. A short distance ahead a trestle bridge spanned the river and Marcus ran towards it.

A figure stepped out from the shadows. Filled with panic, Marcus prepared to take the man on. This was his only escape route. He had to keep going.

But as he drew closer, the figure called out quietly, 'Marcus, stop.'

'Kasos . . .?' Marcus said as the boy emerged from the gloom.

'That's right. I was with the men who saw you come down the hill. I knew they'd block the way to the Boarium. This was the only way left open to you.' Kasos smiled faintly. 'And now you are caught in a trap.'

Marcus braced himself, ready to spring at the boy. Kasos stood his ground but made no move to attack. He smiled coldly. 'Not much fun staring certain death in the face, is it?'

'I won't go down without a fight,' Marcus growled through gritted teeth. 'You can count on it.'

For a moment the two boys were still and then Kasos chuckled. 'Don't worry, I'm here to help you.'

'What?' Marcus was stunned. 'What are you talking about?'

'You could have finished me off easily, and no one would have stopped you,' Kasos said bitterly. 'You spared my life, now I'm returning the favour. Then we're even and I owe you nothing. Now if you want to live, you'd better come with me, over the bridge.'

Marcus shot a look to both sides. More men had emerged on to the wharf in either direction.

'Fair enough,' he said, nodding. 'So let me by.'

'Not so fast,' Kasos replied. 'They know I'm here. I was sent to keep watch. If you escape they'll know I let you. I need a story to tell Milo.' He reached to his waist and the pale slither of a blade gleamed dully. Marcus held out his hands, ready to grapple, but Kasos quickly drew the blade across his own arm.

'What are you doing?' Marcus whispered.

'I'll say I tried to stop you. There was a fight, then you fell into the river and drowned.'

Marcus saw another party had emerged on to the wharf. He recognized Milo and his two guests, both with their heads covered, advancing beneath the light of a torch. He had no choice. He must trust Kasos.

'All right. Lead the way.'

Kasos nodded and turned on to the bridge. The heavy wooden planks sounded hollowly under their boots. They passed far enough over the Tiber to clear the boats rafted up below and then they were over the main flow, a dull, glistening surface that reflected the torches and braziers that flickered across the city.

'Here,' said Kasos as he stopped. 'Climb over the side of the bridge and swing yourself down to hide underneath, in the trestle. Once you're out of sight I'll call the others. I'll use this to convince them you fell in. Got it from one of the barges.' He tapped a small sack of gravel with his boot. 'No one will see you under the bridge. Wait till the morning when it's safe to come out and join the crowd on the wharf.'

Marcus took in the plan quickly. Then he turned to Kasos with a searching expression, still unsure if he should trust the other boy. 'Why are you really doing this?'

'I told you why,' Kasos replied, then gave a soft laugh as he continued. 'Besides, I'll be Milo's blue-eyed boy once you've gone. Just swear to me you'll never, ever return to The Pit.'

'You have my word.' Marcus smiled grimly and offered his hand.

Kasos stared at it briefly and then shook it firmly. 'Now, over the side.'

Marcus clambered on to the rail and carefully lowered himself down until his feet found a grip on one of the supporting timbers. Kasos turned back to keep an eye on the wharf as Marcus worked himself under the walkway.

But before he lost sight of the other boy, he called softly, 'Kasos!'

Kasos turned and looked down.

'Thank you,' Marcus said.

Then Kasos was gone. Marcus found a thick timber support and wedged himself into it. Moments later he heard Kasos shout overhead.

'Over here! I've got him. Over here!'

There was a loud splash from the river below, then the drumming of boots overhead.

'What happened?' Milo demanded. 'Where is he?'

'In the Tiber,' Kasos replied. 'We were fighting and I pushed him over the rail.'

Footsteps sounded directly above Marcus. He kept as still as he could, his breathing shallow as his limbs began to tremble from exhaustion. This might be a trick, after all – Kasos could betray him at any moment.

'Anyone see him?' asked Milo.

There was no reply as the last ripples from the sack of gravel faded away and the river continued its peaceful flow.

'He's gone,' a voice decided. 'Probably drowned.'

'Maybe,' Milo responded. 'But I'll leave a few men here in case he managed to reach one of the boats. Kasos, and the rest of you, back to the wharf and wait for us there.'

Footsteps rumbled overhead once again.

'If he's drowned, then we can continue with the plan,' said Bibulus. 'Caesar will know nothing.'

'Let's hope so,' said the familiar voice of the man whose hood remained up. 'My master will not be pleased if we fail.'

'We won't fail,' Bibulus insisted. 'Soon Caesar will be dead and all the insults and indignities I've endured will be avenged.'

Milo chuckled. 'And I thought the street gangs were the ones who are supposed to have no scruples. Truly, there is nothing more devious and lethal than a politician with a grudge.'

Their footsteps faded away and Marcus was left shivering as he perched on the support beam. His body felt sore and bruised from his tumble down the gully and he was exhausted, but he dared not sleep for fear of falling into the river. So he raised his knees to his chest, wrapped his arms round them and composed his mind to stay alert through the remaining hours of darkness.

24

'Are you certain about what you heard?' asked Caesar. Marcus stood next to the kitchen table, wearing only a loincloth, as Festus cleaned his cuts. Even he had been surprised when he'd taken off his ragged tunic and seen the full scale of the injuries he'd suffered during his escape. His knee was especially bad, a deep gash that had torn the flesh and would leave a nasty scar. He hadn't wanted to remove his tunic in full view, but Festus left him no choice. At least his shoulder faced away from the rest of the room. Marcus prayed that the filth Lupus had applied still disguised his brand.

'Yes, master,' Marcus replied. 'There's no mistake. They intend to kill you once you have announced the senators will be forced to swear obedience to the new law.'

'And you are sure that it was Bibulus you saw with Milo?'

'It was Bibulus.'

'And the other man? He never revealed his face to you?'

'Not once, master. But there was something about his voice I recognized.'

'Hmmm.' Caesar stroked his chin thoughtfully. 'This is quite a turn-up. There's a handful of men I suspect capable of having me killed, but Bibulus is not one of them. He lacks the stomach for it. I thought he was like Cato, all bluster and high principle. Now it seems he has a more ruthless streak. I wonder who talked him into it?'

There was a knock on the door frame and Flaccus entered the room. He looked surprised at the injuries covering Marcus's body.

'What is it?' asked Caesar.

'Publius Clodius is in the atrium, master. He says you sent for him.'

It was the first thing Caesar had done after Marcus returned shortly after dawn.

'That's correct. Show him in.'

'Do you wish to receive him in your study, master?'

'No. Send him here.'

Flaccus glanced round the kitchen before he bowed his head and spoke in a disapproving tone. 'As you wish, master.'

He backed out of the doorway and shortly afterwards returned with Clodius. The young aristocrat clasped arms with Caesar before turning his attention on Marcus.

'Well, well, the spy returns. And quickly too. I take it your mission was a failure.'

Before Marcus could reply, Caesar cut in. 'Certainly not. Young Marcus found out a great deal before he was discovered and forced to flee. We know the enemy's plans in detail now.'

'Oh?' Clodius turned his gaze on Marcus. 'Well, there's obviously more to you than meets the eye, young gladiator. You have done a man's job. I congratulate you.'

Marcus felt his heart swell with pride and he bowed his head in thanks.

Clodius turned to Caesar. 'So what are they up to?'

Once Caesar had briefly outlined the plot, Clodius pondered a while before responding. 'Clearly, you can't attend the Senate with a killer close at hand. You'll have to postpone your amendment until the danger has passed. I always thought it was a step too far to insist on the Senate taking an oath never to repeal the Land Bill. You know how touchy they are when too much power seems to be in the hands of one individual.'

'And you can imagine how touchy I am about politics stooping to the level of murder. My murder in particular,' Caesar retorted.

'Quite,' Clodius sniggered. 'So what do you intend to do about it?'

'I will not show them I am afraid. That would only make them more confident. So it's business as usual. I shall go to the Senate and put my amendment to the senators.'

Festus paused from dabbing the dirt and grit out of Marcus's cuts. 'No, master. Why place yourself in the way of an assassin's knife? You can't take the risk.'

'Any life worth living is a risky business, my dear Festus. But I take your point and I fully intend to reduce the danger posed to me. First, I will have Marcus join me when I attend the Senate. The other side has seen his face, so it would be best if he wore a hood. He is to watch for any sign of the signal he spoke of. The instant that happens, you and your men must close ranks about me, Festus. At the same time, I want Clodius and his gangs to take control of the approaches to the Senate House. We won't give Milo a chance to create any diversion.' Caesar looked round at the others. 'As long as we are all vigilant, there is little danger.'

Clodius chuckled. 'It's your decision, Caesar.'

Marcus wondered if his master was truly as calm as he appeared. But a sudden insight struck him. In some ways, men like Caesar were the same as gladiators. They were raised to face danger without showing fear and, if the need arose, to meet their end with dignity before the eyes of the world. Their contests might be fought in very different arenas, but the stakes were essentially the same: life and glory, or death.

Caesar turned his attention to Marcus. 'Once again, I owe you my thanks. You are as brave as any soldier I have ever commanded, and I will see you are rewarded when the time is right.'

Marcus nodded, his most treasured hope rekindled in his heart. But he knew he must wait until the threat to Caesar had passed, when his master would be as well disposed towards him as possible. Then he could ask for his reward.

Caesar turned to Festus. 'Have you finished with him?'

Festus wrung the last drops of water out of the cloth as he replied. 'Yes, master.'

'Then you can go, Marcus. Get some rest.'

'Yes, master.'

He turned to leave but had taken no more than two paces before Caesar called out, 'Wait!'

Marcus stopped and began to turn when Caesar spoke again.

'Stay where you are. What is that mark on your shoulder?'

Marcus's stomach clenched in icy terror. He heard footsteps behind and then the touch of Caesar's fingers on the scar on his back. He fought the urge to shudder. He licked his lips and swallowed nervously before he dared reply.

'I don't know, master. It has always been there.'

Caesar was silent as he examined the mark. 'It's a brand of some kind. What is that? A wolf's head . . . and a sword . . . I think I've seen that somewhere before. Marcus, turn round.'

He did as he was told and forced himself to look steadily into Caesar's piercing gaze. Marcus felt an icy fist clench round his heart. *This is it*, he thought in terror, *he knows!* It took all his resolution to keep his face as expressionless as possible while Caesar's eyes bored into him.

'Where did you get that brand?'

'I don't know, master. I didn't even know it was a brand until recently,' he replied truthfully. 'I always thought it was a scar.'

'Did your parents not tell you anything about it?'

'No, master.'

Caesar stared at him a long time, frowning. 'I've seen it before. I'm sure of it.'

'I'm told the lad's father was a centurion,' said Festus. 'It could be something to do with that. You know what soldiers are like about their secret clubs and religions, master.'

'No.' Caesar shook his head. 'That wasn't it.'

'Well, I'm sure it's of no consequence now,' Clodius interrupted impatiently. 'We have more important things to worry about.'

'Yes.' Caesar nodded, though he still stared at the mark in puzzlement. He shook his head. 'You're right. Marcus, you may go.'

Marcus bowed his head and left, walking as swiftly as he dared. His heart pounded in his chest. Outside, in the corridor, he slumped against the wall and breathed deeply as his mind raced. The symbol was a closely guarded secret. Only Spartacus and his inner circle shared the brand. How could Caesar recognize it? Perhaps he had seen something similar once. After all, the wolf and the sword were not uncommon symbols. Marcus gritted his teeth as he put aside such hopeful thoughts. The head of a wolf – the beast that had suckled Romulus and Remus, the founders of Rome – impaled on a gladiator's sword revealed an obvious challenge to Rome. Lupus had said as much. Caesar was sure to realize that, even if he didn't know the precise origins of the symbol. Marcus felt sick with dread as he continued down the corridor to the slave quarters.

Lupus was not there and Marcus was relieved to be alone with his thoughts. He lay down on the bedroll and stared at the ceiling. Now he was resting, the aches and pain from his cuts made themselves felt and he winced at the throbbing in his knee. He found himself reliving the events of the previous night with the terror of being caught and tortured for information. He'd been so thankful to return to the safety of Caesar's house, but Caesar had seen the mark of Spartacus and reminded him this was all an illusion. Once Caesar recalled what the mark meant, he would see Marcus's connection to a sworn enemy. Then there would be no reward for Marcus. Both he and his mother would be killed.

He heard a rustle of soft footsteps and looked towards the door. Portia stood in the threshold, her face ashen as she looked down at him.

'By the gods, Marcus. What have they done to you?'

Marcus reached for the worn blanket beside the bedroll and pulled it over his body. 'I'm all right, mistress. Just tired.'

'Where have you been? Festus said you were doing something for my uncle.' Her eyes narrowed. 'Have you been beaten for something? Was it Flaccus? Let me know and I'll deal with him.'

'No, mistress. I just had a fall.'

'A fall?' Portia arched an eyebrow. 'Just the one?'

Marcus laughed, and then winced from his bruises.

Portia stepped closer and crouched at his side, tentatively resting her fingers on his shoulder. 'You're in pain. I should send for my uncle's surgeon.'

'No. I don't need anything, apart from rest,' Marcus replied. 'You shouldn't be here, mistress. If they found you –'

'I would say I'm enquiring after the health of my bodyguard. Perfectly innocent.' She smiled. 'And stop calling me "mistress", please. We're alone – probably for the last time. I'm to marry Pompeius's nephew as soon as this business at the Senate is over. Uncle's arranging a feast to celebrate his success, and my marriage, a few days from now.'

'So soon? I thought the wedding was supposed to be late summer?'

'It was. Pompeius asked to move it forward. Uncle thinks he wants to be sure the alliance between them is secure.'

This was a bitter blow, thought Marcus. 'And what about our plans for taking me with you as your bodyguard?'

She shook her head sadly. 'My uncle won't let you go.'

'You asked him?'

'I did. He said you were far too valuable to him.' She forced a smile. 'It seems I'm not the only one who thinks highly of you.'

Marcus let out a sigh. It was as he'd thought – everything depended on winning Caesar's favour now. And Marcus would miss Portia's friendship.

Portia's chin trembled. 'It seems I must say goodbye to everything I have always known, and you. I owe you something I can never repay. You saved my life.'

'I saved both our lives.' Marcus smiled back.

She stared at him a moment, then leaned forward and kissed him. 'I shall never forget you, Marcus.'

Marcus held up his hand to still her tongue. 'Nor I you. Goodbye, Portia.'

She smiled, then turned away and left the room. Marcus heard her foodsteps fade and then the house was quiet again. Only the distant sounds of other slaves talking as they worked in the garden came to Marcus's ears, above the faint hum of the city. He lay back on his bedroll and stared at the ceiling again, his heart weighed down by yet another burden. Despite all his training, Marcus was suddenly struck with as deep a grief as he had ever known. He realized there was something worse than fear – worse than the terror of facing an opponent in a fight, worse than being hunted through the streets of Rome by a bloodthirsty gang – and that was the knowledge you are alone in the world.

Easing himself on to his side, he curled up into a ball, no longer able to fight the sorrow that had been building up in him for so long.

25

'At least I won't be alone in this,' Caesar announced confidently as they set off from the house in the Subura. Ahead strode ten of Festus's men, while around him marched the twelve lictors who made up the consul's honorary guard. Another ten body-guards took up the rear. At his side paced Festus and Marcus, each armed to the teeth with concealed weapons. Lupus strode a few paces behind his master, weighed down by his satchel.

Marcus decided that any assassin making an attempt on Caesar's life would have his work cut out for him. Even so, Marcus was tired. He had not slept well, troubled by Portia's news and his fear that Caesar might discover the secret of his brand. There had been no mention of it since, and Marcus prayed to the gods that Caesar would not consider it significant enough to investigate further.

The small procession made its way through the narrow streets of the Subura before emerging into the Forum. It was mid-morning and the centre of the city was filled with people. Most were shopping from the stalls lining the main thoroughfares and public buildings, but many men were clustered in loose groups, watching the passers-by as they talked and joked among themselves. Marcus wondered how many of them belonged to the rival street gangs and how many had turned up in the hope of watching a fight.

The largest crowd had gathered around the Senate House and there was an air of expectation as Caesar and his men approached the steps to the entrance. Marcus had been assigned to watch to the left while Festus kept his gaze to the right. The faces surrounding Caesar and his men had mixed expressions. Most were cheering his name and waving. But others were booing and shaking their fists, and Marcus watched closely, looking for the glint of a blade.

The crowd slowed the pace of the small column and it seemed a long time before Caesar and his entourage reached the entrance to the building, away from the danger of the gangs outside. Most of the bodyguards and lictors waited outside the entrance, but Marcus, Festus and Lupus joined the small body of clerks behind the dais upon which the consuls' chairs stood. While the clerks sat on stools and prepared their waxed slates and pens to record the proceedings, Festus and Marcus watched the senators for any sign of the red cloth that the plotters had agreed as the signal for their assassin. Most of the senators had already taken their places on the benches that arced round the dais. While many wore fine togas of white, a few of their number, mostly the younger senators, wore bright colours. Some, like Cato, wore plain brown togas, deliberately chosen to make them appear in keeping with Rome's strait-laced traditions.

As had been the case since earlier that year, Bibulus's chair was empty, and Caesar ignored it as he took his own seat and called the house to order. Marcus took little interest in the usual rituals of prayers and announcement of the agenda. Only when the debate began did he pay close attention to the contributions and reactions of the senators. While Caesar's followers and those of Pompeius and Crassus gave their backing to Caesar's amendment to the Land Bill, the other senators listened in stony silence. At last, Cato raised his hand to request permission to speak. Caesar regarded him coldly and then nodded his assent. 'Be sure not to talk at too much length,' he warned Cato.

Cato rose to his feet and adjusted his toga, looking around at the expectant faces in the chamber. Then he began.

'Those in this House represent the will of the Roman people. But they do more. It is their sacred duty to uphold the traditions that have kept our great republic free from the tyranny of kings, and those men who would be kings. Therefore it is the duty of every man here to vote against the proposal put forward by Caesar. His amendment will make it a crime for any of us to oppose the Land Bill. It would seem that the choice open to us today is to either support Caesar or be declared an enemy of Rome . . .'

Marcus knew that Cato and his allies were fighting to preserve the rights of the rich and powerful, but he couldn't help wondering if Cato was right to warn his audience about Caesar's ambitions. He himself knew that Caesar would stop at nothing to get his own way.

There were angry mutters from the men on the benches surrounding Cato. He let their comments die down before he continued. 'This measure is an insult to everything that this House holds dear. It is worse than an insult. It is a direct attack on the freedom of every one of us. Since when has it been a crime to disagree with the consul of the day? When was it ever a crime to vote against a measure you disagreed with? I tell you now, if we give way to Caesar today, then we pave the way for tyranny tomorrow. It may not be Caesar who presses his boot on our throats, but it will be a man like him. The choice before us is simple. If we value our freedom we will vote against Caesar. If we are little more than craven dogs to sniff at his heels and beg for scraps, then we will vote for Caesar.' He turned to the consul and arched an eyebrow. 'I trust that was brief enough for you. It may well be the last free speech anyone ever hears in this House . . .'

Cato sat down and those around him cheered loudly as they tried to drown out the jeers and howls of protest from Caesar's supporters. Marcus scanned the faces of the senators, but could see no glimpse of the red cloth that was the sign at which Caesar's enemies had agreed to strike. It seemed the attempt would not take place within the Senate House itself, Marcus decided.

The chief clerk rose from his seat and banged his staff on the marble floor to restore order. When the senators were quiet he turned and bowed to Caesar. Marcus saw his master compose himself before he responded.

'My thanks to Senator Cato for sparing us his usual tactic of boring us to death before a vote. His newfound brevity is a welcome relief.'

Caesar's supporters laughed and he smiled as he waved a hand to quieten them. 'I would not need to include such an amendment if there were not so many members of this House who are prepared to oppose a perfectly reasonable, fair and necessary proposal to provide our soldiers, to whom we owe so much, with a decent reward for their efforts. Why should those who have shed their blood for us be denied a small plot of land on which to farm and raise a family? Are we so ungrateful that we would deny them this? We all know why Senator Cato and his companions are opposed to the Bill. They have fine estates built up from the cheap land they purchased when those families the soldiers left behind could no longer work their farms and were forced to sell them.' He paused and his expression became cold. 'That, I find objectionable. I wonder how those who oppose this proposal can sleep at night? But since they can, and I have exhausted every avenue of reasonable debate I am left with only one means of ensuring that our veterans have the meagre reward they deserve. I move that we call a vote at once.' Caesar turned in his chair. 'Clerks, prepare to take the tally.'

There was uproar as the senators realized there would be no further debate, and it took a while before they calmed down sufficiently for the vote to be called.

'Those in favour of Caesar's proposal?' the senior clerk intoned, and his assistants counted the hands raised and agreed the total.

'Those against?'

The number was taken and the clerks conferred before the chief clerk stepped forward to give the result.

'Those in favour of the amendment, two hundred and eighty-five. Those against . . . two hundred and eighty-one. The amendment has passed.'

At once there was a deafening cheer from Caesar's supporters. Caesar stood and stretched his arms out to draw the attention of the senators. Cato and his companions looked on, furious.

'That concludes proceedings for today. The Senate will meet again in two days' time to vote on the Land Bill. Good day to you, and I thank you on behalf of our brave veterans.'

As Caesar turned away, Marcus saw him smile with cool satisfaction. Around him, the scribes and clerks scrambled to their feet. Marcus felt a tug at his sleeve and turned to see Lupus, grinning. 'It's over then. The master has got his way.'

'Not yet. There's the other vote.'

Lupus shook his head. 'That's a formality. If they passed this proposal, then they'll pass the Land Bill. Then it will be over. The street gangs won't have anything to fight about, at least not for a while. We'll have peace on the streets.'

Marcus turned his gaze towards Cato again. There was no

disguising the hatred in the senator's eyes. Marcus couldn't believe Caesar's opponents would give up so easily.

'Come on,' said Festus. 'We must escort the master back home.'

As Caesar emerged from the entrance to the Senate House there was a thunderous explosion of applause and cheering from the crowd outside. Many of the people supporting Caesar were clearly veterans themselves, judging from their grizzled expressions and the scars on their face and arms. For many others, the vote represented a victory for the poor and down-trodden over the aristocrats who had grown rich from the spoils of the campaigns fought by General Pompeius's soldiers. Caesar paused to bask in their acclaim.

'Keep your eyes open,' Festus instructed.

'I will,' Marcus replied, cupping a hand to his mouth to be heard over the din. He was determined not to let his guard slip for an instant. He knew that Milo and Bibulus would stop at nothing to see their plan through. 'I'm ready.'

They waited while Caesar's lictors took up their formation around him and Festus waved his bodyguards into position. Marcus saw Clodius near the bottom of the steps, raising his arm in a circling motion above his head. At the gesture, small groups of men forced their way to the front and cleared a path into the Forum, linking their arms to form a chain that held the crowd back.

Caesar gave a final wave and began to descend the steps. The senators and their supporters moved aside for Caesar and his entourage. This was the moment, Marcus told himself. The assassin would be in the crowd, hand clutched round the handle of his knife as he waited for the signal. Even so, Marcus couldn't believe the killer would get through. Caesar was surrounded by armed men. Clodius's gang members were holding back the public. They had all the angles covered, Marcus decided as he scanned the crowd once again.

Cheering faces, a handful of scowling faces. A few children on their father's shoulders, cheering as they held on tight, a veiled woman standing on the pediment of a statue as she waved, a cripple with withered legs on crutches who had dragged himself to the front to shout his support for Caesar.

Caesar reached the bottom of the stairs and began making his way through the Forum. Just then Marcus spotted a flash of red at the foot of the stairs, among the senators. He snapped his head round to see better. The colour had gone and he found himself staring at the group of men surrounding Crassus. Among them was the tax collector, Decimus.

Only he wasn't interested in the discussion of the men around him. He stared at Caesar, or rather past Caesar . . . Marcus followed Decimus's line of sight and his blood froze. The woman clinging to the statue reached an arm behind her back and Marcus saw the glint of a blade. She drew back the knife and took aim.

Marcus didn't stop to think. He darted forward and snatched up one of the cripple's crutches, thrusting it above his head and between Caesar and the woman on the pediment. At that instant there was a splintering crack and the crutch lurched in his hand, almost knocked from his grasp.

'Marcus, what the –?' Festus shouted.

Caesar was facing in the other direction and had not seen anything. Marcus lowered the crutch and saw the handle of a heavy throwing knife, vibrating where it had struck and splintered the solid support at the top of the crutch. Now Festus saw it too and his eyes widened in alarm. 'Who?'

'A woman, over there on the pediment!' Marcus turned to point but she had gone. 'She was there an instant ago. I saw her throw the knife.'

'Come with me!' Festus ordered.

Marcus snatched the knife from the support and thrust the stick back at its owner who cursed him for playing a stupid prank. Festus forced his way between two of Clodius's men and plunged into the crowd, oblivious to the angry shouts of those he thrust aside. Marcus ran in his wake, knife point held low where it would not harm anyone. They reached the pediment and looked around for any sign of the woman. Marcus grabbed the man nearest him and nodded up at the statue.

'The woman who was there a moment ago – where did she go?'

'What woman?' the man replied. 'Watch that knife, boy! You'll do someone an injury!'

Marcus and Festus asked a handful of other people, some of whom remembered seeing the woman jump down, but that was all.

'She's close, Marcus, I know it,' said Festus as he frantically scanned the crowd. Just then Marcus felt something underfoot. He looked down. A woman's cloak and a veil lay close to the base of the pediment.

'Festus! Look here.' Marcus bent down to show him. 'I don't think we're looking for a woman.'

Festus looked around, but the crowd was too dense to see anyone escaping. In any case, they had no idea who they were looking for. He gritted his teeth in frustration. 'Too late. We'd better get back to Caesar, in case there's another attempt.'

They fought their way through the crowd and Clodius's cordon to resume their position close to their master. Caesar shot them a questioning look, but said nothing as he continued waving at the crowd. It took the party a long time to move through the Forum and it was noon before they entered the narrow streets of the Subura and left the crowds behind.

'What happened back there?' asked Caesar as the hum of the Forum faded behind them. 'I turned away for a moment and you had both vanished.'

'There was an incident, master,' Marcus replied and held up the knife. Caesar took the weapon and examined it.

'Nasty.'

'It was aimed at your throat, master,' Marcus explained.

'Marcus blocked it,' said Festus. 'Otherwise . . .'

Caesar looked down gravely at Marcus and bowed his head. 'Once again, I am in your debt. I sincerely hope it's the last time, for a while at least. Here, a souvenir.' He handed the knife back.

As they turned into the street on which Caesar's house stood, Marcus saw a litter outside the front door. The slaves stood still beside it. An escort of lictors stood around the litter and its bearers.

'There's only one other man in Rome entitled to such

protection,' Caesar mused. 'My fellow consul for the year, Bibulus.'

Sure enough the curtains on the litter parted and Bibulus swung himself out.

'My dear Bibulus.' Caesar offered his hand with a smile. 'It's good to see you abroad. I had begun to wonder if you would ever leave your house, except to make furtive visits to the Aventine from time to time.'

Bibulus's expression was frigid and he ignored Caesar's hand. 'I'll come straight to the point. I've had news that your amendment was forced through.'

'There was a free vote, yes.'

'Free vote? Don't make me laugh.'

'That is your prerogative.'

Bibulus ground his teeth. 'Look here, Caesar, you've gone too far. But I've come on a different matter – to make you a challenge. I have my spies too, and it seems you have a young gladiator from Porcino's school. Is that right?'

'It is. In fact, this is the boy himself.' Caesar stood aside and indicated Marcus. Bibulus stared at him and his jaw sagged.

'I know you. You were at the inn!' Bibulus exclaimed, then shut his mouth immediately as he realized his mistake.

'And a good thing that he was, eh, Bibulus?' Caesar

commented in a dry tone. 'Otherwise Rome might have lost one of its consuls a little earlier today.'

Bibulus's face flushed bright red. 'I have no idea what you're talking about. Besides, I'm not here to discuss that. This boy is your fighter. I have acquired a young gladiator of my own and a fight between younger gladiators would cause more than the usual interest among the public. So, I formally challenge you to a contest between our fighters – to the death, two days from now, in the Forum, outside the Senate House.'

Caesar looked at him shrewdly. 'Before the vote. I see.'

'I have already instructed my men to paint advertisements for the fight on walls across the heart of the city. If you failed to have your boy show up, the people wouldn't like it. They might think you were afraid to accept my challenge.'

Caesar's expression showed dark fury at being forced into a corner.

A sick feeling welled up inside Marcus. The thought of facing an opponent in the arena again filled him with dread. The urge to refuse the challenge was overwhelming. But the price of saving himself would be to lose Caesar's favour, just when he hoped to gain help for his mother.

'Well, what is your answer?' Bibulus demanded.

Marcus took a deep breath to calm his nerves as he saw Caesar fix his eyes on him.

Caesar turned a look of pure loathing on his fellow consul. 'You'll have my answer when I am ready to give it, and not before.'

26

'What are you going to do?' asked Lupus as they sat together in their shared cell that afternoon.

Marcus shrugged. 'What can I do? If the master tells me I must fight, then I have no choice. But I would give almost anything not to have to fight as a gladiator ever again.'

Lupus stared at him and frowned. 'Why? Surely if you hate being a slave as much as you say this might be the quickest way to win your freedom. Of course, it might be the quickest way to be killed . . .'

'There is that,' Marcus responded dryly. He paused, then continued. 'The truth is, the very thought of it fills me with terror.'

Lupus could not hide his astonishment. 'You, afraid? I don't believe it. You risked your life to save Portia, and then you went into The Pit. You're no coward, Marcus.'

'Really?' Marcus smiled grimly. 'I tell you, my stomach feels like it's tied in a knot, my hands clammy and my limbs tremble at times. It's one thing to act on the spur of the moment, like when we rescued Portia, but another to know you will fight someone at a set time and place, and to the death.' Marcus looked away, ashamed. 'I am afraid, Lupus. I thought it would be easier a second time, but it isn't. I feel more afraid than when I faced that bully, Ferax, back at the gladiator school.'

Lupus was silent for a moment before he spoke again, in a quiet, thoughtful voice. 'And yet, you will fight, even if the master offers you the choice.'

Marcus nodded. 'I must. For my mother's sake.'

'Then you are no coward, Marcus. Anyone who lives in fear of such a fight, and is prepared to overcome that fear is a hero in my book. That's what courage is about.'

Marcus considered this and nodded. 'Maybe you're right. Even so, I wish there was a way out of this situation.'

They heard footsteps approaching and Flaccus appeared in the doorway. 'The master wants you in his study.'

Marcus stood up stiffly and flexed his shoulders. He followed

Flaccus out of the slave quarters and across the yard to the main part of the house. Flaccus slowed his pace until he fell into step alongside Marcus.

'You've become quite the favourite around here,' Flaccus said sourly.

There was no mistaking the man's jealousy, and Marcus thought how absurd it was for slaves to turn on each other when they were all victims of injustice.

'I'm a slave, just like you,' Marcus replied. 'Neither of us is special, we're just property. The only difference that counts for anything is whether you are enslaved or free.'

'Huh,' Flaccus sneered. 'There are slaves and there are slaves, boy. Some of us have worked hard and proved our loyalty over many years before we are shown the least sign of favour. But you? You walk in here and you're instantly Caesar's pet. It ain't right.'

Marcus laughed hollowly and raised his arm to show Flaccus his cuts and bruises. 'Do I look like some pampered pet?'

Flaccus glanced at his arm and shrugged. They continued the rest of the way in silence. Marcus could not help feeling angry – what hope was there for slaves while they were divided by petty jealousies and competing for their master's favour?

Unless all those enslaved by Rome recognized their common interest, they would never win their freedom.

They reached the study and Flaccus cleared his throat before knocking on the door frame. 'Master, the boy's here.'

'Send him in.'

Flaccus bowed his head and waved Marcus forward. As he entered the study, Marcus saw Festus sitting on a bench beside their master's desk. A decanter of wine and two finely blown glasses sat between them.

Caesar looked at his steward. 'How are the preparations for the feast going?'

There had already been several deliveries of meats and exotic fruits to the house earlier in the day, and Marcus had learned from Lupus that Caesar planned to celebrate the passing of his Land Bill the same evening that he officially announced the coming wedding of Portia to Pompeius's nephew, provided the vote went in his favour.

'The ingredients for the dishes have been ordered, master. And the wine. I have booked the dancers and the musicians. I am waiting confirmation from the Greek mime company.'

'Waiting?' Caesar frowned.

'Yes, master. It seems they might not be able to script and rehearse the outline you provided for them. One of the cast

281

has fallen ill and they've had to take on a new man.'

'Then you had better inform them they will do as I require, come what may. You might let them know it is unwise to let down a serving consul, if they ever want to have more work in Rome.'

'Yes, master.'

Caesar waved his hand dismissively. 'You may go, Flaccus. Make sure I am not disappointed. Close the door behind you.'

Once Flaccus had gone, Caesar gestured Marcus towards the bench. 'Sit down.'

Caesar poured him a small glass of wine, then topped it up with water from a brass jug. 'Here.'

'Thank you, master.' Marcus took a sip and found the fruity flavour to his taste.

'Not too much, eh?' Festus smiled. 'You'll need to keep your wits about you for the next few days. How are you feeling, lad?'

Marcus considered putting a brave face on it, but decided it was more important to be honest in advance of the coming fight. 'The cuts and grazes are nothing. The bruises hurt, but they won't hinder me. It's only the knee that worries me.'

'Let me see.'

Marcus laid his leg along the bench and Festus carefully

removed the dressing. A wide, blackened scab had formed over the puckered flesh and clear liquid oozed out from one end. Festus drew a deep breath before he replaced the dressing and told Marcus to lower his leg.

'The joint will be a little stiff,' Festus reported to Caesar. 'I doubt that Marcus will have full mobility within the next two days. If he works it too hard, or opens the wound while fighting, he will bleed.'

'That's too bad,' Caesar replied. 'He must fight. I've thought it through and I have to accept Bibulus's challenge. If I back down, then I will look weak.' He fixed his eyes on Marcus and gave him a sympathetic look. 'Marcus, you have to understand my position. I know you are the one called upon to fight, and I trust you will do all you can to win. You will have to, in any case – I dare say Bibulus has ordered his gladiator to show no mercy and ask for no quarter. In all likelihood, it will be a fight to the death, no matter what the spectators want. Be clear about that.'

Marcus nodded. 'I understand, master.'

'I would not call on you to fight if I had any choice. My opponents have been clever and forced me into this. They hope you will be defeated, and that it will reflect badly enough on me to sway the mob in their favour, and also the handful of senators needed to defeat my Land Bill.' Caesar took a mouthful of wine and continued. 'If that is voted down, then General Pompeius's veterans will be denied the land they feel is their just reward. They will put pressure on Pompeius to stand up for their interests. I fear that Pompeius may be prepared to throw caution aside and declare himself dictator of Rome. Marcus, the last time there was a dictator, tens of thousands of people were killed. The streets of the city ran with blood – the gang wars we have witnessed these past months are nothing in comparison.' Caesar winced at the memory. 'That is why we must win the vote, and why nothing can be left to chance. I need you to win that fight, Marcus. The lives of thousands depend upon you.' He stared intently across the table. 'Can you do it?'

Marcus met his gaze coolly. He wondered if Caesar truly had the interests of his fellow Romans at heart. But whatever the truth might be, Marcus knew the fates of other people hung in the balance and that he must fight for them.

In a fight to the death he would do all he could to survive. He was a skilled fighter and Festus had taught him a number of new tricks and techniques. Marcus was as well prepared as any gladiator his age could hope to be. But there was always the element of chance. A slip or an unexpected distraction could lose him the fight. And there was the question of his opponent, who might simply be the better gladiator. Too many factors were involved for Marcus to give a definite answer. He turned to Festus. 'Have they named my opponent on the street notices?'

Festus shook his head. 'He is merely described as the champion of a gladiator school in Campania. I've asked about, but Bibulus has kept him tucked away.'

'Do we know what type of gladiator he is?'

'No. Not even that,' Festus replied with a shrug.

'I see.' Marcus sighed in frustration. He turned back to Caesar. 'Master, I will do my best. That is all I can promise.'

Caesar nodded slowly. 'And that is all I can reasonably ask. I have been more than well served by you, Marcus, and I promise to reward you when our troubles have passed. You shall not find me ungenerous.'

Marcus thought quickly. Here was his chance. In two days' time he might be dead, so there was nothing to lose in making his demands now. Even if Caesar was angered by his terms there was little he could do about it. Caesar needed Marcus, he needed him as fit as possible, and so he dare not punish him. Marcus cleared his mind of all but the most important considerations.

'Master, I will fight as well as I can. I want to live. Also, I understand what is at stake for you and your allies in the Senate. If I win then I shall deserve my reward, and I will name it now.'

Caesar's eyebrows rose. 'You would presume to tell me?'

'Yes, master.' Marcus swallowed his nerves and continued as boldly as he could. 'If I win, then you will have your great political victory. I have saved your life, and your niece's life, twice. I will deserve more than your gratitude.'

'How dare you!' Festus interrupted, outraged.

'Let him speak!' Caesar commanded. 'Now that he has found his tongue, I will hear what he has to say. Continue, Marcus.'

He nodded his thanks. 'You know my story, master. You know the great injustice that my family has suffered. My . . . father lies dead, my mother is condemned to a chain gang, and I have endured the hardship of a gladiator's training. If I win the contest in two days' time, then I shall want my freedom. I shall want freedom for my mother and I shall want the tax collector Decimus brought to justice. Those are my terms.'

'I can promise the first, and I will do what I can for your mother,' Caesar replied. 'But as for the third, I shall need evidence I can use against Decimus.'

'Be that as it may,' Marcus replied firmly. 'I will have my revenge. One way or another.'

'Is that a threat?' Caesar could not help looking slightly amused.

Marcus did not feel a shred of humour in his body as he replied. 'It is a promise.'

Caesar was quiet for a moment before he nodded. 'Very well, I agree to your terms.'

'Then swear an oath to guarantee it, master. With Festus as witness.'

Caesar sucked in a sharp breath and spoke in a low, cold tone. 'Be careful, young man, you may push me too far.'

'Master, I have nothing to lose.'

Festus shifted uncomfortably in his chair but dared not pass any comment. There was a deadpan expression on Caesar's face. Marcus had seen that look before . . . when Caesar was contemplating some ruthless deed.

All three were still and silent. The tension was almost as much as Marcus could bear. He feared he had gone too far, and Caesar might well have him flogged, but there was no turning back now. There was a deep frown on Caesar's brow when he finally spoke.

'I swear it, by the most sacred gods of my family.' He gave

a dry laugh. 'Who would have believed it? A consul of Rome held to account by a mere slave boy. That I have lived to see this . . .'

27

They arrived early in the morning, a full hour before the appointed time for the duel. It had rained hard during the night and the flagstones in the Forum were slick and gleamed dully in the pale light. The air, usually heavy with the stink of the city, was fresh and had a slight musty tang as the morning sun evaporated the puddles on the dirty streets.

Marcus was accompanied by Festus and a handful of his bodyguards who carried Marcus's weapons and equipment, as well as a small litter to take him back to his master's house if he should lose the fight. Caesar had yet to set out for the Senate House, and was conferring with Pompeius, Crassus and the rest of his closest political allies. Regardless of how the duel turned out, the vote over the Land Bill would go ahead and they had to be ready for any last-moment switches in allegiance.

A large crowd of people had already claimed the best vantage points to watch the contest. Once Festus's men had set down the equipment they began to rope off an area in front of the steps of the Senate House to form a makeshift arena, a square of roughly sixty feet on each side.

Marcus stood by the equipment as Festus oversaw them. He was filled with the same dread he had felt at his last fight in an arena – at Porcino's school, months ago now. He felt sick to his stomach and the tension heightened his senses so the world around him seemed drenched with colour, light and shade, and the sounds of the city were more keen and rich in tone. Even his sense of smell detected subtle odours he had not been aware of before. His limbs felt light and tense and they trembled a little.

'Here, take my cloak,' said Festus, wrapping it around Marcus. 'Better?'

Marcus nodded. 'Thank you.'

'Try not to think about the fight itself. Concentrate on your preparation.'

Not knowing what weapons the other gladiator would be using, Festus had opted to play safe and have Marcus fight as a retiarius – a net man. This meant he was protected by a shoulder guard and a studded leather stomach belt, and armed with a short trident with cruelly barbed points, as well as the net itself. This was eight foot across, weighted at the edges and attached to Marcus's wrist by a leather loop, which he could easily slip off if the need arose. Although he would have hardly any protection, Marcus would be able to move and strike quickly.

They had spent the previous day practising in the yard. During the morning, Festus had taken the role of a heavily armed Samnite, constantly trying to rush Marcus and force him into a corner. But Marcus had learned to avoid that trap and darted aside, casting his net to trip Festus, or throwing it high in an attempt to tangle him in its folds. Marcus had been careful to favour his wounded knee and had been knocked down twice, much to Festus's irritation. In turn, he had brought down his trainer three times and Festus had been grudgingly satisfied. In the afternoon, Festus had sparred as a retiarius and it had become a fierce and focused duel in which Festus had used his greater size and speed to hold his own. They had ended the day hot, tired and sweating, with equal honours.

Although he still felt a little stiff, Marcus was ready to face his opponent. His knee had been carefully bound to protect the wound while giving him as much mobility as possible. He felt confident about his weapons and had carefully chosen the most balanced trident from the small armoury at Caesar's house.

291

'Best get you limbered up,' said Festus. He took a pot of garlic oil from his leather satchel and poured some into the palm of his hand. 'Take off the cloak.'

Marcus did as he was told and shivered in the cool air as Festus gently kneaded his shoulders, arms and legs, easing the tension out of the muscles. Once he had finished he handed the cloak back to Marcus – just as Caesar and his closest political allies strode up. Lupus followed a short distance behind his master and offered Marcus a nervous smile as they approached.

'All ready, Marcus?' asked Caesar.

'Yes, master.'

General Pompeius looked over Marcus and sucked in a breath through his teeth. 'Are you certain about this, Caesar? Our hopes are riding on this boy and, well, he doesn't look much like a champion gladiator to me. Isn't he the one who allowed two gang members to kidnap my future daughter-in-law?'

'I know this boy well,' Caesar countered. 'He has the heart of a lion and can strike with the speed of a panther. Trust me, Pompeius. I know what I'm doing.'

'I hope so, for all our sakes.'

As his companions mounted the steps to find a place to watch the fight, Caesar waited behind. He placed his hand on Marcus's shoulder and smiled.

'What I would have given for a son like you . . . May the gods protect you, Marcus. And there's something else.' He reached inside his toga to pull out a small silk scarf. 'Portia sent this to you – for luck.'

Marcus felt his spirits rise as he took the scarf. A sweet scent rose from the material. He carefully folded the scarf into a loose band and tied it securely about his neck. Caesar nodded with satisfaction, then patted Marcus's shoulder affectionately and strode off to join the others. Marcus wondered if the gesture was real, or whether it was merely one of Caesar's tricks to win the loyalty of those who served him.

By now the crowd had swelled and Caesar's lictors joined Festus's men to keep people back from the rope perimeter. Shortly before the fight was to begin, Lupus stood on tiptoe, craning his neck as he stared across the Forum.

'Here they come.'

Bibulus and his bodyguards appeared through the crowd, leading a small procession of allies, including Cato, as well as his fighter and trainer. The crowd parted before them as people tried to catch sight of the other gladiator and assess his form before making bets on the outcome. Marcus strained for his first sight of his opponent, but there were too many people in the way.

Bibulus waited while the rope was lowered, then crossed the open space and raised his hand in greeting to Caesar. No words passed between them, but Bibulus stopped in front of Marcus and shook his head mockingly. 'Is this the gladiator who will save Caesar's honour?'

Those close enough to hear grinned or laughed at the comment, and Marcus felt a flush of rage. He quickly checked the feeling. Bibulus was trying to unsettle him – what had he been taught? He must not let his anger throw him. Instead, he raised his voice as he replied. 'I wonder what this senator even knows about honour?'

The crowd laughed again, some of them cheering, and Bibulus's amused expression turned to anger. He leaned closer to Marcus. 'We'll see who is laughing when my boy smashes you to the ground and plunges his blade into your throat . . .'

He turned round abruptly to address the crowd. 'To honour the noble people of Rome, and as a blood offering to the gods to guide the judgement of those about to vote on the most important legislation in a generation, I offer you this fight between two of the finest young gladiators in the republic! Fighting for Caesar, we have Marcus, from the school of Porcino in Campania. Opposed to him, I give you my champion, from the same school . . .'

He gestured towards the group of men who had accompanied him, and they parted to allow the gladiator to step forward. He was taller than Marcus and well built. He already wore his equipment and was armed as a Samnite, with leg guard, heavy square shield, and a gleaming bronze helmet with two red plumes rising on either side of its crown. Marcus was desperate for a look at him, but his face was obscured by the helmet's grille. He hardly dared think the name he suspected, but Bibulus had said his opponent was from the same school . . .

The gladiator stopped, ten feet from Marcus, leaned his shield against his thigh and reached up, undoing the strap to lift the helmet from his head, just as his master announced his name.

'Ferax, the Celt!'

Of course. Marcus smiled grimly at the sneering boy who had made his life a misery at Porcino's gladiator school. Who else would be so determined to defeat and kill him? Bibulus had made a cunning choice of opponent.

'My old friend,' Ferax chuckled. 'It's been a long time, and not a day has passed when I haven't prayed to the gods for a chance to face you again. Only this time, I win, and you die.'

'Ferax . . .' Marcus whispered to himself. *Why did it have to be Ferax?*

The memory of their last meeting in the arena sent a tremor of fear down Marcus's spine. Ferax had lost and Marcus had spared him, leaving the Celt humiliated.

Festus leaned close to Marcus and whispered urgently, 'Control your fear. Don't show him you are afraid.'

Marcus nodded. He took two steps towards his opponent, drawing himself up to his full height. 'You're still all mouth, Ferax. I beat you last time we met. I should never have let you live.'

'That was a mistake you're about to pay for,' Ferax sneered. 'With your life.'

Realizing there was more to this confrontation than two strangers fighting, the crowd fell quiet and tried to catch every word of the brief exchange. But before Marcus could reply to Ferax, Bibulus raised his hands.

'Let the contest begin! Gladiators, prepare!'

Ferax replaced his helmet, drew his sword and stood waiting while Festus securely fastened Marcus's flanged shoulder guard and, once Marcus had dusted his hands with chalk to ensure a good grip, handed him the net and trident. As he shook his limbs and rolled his neck, Marcus noticed a disturbance at the side of the roped-off area. A small group of boys had squeezed to the front, and almost at once there was a surprised cry. 'Look, it's Junius!'

Marcus looked over to see Kasos staring at him in astonishment. He smiled faintly and nodded a greeting.

'To your marks!' came a voice. The official overseeing the fight stepped forward and used his staff to mark two flagstones, ten feet apart.

Ferax sauntered into place, and turned to tap the side of his blade against the rim of his shield. With a last deep, calming breath, Marcus took up his position and raised his left hand to lift most of the net from the ground. He gripped the shaft of the trident tightly in his right and lowered himself into a well-balanced crouch.

The official glanced from side to side, then thrust his staff into the air as he stepped away quickly.

'Begin!'

28

Marcus stood his ground, watching Ferax like a hawk. At first, Ferax did not move, aside from continuing to tap the rim of his shield. Then he walked forward casually until he had halved the distance between them. Suddenly he lunged forward, and before he could help himself, Marcus flinched back.

Ferax laughed contemptuously. 'Go on, little man, jump!'

Marcus gritted his teeth. He recalled the fear he had lived under as he endured the Celt's endless torments at the gladiator school. *Enough!* Marcus fumed at himself. He was playing into his enemy's hands. He had to shake off the past. He must think of Ferax as his opponent of the moment, and forget anything that affected his concentration.

He stepped forward himself, lifting the net clear of the ground, and began to swing it slowly to and fro. Ferax watched him warily. It was clear that he was no longer the impulsive fighter of several months before. Marcus had been the cautious one then. It gave him an idea – could he use their previous encounter to his advantage? If Ferax was expecting him to be cautious, Marcus needed to do something unexpected to throw him off his guard. Abruptly he rushed forward, stabbing his trident towards Ferax's exposed neck. The blow was blocked with the shield as Marcus had expected and, as he snatched his right arm back, he swung the net out wide to his left, attempting to snag Ferax's sword arm. Ferax twisted and stepped nimbly out of reach, and the two faced each other again, breathing hard as they planned their next moves.

'Come on, Junius!' Kasos called out. A man next to him said something in an irritable tone. Kasos looked surprised.

'No? Really? All right then . . . Come on, *Marcus*! Stick it to him!'

His gang took up the chant and Marcus smiled grimly, then dashed forward again, feinting at his foe's throat. As Ferax's shield went up, Marcus altered the angle of the thrust towards his opponent's leg. The outside prong gashed the other boy's thigh and Ferax let out a cry of pain and anger, before he charged inside the reach of the net and slashed his sword in an arc aimed at Marcus's face. Marcus felt the sweep of air and heard the hiss of the blade as he narrowly managed to duck beneath the finely honed edge, and just had time to thrust his trident under Ferax's exposed armpit. There was not much force in the blow but the prongs gouged three shallow wounds in his side. Marcus sprinted forward past his opponent, then turned quickly, hoping to strike from behind. But Ferax spun round and was on guard before Marcus was balanced enough to use his trident.

They faced each other again. Ferax was breathing loudly through the grille of his helmet, which hid his expression and made him more intimidating. Marcus swished his net forward gently so that it rasped over the ground, trying to unsettle his opponent. Blood trickled down from the small cuts in Ferax's side and thigh but Marcus saw that he was not bleeding enough to interfere with his ability to fight.

'First blood to you, Marcus,' the Celt growled. 'I was going to offer you the chance to end this quickly and painlessly, but now I'm going to make you suffer.'

Marcus did not reply, but stayed in a crouch and began to circle round to one side, forcing Ferax to face him and present his back to the nearest corner. Marcus feinted with the trident and then swung his net low towards his opponent's feet, forcing Ferax to retreat out of range. He repeated the strategy and once again Ferax gave ground and was now no more than six feet from the corner of the roped-off area. Beyond the Celt Marcus could see the faces of the mob. Some were urging Marcus on, their faces contorted with cruel excitement. Those supporting Ferax bellowed with rage that he was retreating.

Ferax sensed he was running out of space and braced himself to attack. Marcus saw him draw his weight back in readiness an instant before Ferax charged forward with an animal roar, his feathers swaying violently above his gleaming helmet. He thrust his shield forward, then made a cut towards Marcus's head with his sword, and then again, always powering forward. Marcus had no choice but to fall back before the onslaught and Ferax gave him no time to ready his net. Now it was Marcus's turn to be pressed back towards a corner and he well knew the danger of such a trap. There was only thing he could do. As soon as Ferax made the next thrust Marcus dived down and rolled under his shield, and rolled over again before regaining his feet, gritting his teeth as he felt the wound to his knee tearing open. Ferax slithered to a stop on the wet stones and turned round as the crowd let out a roar of approval for Marcus's daring move.

The cheering seemed to provoke Ferax and he battered the side of his sword against the rim of his shield as he worked himself up for another attack. With a loud roar, he charged forward, hacking at the shaft of the trident that Marcus thrust back at him. Marcus made to leap to one side and let the Celt rush past him, but Ferax anticipated the move an instant later and swung his shield round to strike Marcus. The corner struck his wounded knee and an intense pain shot up his leg. Marcus scrambled to one side and the two fighters stood a short distance apart, chests heaving as they sized each other up again. Marcus felt something warm flowing down his shin and glanced down. The blow from the shield had torn the dressing aside and gouged open the wound. Blood was welling out of the torn flesh.

'Ha!' Ferax shouted gleefully. 'I have him!'

The crowd's cheers subsided a little as they caught sight of the bright crimson streak on Marcus's leg. He carefully tested the weight and felt the muscles of the leg tremble. A wave of nausea swept through him as the pain took hold and he tottered back a pace, gritting his teeth so tightly that they ached.

'Now I shall have my revenge,' Ferax muttered. He lowered himself into a crouch, ready to make another attack.

Marcus thought quickly. He was at a disadvantage now. Only one thing might save him – he must not give his foe the chance to attack first. Ignoring the pain in his knee, Marcus swiftly stepped forward, slipping the leather loop from his wrist and swinging the net out and above his head, circling it ready to throw, his trident held out with a straight arm as he aimed the points at his opponent's throat. Then he cast the net, hurling it high so it caught Ferax's shield and sword and covered his helmet, before the weights closed the edges of the net around his body. It was a fine cast of the net and the crowd gasped in anticipation as Marcus took the shaft of his trident in both hands and moved forward.

'Get off! Get off!' Ferax shouted as he struggled to free himself. The sword came free from the strands of the net but the shield was still caught in its folds. With a curse, he released his grip on the handle as he let the shield and net drop to the ground. Now he faced Marcus with only his sword, much shorter in reach than the trident.

Marcus feinted and Ferax stumbled away from the barbed points.

'Go on then,' Marcus smiled grimly. 'Jump . . .'

But none of this was funny to Marcus and his expression hardened as he thrust at Ferax in earnest. The other boy parried the trident, and then again as Marcus continued to jab at him. The crowd's excitement reached a pitch as they cheered deafeningly.

'Kill him!' Kasos cried out.

Marcus tightened his grip on the shaft of the trident and made an obvious attack directly at Ferax's chest. The Celt threw up his sword and at the last instant Marcus pulled his thrust, just enough to let the sword pass between two of the prongs of the trident. Then he gave the shaft a violent twist to the side. The sword was wrenched from Ferax's hand and clattered to the ground ten feet away. At once Marcus side-stepped to place himself between Ferax and his weapon, and then moved in, forcing Ferax into a corner until he was pressed up against the crowd. There was a cry of alarm and a man thrust Ferax forward. As he did so, Ferax's toe caught on the corner of the flagstone and he fell face down at Marcus's feet, the rim of his helmet ringing with the impact.

Marcus pressed his boot down on Ferax's back and pushed the prongs of the trident against his neck. 'Don't move!'

Ferax lay still and said nothing, and then a terrible keening cry of rage and bitter frustration strained from his lungs.

'Finish him!' a voice bellowed from the crowd. Others took up the cry. Marcus felt an impulse to thrust the trident home and kill his defeated opponent, and he knew the audience would cheer him for it. Then he recalled the last time he had fought Ferax and the same revulsion flooded into his heart. Despite everything that Ferax had done to him, they were both victims of the same crime against humanity. Marcus leaned forward and spoke urgently. 'Ask for mercy if you want to live! Ferax, do it, before it's too late!'

'Death! Finish him! Kill!' The shouts were spreading through the crowd.

Ferax eased a hand out and lifted it slowly, extending his first two fingers. Now some of the crowd began to call for his life to be spared, and others joined in so that the Forum filled with the din of competing cries. There was no way for Marcus to tell which side was in the majority, so he looked towards Caesar for a decision – and hoped it would not mean Ferax had to die.

His master looked round at the crowd, taking in the disappointed face of Bibulus, then raised his thumb. Relief surged through Marcus as he lifted the trident from Ferax's neck. Slowly, he turned to look at the crowd, deafened by the roar of his name from thousands of throats.

'Marcus! Marcus! Marcus!'

He could not deny the thrill of his triumph and the giddy joy of having survived the fight. Marcus punched his trident into the air, and again as he yelled his name along with the crowd. He turned and saw Lupus grinning at him. Suddenly the grin faded and Lupus thrust out his hand, pointing behind

Marcus. He was shouting something, but his words were lost in the din.

Marcus frowned, lowering his trident, and turning to follow the direction of Lupus's finger. He saw a blur of movement, Ferax bare-headed, a ferocious snarl on his face as he snatched up the sword. Marcus just had time to raise his trident before Ferax crashed into him, smashing him back on to the ground. His head cracked against the wet stone and everything went black.

'Marcus! Marcus . . .'

Slowly the black gave way to light, with a blurred face looming over him. He blinked and his vision began to clear. An agonizing pounding filled his head and he winced.

'Marcus, can you hear me?'

'Y-yes,' he muttered. Now he saw a ring of other faces around him, strangers, looking down. Then he recognized Lupus and Festus staring at him anxiously. He was still in the arena. What had happened? Festus gently lifted him to his feet and supported him round the shoulders. 'Ferax!' He started in alarm.

'Easy there,' said Festus. 'You're all right.'

'Where's Ferax?' Marcus demanded.

'There.' Festus nodded at the ground.

Ferax lay on his side, his eyes wide open and unblinking. His mouth was firmly closed, pinned into place by the prongs of the trident that had impaled him under the chin and pierced his skull. Marcus stared at his body, feeling empty and sick. Festus saw his expression. 'He attacked you when your back was turned. It was lucky you raised your trident in time . . . Anyway, he got what he deserved. Shed no tears for him, Marcus.'

Before Marcus could respond there was another man standing in front of him. Caesar was smiling widely. 'Well done, my boy! A fine victory. I'm proud of you. And grateful.'

Caesar called one of his slaves over. 'A purse of silver for my champion. And give the rest to the crowd.'

The slave bowed his head and then fished into his haversack, taking out a small leather purse the size of a pear that he pressed into Marcus's hands. Then he reached into his bag again and took out a fistful of bronze coins, which he hurled into the air. The crowd cried with excitement as people snatched at the coins, or bent down to retrieve those that had fallen to the ground.

'Caesar!' the slave cried out, throwing out a last handful of coins. 'Caesar!'

The cry spread through the crowd, echoing off the walls.

Marcus watched as Caesar turned back towards the Senate House and climbed the steps at a stately pace. Most of the senators on either side joined the crowd in cheering his name.

Now the fight was over, Marcus felt his limbs tremble with relief as Festus wrapped his cloak over Marcus's shoulders and steered him away, back in the direction of the Subura. 'Festus. I didn't mean to kill him.'

'You had no choice, boy. Listen, we're finished here, Marcus. You need rest, and later something to eat. You may want nothing now, but you will later. Trust me.'

Marcus was in no mood to argue. He let himself be guided by Festus, and was almost oblivious to the pats on his shoulder and the ruffling of his hair from those in the crowd who congratulated him as he moved through the throng. He reached up and with trembling fingers unfastened Portia's scarf. He breathed in the scent, marvelling at how good it smelt. Closing his eyes, he sent a prayer of thanks to the gods. He was still alive.

29

When they returned from the Forum, Festus removed the bloodied dressing from Marcus's knee, shaking his head at the wound, raw and red where the scabs had opened. He cleaned it up, rinsing away the fresh flow of blood, and then put on a new dressing. After that he brought some porridge from the kitchen, hot and steamy, and made Marcus finish the bowl before he ordered him to get some sleep.

Marcus was content to obey Festus. The hard training of the previous day, the anxiety of a largely sleepless night and the frenzied burst of energy and nerves in the fight had left him utterly exhausted. He slumped back on his bedroll and Festus covered him with a blanket and his cloak, then left the cell, closing the door behind him. Marcus stared up at the ceiling, troubled by flashes of images from the fight. Then he forced the dark visions from his mind and closed his eyes, breathing deeply and slowly until he slipped into unconsciousness.

'Marcus . . .'

He felt a hand gently shaking his shoulder, and opened his eyes a fraction. Lupus was squatting beside his bedroll. The room was filled with shadows and only a weak shaft of light from the window high above pierced the gloom. Marcus sat up slowly, groaning at his aching muscles. Lupus remained silent, regarding Marcus with an admiring expression.

'What time is it?' Marcus asked as he rubbed the back of his head.

'Past the seventh hour. Festus sent me to wake you up. The master's guests have arrived for the feast.'

'Did his Land Reform get through?'

'Yes. It was close, though.'

Marcus wearily ran a hand through his hair. Then the crisis had passed. Pompeius's veterans would have their reward and the threat of a dictatorship had passed. Marcus had played his part in making that possible, and he took some satisfaction from that. But the prospect of claiming his reward was uppermost in his mind. Only when he was free could he begin his fight to rescue his mother.

Lupus smiled. 'Caesar always gets what he wants.'

Marcus stared at Lupus, wondering at the other boy's blind faith in his master. 'He nearly didn't, this time.'

Outside the slaves' quarters came the sound of running feet and shouting as the final preparations for the celebration were made. The waft of rich odours from the kitchen drifted down the corridor. Now that he was rested, Marcus felt ravenously hungry. He stood up and stretched his limbs and Lupus scrambled up beside him, anxious to know more.

'That Celt you defeated was a giant.'

'He was bigger than me,' Marcus replied. 'But not as fast.'

'Nor as honourable. Trying to stab you in the back like that.'

Marcus recalled the glare of hatred in Ferax's eyes and shuddered.

'It was a low thing to do.' Lupus shook his head. 'He deserved to die.'

Marcus stared at the other boy. 'He was a slave, Lupus, like you and me. Neither of us had any choice. We had to fight, because our masters made us.' It was not wholly true, Marcus reflected. Caesar had implied that Marcus could turn down the fight, but Marcus wondered what would have happened if he had done so. Perhaps Caesar was shrewd enough to know that Marcus would accept the challenge. And it was better that he went to the fight willingly rather than being forced into it. Marcus smiled to himself, understanding one aspect of his master's greatness – the ability to bend others to his will while they thought they were making their own choices. *Clever. Very clever indeed.*

His mind switched back to his earlier train of thought. 'Lupus, no one deserves to die, just for being a slave.'

Lupus looked at him blankly, then shrugged. 'I heard it was a good fight. Festus thinks you will be the greatest gladiator in Rome in years to come.'

'He said that, did he?'

'Oh, yes!' Lupus nodded eagerly. 'He says that he has never seen anyone with such promise.'

Marcus took little pleasure in such praise. He had not chosen to be a gladiator, and had long promised himself he would win his freedom and never again fight for the entertainment of other people. Yet he was aware of something stirring in his heart – a feeling of pride and, perhaps, a sense of destiny. The blood of Spartacus flowed in his veins and the same anger at the injustice of slavery filled his mind. Perhaps the gods had greater plans for him than he supposed.

'Anyway,' Lupus continued, 'Festus sent me to wake you.

He says you are to attend the master's feast and stand at Caesar's shoulder. That's quite an honour. Now I'd better get back to the garden. Flaccus has appointed me Caesar's cup bearer for the night.'

Lupus hurried from the room and Marcus was left alone. He smoothed down his tunic and his hair and then took a deep breath before he strode stiffly out of the cell, down the corridor and across the yard to the main house. The clouds that had covered Rome earlier in the day had gone and the evening sky was clear, washed with a golden hue. The feast was being held in the garden, where temporary dining couches were set in lines along the paths. The benches and other garden furniture had been placed along the rear wall, out of the way.

The most important guests sat with Caesar at the end of the garden, looking back towards the atrium. Portia was sitting a short distance from her uncle, next to a powerfully built man with thinning fair hair. The similarity of his features to those of General Pompeius were striking. Marcus felt his heart sink as he realized he was looking at the man Portia was to marry.

Oil lamps on tall stands had already been lit, and thin trails of smoke curled up into the evening sky. The guests were halfway through the first course – trays of small pastries containing spiced meats. Slaves scurried from table to table with jars of wine and the troupe of Greek mime actors was limbering up to one side as they prepared to perform. One of the team was busy arranging the props and costumes they would be using in their act.

Festus was standing beside Caesar's couch and saw Marcus approaching. He bent down to whisper in his master's ear. Caesar looked up and smiled, then rose to his feet as he beckoned to Marcus. He reached for his cup and, finding it empty, held it out to the side. At once Lupus, who had been standing several feet back, came forward to top it up from a small jar decorated in gold and silver, and then hurried off to the wine tubs for a refill.

'Here is my champion!' Caesar announced loudly, his voice carrying across the hubbub of conversation, which rapidly died away. Marcus felt the eyes of every guest upon him as he made his way round the couches where Pompeius, Crassus and their closest friends were lying, a few places away from Caesar.

Caesar placed his hand on Marcus's shoulder and gently eased him forward so the guests could see him clearly. 'My friends! Today we celebrate a victory for reason, and the humbling of those who would have led Rome into a new dark age. Bibulus and Cato were defeated in the Senate House and the ruthless gangs of their creature, Milo, have been driven from the streets. But perhaps the sweetest victory was the crushing of Bibulus's gladiator by my own fighter, Marcus. Though the odds were against him, he had the courage, determination and skill to win through. His victory inspired ours, so I would ask you to raise your cups and toast the champion of Rome.'

All around the garden and the atrium the guests hurriedly picked up their cups and echoed his name before taking a sip. As the sound died down and the guests returned to their conversations, Caesar gestured to a spot to one side of his couch. 'Over there, Marcus, where they can all see you.'

'Yes, master.'

Caesar smiled. 'You will not have to call me that for much longer.'

Marcus bowed his head in gratitude before he took his position and stood, arms folded, at the shoulder of the most powerful man in Rome. His heart swelled with pride at his famous victory, but even more at having won his freedom. This was what he had come to Rome to achieve. Now, at last, he could begin the next stage of his quest, to find and free his mother.

Looking out over the guests, Marcus saw Pompeius smiling and laughing with his close associates. A short distance away, Crassus was looking more subdued, and he shot Pompeius a withering glance before turning back to his own entourage. The other guests, mostly senators, tribunes and wealthy merchants, all seemed to share Caesar's cheerful mood. At the opposite end of the garden, the Greek actors, their faces heavily made up, were waiting for the signal to begin the performance. The man minding their equipment had moved closer to the wine tubs for a better view. Marcus saw Lupus approach the wine tubs, carrying Caesar's personal wine jar. The Greek smiled and spoke to the boy, wrapping a familiar arm round the slave's shoulder. He pointed at one of the actors and, as Lupus glanced away, a tiny flash of red from the man's ring caught the light from the flames of a nearby oil lamp.

It was a small movement and at first Marcus wasn't sure what he had seen. But he thought something had dropped from the Greek's fingers into the wine jar. Before he could make up his mind, he heard a shout from behind him.

'Marcus!' General Pompeius beckoned to him. 'Over here, boy!'

Marcus glanced questioningly at Caesar and his master nodded. 'Go ahead.'

He strode over to Pompeius's couch and bowed his head. As he walked he struggled with the sense that something wasn't quite right about the Greek man with the mime artists. There was something familiar about him, despite the theatrical make-up.

'That was some fight.' Pompeius smiled. 'Never seen a full-grown gladiator move so fast on his feet, let alone a boy! Hah! Caesar is right. You'll be a champion to remember. I wonder, how much of that is down to your father? Did he raise you to be a fighter?'

'My father is dead, sir. But you may remember him. Centurion Titus Cornelius. He fought with you in the last battle against Spartacus. He once told me he saved your life that day. One of the slaves had been lying on the ground pretending to be dead. He leapt up after you had passed him and tried to stab you. My father managed to intervene and kill the slave.'

Pompeius's brow creased as he thought for a moment. His eyes suddenly widened. 'By the gods, yes, I remember! That was a fine piece of work. But for him, that cursed slave would have plunged his blade into my back . . . And you're his son. Then how did you come to be a slave?'

317

'My father was murdered by the men of Decimus, a tax collector, sir. My mother and I were kidnapped and sold as slaves. That is how I became a gladiator.'

Pompeius stared at him before replying. 'That is a hard tale, boy. If I had known the family of one of my officers had endured this, I would have intervened. What was the name of the tax collector again?'

'Decimus, sir. But it was his servant who killed my father.'

'And what was the servant's name?'

'Thermon.'

Something stirred in Marcus's memory. The steely rasp of Thermon's voice on the day he had turned up at the farm and killed Titus. A voice he thought he had heard again, more recently . . .

The truth hit home like a hammer blow. The third man he had overheard at the inn. The one who had kept his hood raised. The man who wore a ruby ring on the finger of his right hand . . .

A cold stab of fear shot up Marcus's neck. He swung round and saw that Lupus had returned to his master's side, and refilled his cup once again. The Greek who had been standing by the wine tubs was watching Caesar expectantly. Marcus abruptly turned away from Pompeius and sprinted back towards his master. Caesar drew his cup away from the jar and raised it towards his lips.

'Caesar!' Marcus shouted. 'No!'

30

Marcus's warning was drowned out by the deep booming of drums as the actors ran into the centre of the garden. Caesar paused, as if he thought he might have heard something, then moved the cup to his lips. Marcus hurled himself across the couch and thrust the cup away, so that the wine slopped over and stained the white linen cover of the couch in spatters of red.

'What on earth!' Caesar spluttered.

Marcus firmly took the cup from his hand and set it down carefully on the table. 'It's poisoned, master.'

'Poison?' Caesar stared at the cup in horror. He looked up at Marcus. 'What are you talking about?'

Marcus pointed at Thermon, still standing beside the wine tubs. The Greek was watching them intently. 'I saw him put something in the wine. He's the one who was plotting with Milo and Bibulus. His name is Thermon.'

Caesar glanced down the garden. The rest of the guests were watching the mime artists and only those closest to the host were aware of what had happened. Caesar turned back to Marcus. 'By the gods, you had better be sure about this.'

He sat up and caught the attention of Festus. 'Take that man, the Greek, standing beside the wine tubs. Do it quietly, and put him in the cellar in chains and watch over him. I'll come to you as soon as the party is over.'

'Yes, master.' Festus turned and walked quickly round the line of tables, gesturing to the men he had placed around the garden to join him.

But they were too late. Thermon had seen Festus heading for him and he suddenly made a run for it, towards the wall of the garden.

'Stop him!' Caesar cried out. 'Festus! Don't let him escape!'

Faces turned towards Caesar and the actors paused in their performance. Marcus watched as Thermon sprinted for the wall, wondering how he hoped to scale it. But as Thermon rounded the corner and struck out towards the stacked benches, it was obvious. Festus broke into a sprint. But he was too late. Thermon reached the benches, clambered up and swung himself on to the wall, kicking the benches away as he did so. He rolled over the top and was lost from view.

Festus abandoned any idea of pursuing him over the wall and shouted orders to his men to get out into the street to try to block the Greek's escape. They raced out of the garden, leaving the guests staring after them. Caesar hurriedly called for their attention and assured them there was nothing to worry about. A petty thief had been caught in the act, he said, before calling on his guests to continue the feast. After a moment the mime performance continued. Once he was certain the incident wouldn't disrupt the celebration, Caesar turned to Marcus with a cold expression. 'Go to my study at once. Wait for me there.'

Marcus sat in the gloomy light cast by a single oil lamp. He was trying to think through what this all meant. Thermon was the servant of Decimus, who in turn was the friend of Crassus, one of Caesar's closest allies. Why would Thermon have tried to kill Caesar – twice now? It didn't seem to make any sense.

The feast ended late in the evening and Marcus heard the guests begin to leave, talking noisily as they passed by the door of the study. Gradually the sounds died away and there was a long delay before footsteps sounded outside the door. Festus opened it and stood aside to let his master, Pompeius and Crassus enter the study. Marcus rose up from the stool. Caesar and his two political allies sat themselves down on the more comfortable chairs round his desk, while the two slaves remained on their feet.

'What is the meaning of this?' asked Crassus. 'Why have you called us in here?'

'There's been another attempt on my life tonight,' Caesar replied tonelessly.

'Ah!' Pompeius slapped a hand on his thigh. 'I wondered what that fracas was. Did you catch the man?'

'No. He got away. But I have his name. Thermon. That's right, isn't it, Marcus?'

'Yes, Caesar.'

'And what exactly do you know of him?'

Marcus pursed his lips. 'Not much. He was the man who killed my father and kidnapped my mother and me from our farm on Leucas.'

'Then what is he doing here?' asked Pompeius. 'Why would he want to kill Caesar? Who is he working for?'

'I can't say. He used to work for a tax collector by the name of Decimus.' Marcus glanced at Crassus. 'The same Decimus

I saw you with outside the Senate House earlier this year, sir.' Marcus turned to Caesar. 'And the same Decimus who gave the signal for the attempt on your life, master.'

Caesar stared at him intently. 'Are you certain?'

Marcus knew he had no firm evidence, but he had to tell Caesar his fears – if Crassus was in league with Decimus and Thermon, he was also in league with Bibulus and Milo. Caesar's life was still in danger, and Crassus wasn't really an ally at all. He was a deadly enemy. 'It was Decimus, master. I am sure of it.'

Caesar turned to Crassus. 'It seems you owe me an explanation, my friend,' he said firmly.

Crassus folded his hands together in his lap and replied casually, 'Decimus is a business associate of mine.'

'Where is he now?' Caesar demanded. 'I demand to speak with him.'

'He left Rome recently. I believe he was returning to his estates in Greece.'

'I see . . . How convenient.' Caesar continued to stare at Crassus until the other man's gaze finally wavered. 'And would you mind telling me why the servant of a business associate of yours would try to kill me?'

'I have no idea. You'd have to ask this, er, Thermon. If you find him.'

'Or perhaps I should have a word with Decimus, once I've tracked him down?'

'You could, though I doubt whether an honest businessman like Decimus would know anything about an attempt on your life.'

There was a brief, tense silence before Caesar sighed. 'Crassus . . . What are you hiding from me? What do you know about all this? The three of us have entered into an alliance. We swore an oath to look after each other's interests. We said that we would discuss any grievances we may have openly, to avoid the danger of conflict. We are supposed to be equal partners.'

'Yes, that was my understanding,' Crassus replied coolly. 'But since you mention equal partners – why did you give your daughter to Pompeius as a bride? And why are you now strengthening your ties to Pompeius by marrying your niece into his family? A reasonable man might question the motives behind such moves to tie your political fortunes more closely to each other.' His lips compressed into a thin line. 'Caesar, from where I'm sitting, it looks as if the two of you are trying to make me into the junior partner of our agreement.'

'Preposterous!' Pompeius snorted. 'And if marriage helps to cement relations between me and Caesar, then so much the better for all of us. You're jumping at shadows, Crassus. Just like a freshly minted junior officer!'

Crassus's eyes narrowed for a second before he continued in a quiet voice that Marcus found menacing. 'You must think me a fool. I know what your game is and I won't live in your shadow. Nor Caesar's.'

'Is that why you plotted to kill me?' Caesar asked bluntly. 'You would have me murdered just because my family and Pompeius's are linked by marriage?'

There was a long tense silence before Crassus replied. 'There is nothing more to be said. You can't prove anything. I have better uses for my time.' He stood up. 'My dislike of the situation is not personal, Caesar. Ours is a business relationship. You should never forget that. It only works if we share the profits and business opportunities equally. If a man goes into business with me, and tries to take advantage of me, then he will suffer the consequences. I suggest you remember that. And you, General Pompeius.' Crassus smiled coldly. 'I wish you luck in catching your would-be assassin, Caesar. I bid you goodnight.'

He strode from the room, closing the door hard behind him. Pompeius stared after him in astonishment as the sound of his footsteps faded into the distance. At length Caesar cleared his throat. 'From now on, we'll need to handle our business partner carefully, my dear Pompeius.'

'Are you mad?' asked Pompeius incredulously. 'The man tried to have you killed. He's your enemy, and therefore mine. We have to do something about him, double quick.'

'He's not an enemy; he's a politician. He's played his hand and lost. I suspect he will think hard about this and realize he has to accept our arrangement over Portia. Even allowing for that, Crassus has much to gain from our alliance. Hopefully, he will see that.'

'If not?'

'Then we may have to deal with him at a later date. We're playing for high stakes, my friend.' Caesar stroked his chin thoughtfully. 'Perhaps it is true what they say. Two is company; three is a crowd. There may well come a time when there is not room enough in Rome for three men such as ourselves. Until then, we'd better watch our backs . . . Under the circumstances I think that Portia's marriage to your nephew is, how shall I put it – improvident.'

Pompeius frowned. 'What are you saying? That we call it off?'

'Precisely.'

Pompeius's eyebrows rose. 'But what about all the preparations? What will we say to people?'

'I don't care what people think,' Caesar replied curtly. 'The risks outweigh the advantages. We can't afford to lose the support of Crassus. Not yet.'

Marcus and Festus witnessed the exchange in silence. Marcus could hardly believe it. There was little doubt that Crassus was behind the attempt on Caesar's life. And yet Caesar refused to act against him. Marcus couldn't help wondering at the heartlessness of this trio of powerful men. For them, marriage, politics and plotting were merely tools for the pursuit of personal ambition. They were utterly ruthless and more dangerous than Marcus had ever supposed.

Again, he was seeing another kind of gladiatorial combat in the world of Rome – one that was every bit as dangerous as those fought in the arena. He didn't know what this meant for his plan to seek vengeance on Decimus, but if Caesar wouldn't help him, he would find a way himself.

Pompeius reflected on Caesar's decision and then stood up. 'It's been quite a day. I'm tired and I've had too much to drink. We'll talk again when the air's cleared.'

'Yes.' Caesar nodded. 'That would be a good idea. I'll see you out.'

'No need, my friend. I know the way!' Pompeius smiled. He made his way round the desk and stopped briefly in front of Marcus to pat him on the cheek. 'What a soldier you would make. I miss good honest soldiering. Now that's an honourable trade. Not like the double dealing that goes on in Rome, eh?'

He lowered his hand and made for the door, nodding a brief farewell to Caesar before he closed it behind him. Caesar let out a long sigh and seemed to deflate slightly.

'Caesar,' Festus spoke gently. 'Do you wish us to leave you?'

'What?' Caesar looked up. 'No. Not just yet. There's one final duty to be performed tonight.'

He reached down into the document chest lying open under the desk and drew out a small lead plate. He straightened up and held the plate in both hands for a moment before he spoke. 'I had this prepared yesterday, to help bolster my confidence that you would win the fight, Marcus. It's your manumission.' He looked up. 'This is your freedom. You no longer belong to me. I cannot think of any slave I have ever known who has earned this as much as you.' He stood up and held out the brass plate. 'Here. Take it.'

Marcus stood still, not quite able to believe it. Everything that he had fought for, all the suffering endured at Porcino's school and the dangers faced in Caesar's service had been leading up to this moment. He had thought it would never happen, that he might be condemned to spend the rest of his life as the property of another.

He took a deep breath and stepped forward to take the manumission, a plain slate of cheap metal with words etched upon its surface. It had little value in itself, but to Marcus it was the greatest prize of all.

'I thank you, Caesar.' He choked back the raw emotions engulfing him.

'No, Marcus. It is I, and Rome, that owe you thanks. Now go and sleep. In the morning we can discuss the first steps in finding your mother.'

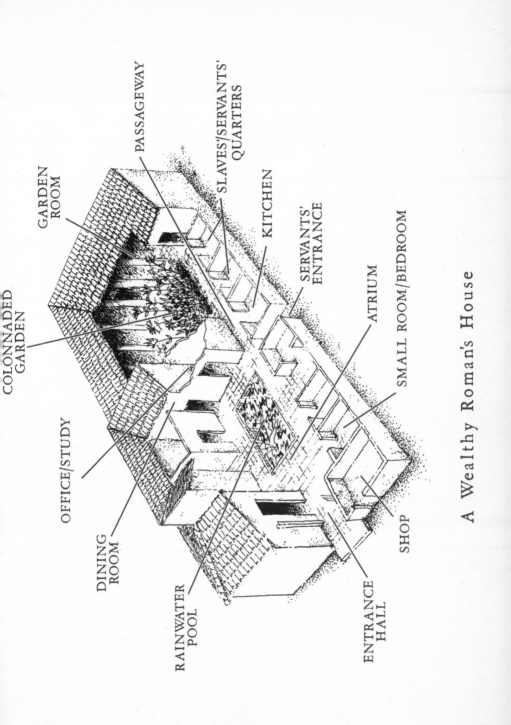

COLONNADED GARDEN

GARDEN ROOM

PASSAGEWAY

SLAVES'/SERVANTS' QUARTERS

KITCHEN

OFFICE/STUDY

SERVANTS' ENTRANCE

ATRIUM

SMALL ROOM/BEDROOM

DINING ROOM

RAINWATER POOL

SHOP

ENTRANCE HALL

A Wealthy Roman's House

BRUTAL.
BLOODTHIRSTY.
BRAVE.

MARCUS'S HEROIC FIGHT CONTINUES - DON'T MISS THE NEXT EPIC ADVENTURE.

COMING IN 2013

Enslaved by empire, he will rise a hero . . .

Have you read Marcus's first adventure?

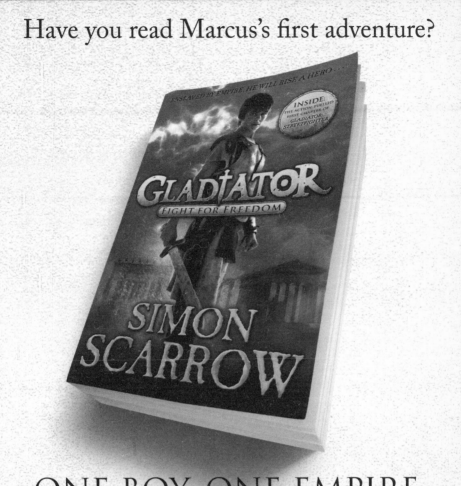

ONE BOY. ONE EMPIRE. ONE ALMIGHTY BATTLE TO SURVIVE . . . HE WILL RISE A HERO.

'This is your new home. Forget your past lives.
All that remains is to learn how to fight and survive.
If you survive and succeed, you will fight, and maybe die, like real men . . .
Learn all you can and you may be rewarded with fame, glory and riches.
Think on that tonight and in the morning
your training will begin . . .'

IN THE
ARENA

FIGHTING STYLES

The gladiators' public contests were carefully planned to show off their fighting skills. Even if they were fighting to the death the spectators wanted to see a good display before the loser was killed. Often two gladiators with different fighting styles were paired together. When the Capua novice gladiators had finished their initial training, the instructors decided what kind of combat they should be trained in.

RETARIUS

(net fighter)

Wore light armour because his fighting style depended on agile movement and speed. Used a net, trident and dagger to trap and kill opponents.

BESTIARIUS

(animal fighter)

Fought wild animals, such as tigers, leopards and lions. Bestiarii had their own training school but some of the Capua slaves were trained to fight animals and Marcus confronts wolves in his first fight. Wore light armour and a helmet with a visor, and used a spear or knife, a whip and sometimes a cage. The animal fights were extremely popular with the public, and the rewards for the animal fighters were high and for skilled animal fighters the fights could be less dangerous than combat between gladiators.

CROWD CONTROL

Gladiators' survival depended not only on beating their opponent, but also on pleasing the crowd. A gladiator who lost a fight and was about to be killed could be saved if the crowd thought he had fought well and gave him the thumbs-up signal.

The thumbs-down signal, on the other hand, meant he was doomed to die. The spectators placed bets on their favourite gladiators and Marcus learns that a gladiator who is the crowd's favourite to win will certainly die if he loses, because his supporters will be angry that they have lost money.

• Watch the **mind-blowing trailer**
• Find out more about the **real gladiators**
• Free **downloads**
JOIN THE
FIGHT
FOR
FREEDOM
NOW AT
www.gladiatorbooks.co.uk